The Legacy:

A source of hope for the 22nd century

Eileen L. Ziesler

Thinking of our great-great-great grandchildren!

Ei—

Toad House Publishing

Dedicated to my father, Louis Havluj, Jr.,
the land that he lived on,
and the water that sustained him.
ELZ

Text copyright 2011 by Eileen L. Ziesler
Cover photograph 2008 by Gary Hoagland
Author photograph copyright 2009 by Peter Olson

Second Edition 2014
Printed in the USA by Publishers Express Press, Tony, WI

To purchase a copy of this book, to contact artists whose work appears in the book, or to schedule author events, please contact eileen@toadhousepublishing.com.

Summary: Matt and Amy are two lonely graduate students from the 22nd century who meet in a virtual encounter. They begin life together on the seemingly untouched land at the confluence of the Chippewa and Flambeau rivers in Northern Wisconsin. Matt learns of his rich ancestry and his connection to the land. With his help, Amy uncovers a sinister government plot to control life and death and this changes their lives forever.

ISBN: 978-0-9818831-8-2

Acknowledgements

I wish to thank the members of the Writers Exchange in Ladysmith, Wisconsin for supporting my efforts by reading their own stories and listening to mine.

I would like to thank Yasmine Ziesler, Carole Lee, Arian and Arlene Knops, Ruth Ralston, and Phyllis Stevenson for contributions to the early edits of the story.

Thank-you to Joanne Leary for a muddy hike into the woods of Flambeau Mountain, an area of Rusk County, Wisconsin with a geological history as old as the Blue Hills.

I am grateful to Al Manson and Colleen Peters for their friendship and work on the careful editing of the final manuscript.

Thank-you for the contributions to the book from members of the Rusk Area Arts Alliance. Gary Hoagland's beautiful photograph of an old pump has become the cover of this book. I have long since forgiven Peter and Anney Olson for waking me at 5:30 in the morning to capture the author photo taken on my father's land. The early morning mist in the background was worth the inconvenience!

Other friends, artists and photographers, contributed their work to give visual transitions to the 275 year span of the story: William C. Fucik, Andrea Korpinen, Phil Ruege, Jennifer Newell, Peter Olson, Karen Koehler, and Bonnie Ohmstead. Thank-you to all my talented friends.

Most of all, I would like to thank Tony Ziesler, the 'idea man' for whom any idea can become reality. ELZ.

List of Artwork

Cover Photograph by Gary Hoagland
Author Photograph by Peter Olson

<u>Desolate Serenity</u> acrylic by William C. Fucik

<u>White Tail Fawn</u> watercolor by Andrea Korpinen

<u>One Tree</u> photograph by Karen Koehler

<u>Legacy</u> pencil drawing by Jennifer Newell

<u>Ice Vertical</u> photograph by Peter Olson

<u>Felsenmeer</u> photograph by Peter Olson

<u>Wagon Wheel and Dry Brush</u> photograph by Phil Ruege

<u>Winter Splitting</u> acrylic by Bonnie Ohmstead

<u>Trailer Trash</u> photograph by Karen Koehler

Preface to the first edition

One must consider the past to understand the present and positively impact the future. AJZ

Writers draw upon their own history and family stories when they create tales of fiction or fact. I live upon the land that was farmed by my parents, grandparents, and great-grandparents. My own children were raised on this land. The stories in <u>The Legacy</u> of Bess, Edward, Elly, James, and Callie are fictional, but they arise from the stories I heard as a child.

Leaders in my community, state, nation, and the world face decisions regarding the protection or degradation of natural resources. Global warming and the related climate disturbances, the dependence on oil, and the shortage of clean water are some of the problems of today's world. How our leaders handle these problems not only affect the quality of our lives today, but the quality of life generations from now.

I give you this story, a combination of fact and fiction, to consider how today's choices may affect tomorrow. I hope our leaders have the wisdom to make good choices.

In the early 1920's Bess and Josh Bordeau moved their young family by horse and wagon from Haugen, WI to the confluence of the Chippewa and Flambeau Rivers. They were lured by the promise of rich farmland and pure water. But the well went dry and the family dug a new well in the location witched by Lemon Extract Paul and sanctioned by Bess.

Thus begins the history of the land and the people, placed in a time capsule by Callie that would be opened in the future by Matt and Amy, two lonely graduate students of the 22nd century. <u>The Legacy</u> spans three centuries of a family's history and their relationship to the cherished water from a hand-dug well.

This fictional work follows our world's trajectory regarding overpopulation and the scarcity of clean water and suggests this takes place under the ever present and watchful eyes of those in power. ELZ

Disclaimer: All facts and figures in this novel have been thoroughly researched and corroborated by the author and editing team. However, it is left up to the reader to determine the factuality beyond an unreasonable doubt, as suits their belief. AJZ

Preface to the second edition

On the eve of another election, I have considered the responses to the book from the readers of the first edition. The general theme of their responses related to how the story gave them the opportunity to consider the future and what it might hold.

Book clubs offer readers an opportunity to share these thoughts with others, exploring the topics suggested by the content of the book.

It is with these thoughts in mind, rather than reprint the first edition, I have chosen to add questions at the end of the book to stimulate thoughtful discussion for a second edition. I hope this will lead to a better understanding of how each one of us, by exercising our right to vote and by making life choices based upon our values, has the power to impact the future.

Eileen L. Ziesler

The woman in the waiting area closed the notebook and stared into the distance through the people passing by. She sighed deeply as if loath to come back in time from where she had been for the past two hours. She placed her pen and notebook in her purse. Her row was called and she boarded the plane.

THE FUTURE

Matt slouched in the chair of his workspace, stifling a yawn. The droning low tones of the professor's voice didn't help and he tried to will his spine to straighten, his eyes to look alert lest someone would see his lack of attention. He heard without comprehending the words: Ethically Responsible Bioresearch. Why did he ever sign up for such a class? His interest was in bio-chem engineering. This was an elective, intended by the great heads of the chemical engineering department to broaden the narrow minds of the graduating engineers. He should have studied historical literature for all this was worth to him.

Professor Bracken's life size hologram was no more than five feet in front of him. As the professor paced the floor, the hologram danced in the space of Matt's den, sometimes sharing the space with the piles of books and papers, sometimes walking through Matt's half-eaten nut butter sandwich or yesterday's coffee.

Unable to focus on the professor, Matt scanned the visuals: a list of Supreme Court rulings and a list of environmental research deemed borderline ethical by the professor—whatever that meant. Getting nothing from the visuals Matt played with the console. He skimmed down the list of class enrollees. They were listed by numerical code, not by name for a reason Matt couldn't fathom. With everyone on line, connected by a wireless network of holocams, computers, and satellites, the college experience was remote, individual. No sparkling social life here like in the old movies he had seen. In the current college experience, something was lost, something was gained. He had his pick of graduate classes and the very best professor his money and documented status could buy. His relationship with his professor and his peers was non-existent.

Matt selected his own code and Matt Bordeau's bored-looking holographic twin appeared next to the professor. There he was with his combed hair and clean but rumpled shirt. Matt studied his own image, a serious, dark, clean-shaven face, and straight black hair. He noticed his hair was thinning slightly and he zoomed in to the top of his head. Oh God NO! A silver gray hair. And then another! Could it be? He was only 23 and shocked at the realization that aging was beginning before he had even started to live.

Unhappily, he panned back to the professor who was calling for a debate of sorts on the topic. Well, someone was enjoying the class, he mused. A girl, seemingly very young, took up the professor's challenge and her hologram appeared in his room with the professor. Matt perked up. This finally might be interesting. He might learn something here or it might be a wonderful little diversion. He stared at the young girl with complete absorption. She was speaking and gesturing with great emotion.

"Research and the news media MUST accept responsibility. The truth alone is only what is important in today's world." The girl's ponytail bobbed up and down and swung from side to side as she became more animated and agitated working to make her point.

Although Matt wasn't particularly taken with the argument, he could not deny his interest in this seemingly very young graduate student. He did not doubt her ability, knowing how he had nearly not made the IQ cut-off for this class.

The professor responded with statements about permissions and the need to follow logical sequences, and other facts well-known to any of the members of the class who were able to stay awake. He droned again, pathetically it seemed to Matt. Matt looked at the pony-tailed opponent. She was clearly agitated, wanting to speak and being unable to pierce the thick wall of power surrounding the professor.

"What do you believe is the truth concerning your research," the professor calmly asked, apparently having dealt with other passionate graduate students in his lengthy career. "Are you willing to share with us and the 'cam'?" (Here the professor smiled, thinking he was making a little joke, lifting the atmosphere from the animosity he was feeling from the girl who was most probably one-third his age.)

The ponytail became very still. The girl took a deep breath. "With due respect sir," she began, "my research points to a governmental cover up. The Governors of Earth Security are promoting the prepackaged food as the only food that is safe. They are banning and imposing fines and persecuting those who attempt to market any other food. As an example, this is the only available drinking water and is it really safe?" The girl held up an empty water bottle with a familiar label. "Can we trust the Governors? Or do they have a sinister plan to erode the health of the lower and middle classes so that the wealthiest will live in health and prosperity and the poor will die early to eliminate the cost of caring for them in their later years?" The girl had become pale as she spoke and when she was finished and quiet, Matt was aware that his own heart was racing and his breathing had become shallow.

The professor looked at his watch. "Well, that was a wonderful bit of fiction there, very compelling and emotional -- but factual, I rather doubt. We will see you all here next Monday, same time, same station." He said the last sentence chuckling a little as though he had made another good joke. The holograms of the professor and the pony-tailed girl faded and Matt's class schedule, assignments, and dinner menu appeared in the air a few feet in front of him. Matt looked at the visuals blankly. He saw not his choices for dinner but rather the passionate face of the girl with the brown ponytail.

Matt replayed the class, arguing with himself that he did this to better understand the professor's lecture. In truth he replayed it to watch that girl. Leaning back in his chair, he reached unconsciously for snacks and a drink. He was about to open the bottle when he realized his drink of choice had the very same label, Thundering Waters, as the bottle that the girl had pointed to in her discourse on the by-product of the war on global warming. Turning the bottle over he read the fine print on the label. It was bottled, the fine print proclaimed, in Canada in a town called Thunder Bay by a well-known company, Purefz. Looking up Thunder Bay, he learned it was situated on the shore of Lake Superior. Matt broke the seal and took a sip. He never before had attempted to taste water, but that is what he determined to do now. The tepid water on his tongue tasted to him as it always tasted. "Nut case," he said to himself as he took a drink, but he didn't finish the bottle.

Matt paused the hologram discussion between the girl and the professor. He selected just the girl and requested her numerical code, storing the code in his menu of visuals. He cleaned up the leftover snacks, cold coffee, and dumped the water. Selecting a juice drink from the food keeper and donning running shorts he left his abode, slamming the door behind him.

Amy was livid after class. She considered dropping the class, dropping the program. "The hell with it!" she said to herself. To cope she changed into her running clothes, placed a sounder in her right ear and started off on a fast jog to town, two miles away. A quarter mile down the road she yelled out her frustration at the realization that she had forgotten her water bottle. It was hot -- the hot dry June that Wisconsin had come to know in the past hundred years of climate change. Amy turned around and ran back home. Once inside she found there was little water left in the large water dispenser on her kitchen counter. She drank the last of it and gave up on the run to town. Grasping the waiting sprinkling can she backed out of the doorway into the bright light of the outdoors. She sauntered with deliberate casualness to the bench shaded by the large oak tree. Adjacent to the shade of the tree was a bramble of brush and to the side of the tree there were a few straggling clumps of coneflowers, pink and withering in the heat. Although there were only a few drops of water in the can she stood next to the flowers and offered them a false sense of cool wetness for their parched roots. Then she sat down on the bench and put the watering can next to the large oak.

Amy listened for the road noise of approaching transports and sounds from the sky. Hearing none, she dropped off the bench to her knees and placed the watering can ahead of her, parting the brush. In the shade, the ground felt damp and cool. Her own skin, hot and dry a moment ago, was clammy.

She pushed the can through a small opening in the brush. Ahead of her was a small block building with a sturdy door built as if for a dwarf. She opened the door, feeling for the cold piece of ancient stainless steel equipment she knew so well. It was wet with condensation from the dampness in the building. She felt along the length of curving arm and reaching the end she pushed the arm up as far as it would go and down again, repeating the motion until she felt resistance. On the next downward pull water gushed from a spout in the darkness. Amy thrust her arms and hands under the cold water, lifting the sweet wetness to her face and lips. She closed her eyes and her mind spoke a prayer of thanks for the forbidden gift.

Positioning the watering can under the spout she pumped again filling it three quarters full. She set it outside of the building with the dwarfish door. Closing the latch she resumed her vigilant listening. Hearing nothing, she pushed the can through the opening in the bramble following on her hands and knees. She straightened up and placed the watering can where it had been before on the innermost edge of the bench closest to the trunk of the large oak. Using a piece of dead brush she scratched the path she had made through the brush, pulling the brush together to hide the opening. She listened intently. Still no sounds. With difficulty, she carried the watering can to the house, trying to appear as if it were light and empty.

Amy brought her precious water into her abode. "Safe," she told herself, as she filled the countertop dispenser and one glass. She brought her glass with her to her study; she switched the browser to the NASA satellite site. Within seconds she zoomed the view to her house and selected the twenty minute review. The mini hologram, viewed from the top of her head came into view. She saw herself watering the coneflowers and retreating to the bench, disappearing in the shade of the large oak. Amy stared at the canopy of trees and brush for any movement or flashes of light. The minutes ticked by. She saw herself walking away from the bench back to the house. Amy smiled with amusement at the way she looked walking back with the heavy can. It was impossible to see anything unusual. She sighed a big sigh and drank big steady gulps of the icy water until her throat was paralyzed with the cold.

Reviewing the act of pumping the forbidden water was a daily ritual for Amy. In the winter it was more difficult with only a few gnarled pine and spruce boughs providing cover on cloudless days, and of course she could not pretend to be watering flowers. She did her daily errand at dusk in the winter on clear days because she learned the satellite images were blurry. She made it look as if she was getting something from her run-about and she carried a large bag in which she hid her jerry can. She wanted to appear normal to any NASA employee of the division of World Security who happened to be poking about in this sector of the world. Of course, she would tell no one of her clandestine operation. Indeed, her fellow man would think she was mad.

*****

It was Monday and a quarter of an hour before class, the same class in which a young passionate girl sparked Matt's interest a week ago. Matt became conscious of his attachment to 574A187632F after reviewing the hologram for the tenth time. He was amused at his own infatuation, not really embarrassed. He memorized her voice, her bouncing ponytail, and her passionate words.

He came to the console earlier than usual today, intending to bring up the girl's image at the onset of class. Scrolling down the list he came to her code and requested the image. There she sat, life-size in his room along with the bulk of life-size standing professor. The professor cleared his throat and began.

It seemed to Matt that the girl must have dismissed the confrontation of last week for she looked fully engaged with the professor's lecture, unlike himself. He studied her image. As in last week's class her hair was in its place, pulled back in a brown ponytail. She still appeared to him too young to be in this class and his hand went absentmindedly to the top of his head, his fingers drawing through the thinning and yes, graying hair. Matt imagined what it might be like to have a conversation with her, walking say along a beautiful stream, their voices in agreement concerning ecology and the environment. They were, in his imagination, having a deep conversation concerning government imposed sanctions. As Matt continued to watch her, tuning out the professor, he realized she wasn't paying attention to the lecture as he had previously supposed. She was playing with the console on her machine. "Oh my God! She knows I'm watching her!" Matt quickly clicked off her hologram, embarrassed that he had been caught. In his haste he also clicked off the professor. Since he hadn't heard a word the professor had said, he closed out this class session, promising himself to connect for a session review after class was over. Agitated, he pulled on running shorts, grabbed a bottle of the questionable water and slipped outside for a run.

Amy turned on her console to participate in this class that was required for her medical degree. It should have interested her greatly, but it didn't. She felt irritation towards the professor and embarrassment in having tried to express her views to this dispassionate man. Her thoughts roamed around and around themes of irritation, passion for her research, embarrassment, anger, and back to irritation again. Though she tried to trick herself into listening, she couldn't process a word he was saying. She fiddled with the console and the menu. She was shocked to see someone had called up her hologram. Her brows knit in concentration as she moved quickly to learn who was spying on her. Just as she opened the menu, the onlooker was gone. Was it the prof's graduate student, scanning the class for wayward minds or her mind in particular? There was no way to know now. The discomfort was so strong she realized she would not hear another word of the lecture. She switched off.

In her kitchen she dispensed a mug of water and placed it in the ancient food preparation device to heat. Chamomile would be calming she told herself. As the water began to boil Amy opened the cellobag and pulled out the mesh tea bag. Lifting it close to her face she inhaled deeply. Ah yes, chamomile. It began to work its magic upon her nerves even before she immersed it into the heat of the water. And when she did, the clear water turned pale yellow with the sweet flower. She lifted her cup with the steaming fragrant chamomile to her nostrils. Smells always brought waves of memories to her, both happy and sad. Today the sweet chamomile reminded her of her mother, long ago. Her mother always gave her chamomile when she was a little girl. She would read stories to Amy from a different time, stories of Peter Rabbit and Mrs. Tiggywinkle. Waves of sadness overtook Amy. She curled up in the corner of her sleeper with a soft blanket, the hot tea drawing memories out of her. She, who could be so strong and determined, reduced to a sad little teenager, held in a dying mother's arms. They had sipped their hot chamomile together that last day. Now Amy let her tears mingle in the pale yellow liquid. Today there was no comfort in chamomile.

*****

Running his usual seven miles gave Matt time to reflect on his unusually consuming interest. The fresh air cleared his thinking. He created a plan in the last hour of the run. It was bold. He might fail, but he'd carry it out anyway. He would contact this girl with the energetic ponytail. He mused that it was his destiny.

After a shower and a meal his resolve started to weaken. He could be such a fool he complained to his inner self. Before he weakened completely he turned on his console and selected the code number for the girl. She wasn't online. He felt both relief and disappointment. Continuing on his promise to himself he composed a brief message:

> Hello classmate,
>
> I'm sure this seems awkward and pretty bold to you. It feels the same to me. However, I heard you speak last week during Professor Bracken's lecture. I did not understand everything you were trying to convey, but I am interested in learning about your research and would like to better understand what you were speaking about. I was moved by your commitment.

(Here Matt added 'and passion' but then he thought better of it and deleted this choice of words.)

> If I've not freaked you out totally, would you contact me to discuss the class and your research?
>
> Sincerely,
> Matt Bordeau, 634C348632M

In another moment he sent the message. "Oh brother," he thought, "what am I doing? I am deep in debt with school, running behind in my classes and I don't have time for a social life." But then he clicked on "review class" and there she was.

Where you live on this earth in 2187 does not limit your experience in life. With holograms and high-speed transports, you can go anywhere, at least anywhere you can afford to go. Students are in the position of being neither too poor (education and support of the brightest is subsidized by the state) nor too wealthy to take it all for granted. The Governors of the Earth value their engineers and medical researchers. The carrot of success is there to entice the best brains in the world to learn and to provide a return on the Governors' investment. Ultimately, this is absolutely necessary for life as it exists in the twenty-second century to continue and to evolve.

Both Amy and Matt were able to tap the vast wealth of the Governors of the Earth. Neither came from wealthy families nor did they experience the level of poverty and disease prevalent in the majority of the earth's population. Really, they were hardly aware of the lives of their counterparts in poverty, so consumed were they with achieving their own goals and dreams. Yet, they both lived with embedded memories and fears from the mythology of the masses. The average life span of the masses on some of the continents reached into the mid-forties. On other continents, the life span approached only thirty.

When Matt found a strand of silver hair, he could not easily forget that he was aging. Matt's parents both died before he started graduate school. They dreamed for him the dream of success and achievement. He was an only child. His mother sang and read to him in the womb and in his infancy. The old books of the twentieth and twenty-first centuries filled his home and the concepts enriched his gifted mind. His father provided and supervised countless physics and chemistry experiments for him, presented in a way that enticed the little boy and let him use his own talents as he grew. They dedicated their lives to pulling and pushing him into a better life, dying before seeing the fruits of their labor.

What they did not give Matt was a sense of family history. Perhaps they were embarrassed by their own outcome in life or perhaps the history contained information they felt would hurt their son. They preferred instead to keep the little knowledge they had of the ancestry of the Bordeau family away from their only child and let it die with them.

ENCOUNTERS

Amy looked through the window of her abode mid-morning, reflecting on how the sunlight changed her thoughts and emotions. Last night, she remembered her mother in grief and sadness. This morning the beauty of the sunlight lifted her spirits and she could think about her mother and all the enjoyable times they had together rebuilding this little nest. Her mother bought the property after receiving an inheritance. It was most likely a spontaneous expression: to be free of the confinements and of the expectations of city life. Or perhaps it was a place to teach Amy about the natural world. Maybe it was something else.

It was an old farm home with no trace of the barn or original outbuildings of the twentieth century. The first task they had was to decide what to do with the house that was still standing. First they had gone through the decayed building, picking out the things they could save. Then the salvage transport came and after removing some building materials, vaporized the remaining structure. Amy and her mother decided to keep a portion of the basement. It had been hand built with stone and small boulders from the surrounding land. Shaking his head at the silliness of the two women, the contractor reinforced some of the wall section and created a supporting wall divider before filling in the portion of the basement that would no longer be used. An old fashioned kitchen and a small library facing the oak tree was built over the refurbished basement. Finally, an ordinary functional pod was ordered and installed next to the kitchen at the back so that it was not in view as you arrived from the road. Functional pods provided for a small food preparation and consumption station, a lav, and a sleeping compartment--all that was required for life in the late seventies of the 22nd century. Amy and her mother were overjoyed with the look and feel of their creation. They gave it a name, combining her mother's formal name, Wilamina with her name, Amy. Wilamy, the little getaway in the outskirts of the town of Flambeau, was a combination of the old and new. It became a joy to visit Wilamy, but their joy lasted less than a year. Her mother died in July and Amy no longer used the name they had made up together.

After the funeral, Amy went to Flambeau for three weeks to decide what to do next in her life. She was in her second year of college and she almost quit before the end of the term, her grief was so great. Her mother's death had left her without meaning or focus. However, during the three weeks Amy stayed at Flambeau, the blackberries close to the oak were ripening. She crawled deep into the bramble picking berries and this was how she came upon the little building that housed the well that gave new meaning and new direction to her life.

As Amy reminisced, the Flambeau water transport with the logo, Purefz, lumbered into her yard and connected to the water tank. A boy, apparently her age, made the connection. Amy had seen him many times in the past. He was dark and sweaty with the work. Amy felt glad for the visual barrier that allowed her to look out upon the world while protecting her from prying eyes looking in. As she watched, he filled out his electronic tracker and then looked, or so it felt, directly at her. He kicked at the dirt with his boot; a small dust cloud rose up. Then he walked to her door, placing his hand upon the ID screen. A voice in the abode announced Ned Nader. Amy would rather not answer the door for anyone, but this kid her age whetted her hunger for human contact.

She smoothed the hair that led to the ponytail, and smiling, she opened the door. The boy looked up, actually surprised a person had come to the door. "I just thought I'd let you know," he hesitated, unsure of what he would say next.

Amy smiled encouragingly, "Yes?"

"Ya haven't used your full ration for the last five weeks. It could get cut you know. I can't fake the report." He blurted the last bit out.

"Oh, it's okay." She heard herself say. And then to steer his prying eyes away from her kitchen and water dispenser she stepped to the side of the entryway and said, "I've been away visiting my mom this last week." Here she deliberately lied. "Did my laundry at her house."

"Well, I just wanted you to know. They'll average out the use and cut you down by some predetermined percentage. Just water some of those pretty flowers over there for a few days but don't let anyone see; its not allowed. Your allotment won't change then."

"Hey thanks for the good advice," and before she could catch herself she was saying, "I'm Amy, I'll see you around. Really, thanks for your concern."

The boy looked at her curiously. She wasn't an ordinary citizen of Flambeau. He could tell that she was a student, a girl with a future that didn't include people like himself. But he didn't say that. He said, "Nice to meet you Amy, I'm Ned. See ya next week." and he added to himself, "I hope."

"Okay."

"Bye."

He was gone. Amy bit her tongue. "Why had she been so friendly?" she wondered.

Still wondering, she resolved to review the class. She switched on and saw five new messages. She ignored the pull to open them and instead brought up the class and the professor's transparent hologram. Amy stared through him and used every bit of determination to connect with his words, to make sense of what he was babbling about. For the next hour, she took in what she could, cataloging the ideas she might need in order to pass the class, and then she clicked off.

She scanned the senders of the five unopened messages; two from classmates, one from her father, one from the water company, and one unknown. Continuing the theme of duty first, she opened the message from the water company. After her encounter with Ned, the water boy, she wondered if it would be a rationing notice. But no, it was just a bill. One touch here and it was paid from the governor's student living allotment account. Next, she opened the message from her dad. His hologram appeared in her room and she smiled as he blew her a kiss and told her about his adventure. He admonished her (as he did in each message) to give up her country living and join him and his new wife in Chicago. "Plenty of open space!" he bragged and did his best to sound convincing. Ann, the new wife, came into view and echoed his concern that Amy couldn't possibly be happy stuck in the woods of northern Wisconsin. As they continued, trying to sound convincing, Amy went to her personal lav. She splashed water on her face and hands and touched up her hair. Two minutes later, Ann and Ralph were still enumerating reasons and concerns about her lifestyle choices. When their message was over, Amy hit reply and began her happy speech to her father and Ann with words of thanks for their concern. She ended as she always did, with a firm statement of how she was enjoying her life. She gave assurances that she would visit soon. She chose not to extend an invitation to them to visit her. It would have been useless. They would only feel badly and make excuses for not being able to come. In truth, they were frightened by open spaces, woods, and the occasional rabbit or squirrel they might see.

Amy was careful to keep the holocam focused on her and prevent the default scan of the room. She didn't want her father to see the smallness of the room, the piles of papers and books. Finished with her reply and satisfied with her firm stance, she sent the message. Next she previewed the messages from two classmates and decided there was nothing of significance for her to reply. Then she studied the code of the unknown sender, and requested a match from her own files. Nothing.

With sudden inspiration, she requested a match from the ethics class. There it was, number 634C348632M. When she opened the message she did not get a hologram as in the message from her father. This time it was a typed message. She read, and reread, curious, but undecided.

The isolation of living in this small community while pursuing her medical degree was about to end. In less than one day she had exchanged names with a local water supplier and now was about to reply to a classmate from somewhere, out there in the world. Amy paused on this thought before replying to the e-mail.

"Hi Matt," she typed, "I'm Amy. Sorry I didn't make any sense last week in class. I reviewed what I said—I was really rattled by the prof—and maybe a bit angry too. If you are at your console at 8:00 CST we could try to connect although I doubt I will have improved in my ability to communicate. If this time isn't convenient, send me another possible time." Here Amy stopped and considered how to close this e-mail. Nothing sounded right: 'Yours truly' or 'Your classmate' or 'Sincerely'. Finally she just typed "Amy" and sent the darn thing off.

She would rather have forgotten that she even made that speech a week ago. Time had diminished her blunder; this message revived it. Amy was not a person who would ever back away from a challenge, be it the challenge of being embarrassed or the challenge of being proven wrong. So as much as she would have liked to let this go, she preferred to tackle Matt's questions head on.

Amy went outside and opened the hose leading from the water tank. She just let it spill on the ground, not taking Ned's advice concerning the flowers. It soaked immediately into the parched earth below. Amy hoped the new green growth wouldn't alert Ned. She needed him on her side. After a minute or two she turned the hose off and went in to get her watering can. She repeated the twenty-minute sequence from the day before, ending with the review of the NASA site for any telltale signs of her covert operation. She had almost 3 hours left before she would meet and chat with Matt. Maybe there was time to get in some physical exercise. Remembering her water bottle, she filled it from the dispenser and stepped outside. The sun, though lower in the sky, was still burning hot. Amy sat on the dry grass, mindless of the brittle spikes poking into her bare legs. She stretched and thought. She imagined her classmate to look like Ned, brown and taut with the heavy work he completed every day. She wondered about Ned. What was his life like? She never really had any relationship with others of his standing. Amy stood up and stretched her body from one side to the other. She opened her water bottle and took several swallows. Then she took off down the road in a slow jog.

Matt received the e-mail as soon as it was sent. He hadn't turned the console off but had paced back and forth between the den and the kitchen. First Matt read the message and the sending details quickly, realizing that this Amy person lived in the same time zone that he lived in. Then he studied it more slowly, suddenly feeling uneasy. He had invited a stranger to enter his abode via holographic image. It wasn't like he needed to clean house for real company. Dirt and dust didn't image well with the current holographic technology, and by nature he was neat and organized. His books were shelved by size and subject, the few that he owned. The console upon his desk was square to the desk edge. He didn't have anything more than a few leftover snack remnants and the ever-present bottle of water. That water bottle, the same Thundering Waters brand she held up in class, would have to go. No jackets or less mentionable clothing items lay about. No messy room he may have felt anxious about. It was, rather, the uneasiness of inviting someone to look through you into your soul. What would this Amy see? Simply a transparent being with no inner life?

Thinking about his lack of personality depressed Matt. He decided to ignore his inner dialog and make the most of the few hours by showering, eating, and relaxing. Matt collected the water bottle and leftover snacks before showering. He undressed methodically, placing his used clothing in the laundry hold. He set his typical shower sequence: moist heat two minutes, soap hard spray three minutes, rinse soft spray five minutes, warm blow dry two minutes, one minute light scented mist, and normalize one minute.

He stepped inside the enclosure and pushed start. When the soapy cycle began, Matt rubbed his skin with a synthetic shower mitt. A slightly medicinal smell filled his nostrils and he felt more in charge of the events that would unfold in the next few hours. He mused that the artificially scented smell he associated with himself would not be transmitted via the holocam. He cut the rinse short and eliminated the final, perfumed mist allowing the medicinal scent to linger. When the cycle finished, the door unlatched and opened automatically. Matt stepped out and considered what colors to wear. Yellow was too bold and bright-- gray was more to his liking. In the end he chose a gray-green shirt and gray slacks. Color would be transmitted quite accurately and he wanted to make the correct impression. What that impression would be he didn't know. He wasn't even sure of who he was or who he wanted to be.

As Amy jogged along, she considered how the day had gone so far. It had been a roller coaster sort of day she thought, reflecting on the gamut of emotions she had experienced. Amy ran down the hill of the driveway and out to the road for the steady climb up to Flambeau Mountain. It was no longer a mountain, just a good size hill in the middle of a large valley created by the confluence of two large rivers. Her heart responded, increasing the beat and keeping a steady blood supply to her muscles and brain. "I am SO ALIVE!" she joyously exclaimed to the road ahead of her. She paced herself at a eight-minute mile, fast enough for a nice workout, steady enough to arrive home, shower, and eat before eight o'clock.

Coming up on the third mile her mind wandered to the mother's early death. It was not fair that her mom, who had always chosen a healthy life style, should be hit so abruptly with cancer of the thyroid. It put her body into an accelerated aging process and she looked to be in her sixties when she had just turned forty. Her blond hair turned white almost overnight. Her pale skin took on a gray look. Her father was the complete opposite of her mother. His hair and skin were dark. He drank more wine than water and didn't waste his precious time on exercise or his money on health foods. And now at age 53 he did appear to be aging. She noticed more gray hairs at his temples though his skin looked younger than his fifty years. At least he seemed happy with his new wife and his city life. Her father had shut himself off from Amy and her mother when the cancer set in. He was in the room when she died but not emotionally present. Amy thought to herself that she never really knew what kind of life her parents had before she came along.

Amy checked her GPS. She would have to decide whether to turn back and do an even six or forge ahead for seven and a half. Soon the path would appear that would lead her up to Flambeau Mountain. She checked the time and her pace. The sun was bright, the temperature pleasant. From the top of the hill she would be treated to a view of the rivers and treetops—the view her mother loved. Today it would be the longer run. She turned off the road and onto the path, her heart increasing its rate as she maintained her pace.

Amy ran the last quarter mile to the top in a more labored fashion. She knew she should stop for a drink but her thoughts pushed her onward. At the top she gazed briefly through a notch in the trees where she and her mother often stopped to look upon the joining rivers, a place of great beauty. Since her mother's death, the abode had become the place where Amy stored all the sorrowful and joyful memories of her mother. When she began graduate school she decided to live there full time. It was a spiritual place, and the countryside around where she lived seemed deep with history and meaning. Being a full-time graduate student left her with little time to ferret out the hidden history. She realized she had chosen to live as an outsider in a community of the impoverished or so it seemed from the little contact she had with the people in the nearby town of Flambeau.

She rarely saw people and she rarely saw any wild life as she ran, even though her paths took her through woods and fields. Perhaps the little rodents and toads watched her; perhaps there were deer, raccoon, and an occasional fox that stood still and watched her as she ran by. Today was different. Today, as she rounded a corner, a large deer stood in the path, not ten meters ahead. The deer, alerted to her presence, pawed the dusty path and blew a warning snort from its nostrils. Amy stopped and held her breath, "A blessing!" she murmured to herself. With her abrupt stop, the sweat accumulated and dripped from Amy's forehead into her eyes. She felt the steaming wet cloth on her skin. Her heart raced and pounded as if trying to escape her body.

Amy tried consciously to slow her racing heart and to keep her breathing silent. The deer tossed its head, stamped and snorted once again. A light breeze cooled her skin under the wetness of the shirt.

Both deer and girl stood their ground looking at each other. Amy's tongue licked her parched lips. She knew it was not safe for her to stop running so abruptly but she was loath to disturb the deer and the beauty of this chance encounter. In her right hand, almost forgotten, was her water bottle. With the awareness of the weight of the bottle, Amy became aware of her thirst. Very slowly she brought her left hand to the right, reaching for and turning the cap. She refrained from immediately taking a drink for fear of spooking this lovely creature. The deer stamped again but instead of snorting, flung its head to the side and nipped at a biting fly. A full minute passed. Slowly and deliberately, Amy raised the bottle to her mouth. The deer seemed unconcerned with her movements. Amy drank several large swallows of the cool water and then smiled. She spoke to the deer, "You needed to chase away that pesky fly and I need to take another drink." Steadily she raised the bottle again to her lips and without taking her eyes off the deer drank the rest of the water. The deer put its head down and nipped off a mouthful of grass, chewing. It watched Amy.

They stood, the deer and the girl on the wooded path, neither making a move. Then some signal, unknown to Amy, occurred and the deer gave up watching her, stepping off the path into the woods. Amy closed her empty bottle and was about to take a step when a movement on the other side of the path caught her eye. "Oh" she voiced, barely audibly. A spotted fawn stepped out of the wood. It gazed with its large eyes, its ears bent towards Amy. The fawn having taken a cue from the other deer, now known to Amy as its mother, was unafraid and after a look of curiosity at the being in the blue shorts, stepped delicately onto the path followed by a second fawn less interested than the first. The two little ones followed the doe into the woods.

Amy waited five minutes more, mesmerized by what had just happened, almost waiting for another creature to cross her path. She began to walk and her leg muscles gave way to sudden and painful cramping. After a dozen or more steps Amy sunk to the ground, her eyes watering and her calve muscles in full revolt. The pain was more than Amy felt she could bear and she screamed out through the trees. Ten minutes later she sat up rocking and rubbing her angry muscles. She wished she had more water to drink. She wished there was someone here with her to help. For the first time since she had moved to this area she felt alone and afraid. Another ten minutes passed. It was 6:50. She had more than two long miles to go. She could have easily run it in 20-25 minutes but not like this. Amy stood up, hobbling along the path, grimacing with each step down the other side of Flambeau Mountain. Stepping, painfully, bit by bit, she turned into her drive and into the house. She would have five minutes before meeting Matt and she briefly considered not connecting with him at this time, but the future explanation would be worse than simply getting this over with now. She hobbled into the kitchen, filling a glass and drinking it all before filling another to take to the study. She selected an apple, and holding it in her mouth, she pushed the door to the study open and flipped on the console on. Ruefully she thought, "Well Matt, you are about to meet the real Amy Anderson." It was a minute before 8:00.

In another moment, Matt and Amy were connected, the

hologram of each other sitting a few feet away. He—clean, cool, ordered. She—sweaty with a dirt streaked face, holding an apple in her mouth. They sat for a very long moment looking at each other.

When you visit with someone in real time using the holocam, the person you are visiting appears directly in front of you. As you look into the holographic image you feel as if you are looking into your partner's eyes and they feel the same, because your hologram is sitting in their space. Sometimes you might be distracted by real objects in your own physical space, not present in your partner's physical space. As an example, you might reach through the body of your partner to pick up your cup of coffee or a cookie. It can be very disconcerting until you get used to it.

Matt broke the ice. "Looks like you've just gotten back from a run," he said.

"Oh, I am so sorry for the mess. I planned enough time to clean up after my run, but I've just had the most amazing experience which turned into a painful experience."

"Not a problem." Matt laughed, comforted by her warm voice and humbled by the fact that she would choose to appear to him in her present shape. He thought he might have canceled had the shoe been on the other foot. "I run also. How far did you go?"

"Well, I completed, if that's what you call it, my regular long run, seven miles. But I did it in record slow time!" Amy relaxed into the conversation with someone with a shared knowledge of running.

"You didn't get a sprain, I hope?" Matt sounded concerned

"No—not a sprain—severe cramping. And I should know better, I'm trying to be a medical student." Here she went again, sharing more information than she wanted.

"Ah, dehydration?"

"Yes, you guessed it."

"Say, if this isn't a good day, we can connect tomorrow or the next day," Matt said.

Amy laughed, "Actually, if you don't mind the real me," And here she gestured intending to mean how she looked, "This really is a great day."

"Can you tell me about it?"

"How much time do you have?"

Matt looked at the girl with the ponytail, returning her smile, "As much time as you need to tell a good story."

"Well," Amy hesitated, thinking she would feel more relaxed if she could wash her face.

Matt interrupted as if reading her mind, "How about if you take some time for yourself? I'll get a beer, stay online, and settle in for a good story."

"Hey thanks! I'll be back in a flash."

Amy left the room but didn't disconnect. Matt was left facing a hazy and transparent empty study filled with books and collections of things he didn't understand. As he looked around the space projected by the cam he became curious and wanted to ask Amy why she had all these things. However, he promised himself he wouldn't ask—not this time. So he got up and brought a beer to his den. She was back when he came in. "That was quick."

"I just needed to wash my face."

"So, tell me about your day."

How much to tell, Amy wondered. She smiled and took another drink of water. Then she took a breath. "Well, you are the second person and the fifth being I have seen today. Usually I am alone. First the water transport guy came to the door to give me some information. Then, five miles into my run I made a turn on the path and this huge deer was standing about 10 meters in front of me. It stayed for the longest time and even took a bite of grass as I was taking a drink. After that it stepped off the road into the woods and two fawns followed. So it was a doe." Amy was lost in her own mind, reliving the event and almost unaware that she was speaking aloud to Matt.

"Phew!" Matt said "That was amazing. I've never seen a wild deer. Just ones in a park, contained like in a zoo."

Amy was brought back to the present by his comment. "I was standing there without moving for a long time. When I tried to walk again, my calves and quads went into spasms. It was so painful I almost thought I wouldn't make it back."

"Well, I'm glad you did! Say, where do you run that you have a woods?"

Amy felt caught in a downward spiral; she had begun something that wasn't easy to end. But even if she could have released herself from this conversation she wasn't sure that she would have. Still, one needs some measure of protection. "I live outside of a small rural community. There are woods and unused farmland fields all around me."

"Wow! I didn't know one could live in places like that and still have ways to connect for school."

"Where do you live?" There, she had opened the door. He would either sidestep her question and she would refrain from getting in any deeper with him, or he would tell her something about himself.

"I'm currently living in a student housing pod. It's really a cluster of pods that the university provides. It's nice in some ways but just as you said about being alone, I'm alone in a place where there are many who are alone. I'm in a greenspace or so they call it, just north of St. Paul, Minnesota. I noticed we are in the same time zone. Are you in Minnesota also?"

"I lived in Minnesota as a child, actually in Brainerd. I lived there until my mother died. She purchased the land I now have in Northwest Wisconsin and she and I would come for vacations after we rebuilt this place, keeping the old-fashioned kitchen and a study and adding on a pre-fab pod. We tried to grow some food in the areas that were probably once gardens. I really loved it so I guess that's why I'm here."

"It must be beautiful."

"It is, but like me—messy and with its own problems and history, but I really like the smell of clean, outdoor air." Amy, of course, didn't mention the water.

Amy and Matt talked for three hours. The time flew by. Matt learned about the community of Flambeau and some of Amy's life in the country. He learned more about her educational goals. He learned that the near-by larger community of Chippewa Falls had a grant from the Governors to produce a carbon scrubber plant and produce water on a small scale. It was to emulate the one in St. Paul. The Chippewa Falls scrubber was scheduled to open in about a year. This interested Matt a lot. He had wanted to get a work-study in his undergraduate days at the mega-plant in St. Paul but wasn't able to land it.

Amy learned many things about Matt. She learned about Matt's interest in running and biking. She was impressed with his self-discipline and his organization when it came to these things. She picked up some pacing strategies that she felt would prevent the severe cramping she had experienced. She learned that his parents had died early and that as children, their mothers had read to them many of the same older books from the twentieth century. She was impressed with his father's role and how Matt had learned so much about chemistry and engineering before even starting college.

Matt was impressed with Amy's understanding of the natural world. He was in awe of how much she had accomplished in a very short time. Indeed she was beyond being just a medical student, she was ready for her residency in medicine. He was energized by her commitment to her research.

Matt was about to ask another question when he noticed Amy stifling a yawn. "Well, I've kept you up far too long. I'm so sorry. I had a great time meeting you and I'd like to meet again." There, he said it. He only hoped she didn't see how really interested he was in her.

Amy was startled by Matt's shift in conversational tone. She smiled outwardly but inwardly wondered if she had bored him. "I'm sorry I seem so tired. I also had a really nice evening." Amy looked into the eyes of Matt's hologram and Matt looked at her. There seemed nothing else to say and these two gifted geeks who had little practice socializing with the opposite sex just looked at each other until both were feeling a little uncomfortable.

Amy inhaled deeply, "Well, see you in class," She said glibly.

Matt forced a laugh, "Yes." And then he remembered, "—oh I never did ask you to explain what you were talking about with

Professor Bracken!"

They both laughed, a little more comfortably. "Bye Matt," Amy said when she stopped laughing.

"Bye, Amy Anderson." Matt quickly flipped off the console, almost afraid he'd never find a way to end the conversation if by chance Amy didn't turn hers off. He tipped his console chair backward to the point of almost tipping over. "OH MY GOD!" he yelled to the ceiling and the few family pictures around his room. There was no one to tell how he felt, how much he had fallen for that girl with the ponytail.

Eileen L. Ziesler

TREES

The technology for scrubbing carbon dioxide out of the air had been around for over a hundred years. Back in 2010 there was an experimental scrubbing operation, a small-scale plantation of metallic tree–like structures which pulled air through a network of electrically charged wire. The cost was high but it was able to remove more carbon dioxide from the air than the amount of carbon dioxide produced by the electricity it used. The scientific community was divided on whether this technology could evolve to remove carbon dioxide on a large scale. The environmentalists of that time in history promoted the planting of huge quantities of trees as ecologically more sound than the building of these tree-like scrubbers. They hoped to replace the trees that had been harvested from the rain forests in the late 20th century. The tree-like electrically dependent scrubbers did improve somewhat between 2020 and 2040, but not to the scale that the physicist inventor had envisioned.

Storage of the CO_2 from the tree scrubbers and other experimental technologies that captured carbon dioxide from the air sent technology in another direction. Some thought the CO_2 could be buried deep in the earth. In the first quarter of the century Texas became the graveyard of CO_2. It was pumped into abandoned, depleted oil wells. This strategy, like the process of producing landfills of trash, fizzled out because not enough abandoned wells were found that could safely hold the continuing build up of CO_2. In addition, demonstrations by Greenpeace halted any continuation of this approach.

Then, in June of 2043, a major breakthrough for the environment occurred when chemists invented a polymer of photosynthetic material. Imitating real trees, its upper-branched web extracted the carbon dioxide from the air in tremendous quantities. The by-product of this extraction process evolved as a food source for animal life and for the manufacturing of additional polymer products used in housing, computers, and clothing.

The downfall of the polymer web was that it did use vast amounts of electricity. Nuclear plants sprang up almost as fast as the tree plantations. The growth of the nuclear industry needed to meet the demand for energy created another obstacle. The power plants used most of the fresh water available in the greater vicinity of the plant for cooling. Water became the most valuable commodity traded on the world market. Arid regions of the earth where people depended upon bottled water during droughts could no longer sustain any human activity. Millions of people died, their deaths unnoticed in a world population of 9 billion. They died without a whisper of concern. The wastewater from the cooling of the reactors was tainted and could not be economically sanitized nor could it be reused for cooling the nuclear reactors without expensive treatments.

At this point in history, there were two challenges facing the environmental scientific community: the lack of fresh potable water for the growing world population and for the cooling of the nuclear reactors; and the safe and adequate storage of carbon dioxide that was still in the form of a gas.

A world government sponsored symposium was held to bring together the best minds in the scientific community. Entry to the symposium was based upon the submission of proposals to meet these challenges. The symposium was geared toward 'out of the box' thinkers—scientists unrecognized for their achievements in the global community. Out of this symposium sprang an idea well suited to the government's needs. Within a few years, carbon dioxide from the scrubbers and other emission control sources was being combined with the slightly tainted water supply from the cooling of the nuclear reactors. The process produced an imperceptible carbonation to the water. This new water shared virtually all the physical properties of water. Clarity, viscosity, and the transformation between gas, liquid, and solid states at essentially the same temperatures as real water. It was slightly carbonated but pleasantly so and the end result tasted like real water. The small quantities of radioactive particles and carbon dioxide had a significant purifying effect; thus no additional chlorinating was needed to keep the water safe from biohazards, germs, and bacteria. The government put a high priority into testing the product for safety. Indeed more money was tossed at this plan than in any other scientific venture of the century. After five years of extremely positive test results, the FDA gave its initial stamp of approval for human consumption and the new 'Purefz' water was marketed on a global scale.

When Monday finally came again, Matt was prepared for class. He'd completed all the assigned readings and then some, in the days since he and Amy talked. Time crawled that Monday and Matt was anxious, waiting for the right time to connect to class via holocam. He imagined himself volunteering an argument in class and he imagined Amy would be there, watching him.

He signed in fifteen minutes before the professor would start the lecture. Very few of the 400 or more enrollees were online; neither was the professor. Matt felt butterflies in his stomach. What if Amy skipped today? He watched the list grow as more and more students logged on for today's lecture. He held the cursor close to the place where Amy's number would appear. The professor was online and his large holographic image lumbered around Matt's den, shuffling papers, working on his console. Matt stared at the professor for a moment and then went back to monitoring Amy's arrival on the growing student list. There it was! Amy's number, so similar to all the other numbers, almost jumped off the screen at Matt. Unable to wait any longer Matt clicked on her number and she appeared before him, alongside the professor.

She was glued to something on her console and unaware of Matt's virtual presence. He in turn was disappointed. He had hoped and even assumed that she would be as eager to see him as he was to see her. He studied the holographic image in his den. Part of her face was hidden behind the screen of her console. Suddenly a change came into her eyes. If Matt could have seen her mouth, he would have seen her smiling. But he didn't need to see her mouth, her eyes told him that she knew that he was there. She didn't look up at him but raised her right arm and her hand shaped the universal sign for 'okay'. Matt laughed and noted that his hologram was in her study. A text message rolled across his screen, "Class now. Talk later?"

Matt typed, "Yup."

Matt didn't volunteer in class as he thought he might and neither did Amy. After class they met again and talked and argued about the lecture. Matt learned about Amy's research and Amy learned about Matt's dream to work for Global Environmental Concerns as a chemical engineer. When they both were hungry they agreed to have a hologram supper date, each bringing food to their respective work areas. It took Amy much longer than Matt to prepare her supper and when she arrived back, Matt could see why. He had simply collected various containers of choice from the food keeper and a bottle of juice. Amy had a plate with lettuces, cheese, tomatoes, and bread. She brought in a ceramic mug with something steaming. "Hmmm, looks better than my dinner," he teased.

"You come here and I'll cook something for you, just like your grandma would have done!" Amy returned in good humor.

Matt thought to himself, "I'd really like that, but I wouldn't come because of the offer of food." Aloud he said, "I'll take a rain check on that."

"Sure thing." Amy replied between bites of tomato and cheese.

What else did they talk of that evening? They talked of things as all young people have talked through centuries past. Each read between the lines of what was said and when they were too tired to go on, they each knew more about the other than they knew of any other person on this earth. Another dinner date was set for Wednesday. Amy promised Matt to be prompt. Matt promised to make a salad from scratch, though he wasn't sure how he would find ingredients to accomplish that. All the food he ever ate was delivered to his food keeper automatically. It was prepackaged and ready for him within minutes.

Both Amy and Matt led lives fairly typical of other graduate students. Over the next two days, both young people attended classes, ran for exercise and the release of pent up energy, studied, read, and wrote papers. Amy, for her part, consciously shelved thoughts and feelings about Matt while she was actively engaged in 'education' and brought them out to be studied and considered during her leisure times of cooking, running, and the time before she fell asleep. If Amy could have remembered her dreams, she would have found that images of Matt were present and his form was more real than the transparent hologram.

Matt's experience was different. Mental images of Amy and sound bites of their conversation were present in everything he did. The images energized him and pushed him to work efficiently. His writing for his dissertation took on a new quality. In addition to the highly factual data he collected and wrote about, there was a more compelling, urgent undertone driven by a strongly focused effort to finish his time as a student and begin real work for the greater good. His research was about small-scale operations involving carbon scrubbing. A dream to bring these operations to all small communities on earth began to evolve into a dream of bringing it to one small, remote community in northwest Wisconsin. Matt went to sleep Thursday night, ticking off the tasks he completed that day, and organizing his tasks for the day ahead. He woke up remembering pleasant dreams of the girl with the brown ponytail.

The only new thing Matt did before the Wednesday dinner

date was to go shopping for food. He hadn't gone to a world food market since he was a small boy. He had learned as a child to use the console to plan and order his food consumption. It was auto-delivered to his pod on a regular basis and shelved. To prepare a meal, he simply picked up the containers and placed them all together on a tray in the food preparation device, the FPD. It sensed which foods to rehydrate, which ones to chill or freeze, and which ones to heat. The FPD completed its cycle in two to three minutes, just enough time to use the lav and choose a drink. If he was detained, the FPD automatically maintained temperatures for up to 30 minutes; however, the quality of the food quickly diminished. If he happened to be detained beyond the 30-minute mark, the it went into lock mode and vaporized everything on the tray. Because of the high cost of food, Matt learned quickly to be organized for mealtime.

Matt was determined to make a good effort at producing a salad from scratch for dinner as he had promised. He chose to go to the outlet at the end of his short run and felt he could use his time during the day more efficiently. He adroitly plotted his 5-mile run on his mobile GPS placing the outlet at the 4.5-mile mark. When he arrived at that mark he found a large warehouse and a small sign proclaiming, World Food Market Division--WFMD. He walked in and was faced with a console welcoming him and requesting him to select from the visual menu. None of the choices included shopping for fresh produce. He stood there puzzled and after a moment selected 'request help'. After choosing 'English' and 'live chat' a woman's voice came on and requested he sign in by placing his index finger on the fingerprint reader. Matt felt a growing impatience and irritation as he complied. Once signed in, the woman asked, "How can I help you, Matt?"

Matt took a big breath and said, "I would like to pick out my own produce." Matt thought he heard a hesitation in her voice.

"Matt, I'm sorry, that is no longer an option available at the World Food Market Division. We carry only government sanctioned safe and deliciously prepared food for your dining pleasure. You may use the console in the inner foyer to make your selections and your order will be processed and delivered in eight to ten minutes. You can use the wait time to peruse the holograms of our other food preparation and delivery facilities. Thank you for your question." A soft click indicated the woman had closed the connection.

Matt stood, staring at the console, completely baffled by the response. It was true that he had not been to a market in over 15 years. He was just a small boy with his mother at the time. He never had the need to try to shop like this. Food was always delivered to his pod and if he didn't remember to order, food came anyway, though not necessarily what he would have preferred to eat.

Matt was not in the mood to give up the search for fresh lettuce and other salad vegetables; he had promised Amy. He slowly turned around, leaving through the same small door he had come in, considering what to do next. The answer came in the form of a young, dark-skinned woman seeming to be in her twenties. She was dressed in an unusual style and her clothes appeared not exactly clean.

"Excuse me," Matt ventured. The woman's eyes looked up at him in fear. "I'm sorry to bother you." Now her eyes held bewilderment. "I was searching for a place where I could go to pick out and purchase my own produce. Do you know of anyplace in St. Paul?"

Matt must have seemed comically helpless to her, a resident of this area. She smiled a little and ventured the information. "The only place I know of is across the Mississippi in South St. Paul. A collective of people meets there to trade various commodities. You might find something there." The look on Matt's face gave her the courage to venture more information. "Take the 400 Rapid T from the station five blocks down this street." The woman pointed in a westerly direction. "It won't pay to find a seat, you'll be off before you know it. You will see some semi-circular metal structures. This is where the people congregate with things they want to trade." She studied Matt, seeming to want to offer more information. But instead she said, "Well, good luck."

Matt checked his watch. He had over two hours before his supper date with Amy and he wasn't about to give up on finding ingredients for salad. He took off on a sprint to the station. Checking the schedule he found he would not have long to wait for a transport and there would be one coming back to this spot, the closest to his pod, on the half-hour. Sliding his pass card at the gate he entered the platform. There was an odd assortment of people waiting with him. Some, he guessed, were people like the young woman who had helped him, workers in factories or in the service trades. Some were businessmen and women, well dressed, probably on their way to Chicago, the main destination for the 400 Rapid T. Some were more difficult to categorize. They may have been students like him, or people unscheduled for work. He didn't feel ill at ease, just curious.

The 400 Rapid T appeared, silently, from the north. Passengers exited and those waiting with him entered the transport. Following the suggestion from the young woman, he stood, prepared for a slight sensation of forward movement. Other passengers sat in bench seats and opened their portable consoles. All around him the faint transparent holograms shared space with seats and walls and passengers, the conversations unavailable to all but the individuals who were connecting. As silently, and imperceptibly as the transport had started, it came to a stop. Many people exited. The well-dressed passengers remained.

Matt made his way to the semi-circular sheds he had observed from the transport platform. As described to him, small groups of people were milling about makeshift tables. More tables and people were under cover of the open sheds. As Matt approached he could see that the tables contained assortments of what appeared to be clusters of plant matter held together with string or bands. Some had root systems, some were cut. A wrinkly-faced woman in brightly colored clothing had a table with containers out of which flowers of all colors were available. Inspired, Matt walked to her table and asked to purchase a bunch of particularly lovely pink and yellow blossoms. He held his pass card out to the woman. She looked at him in disbelief, studying his manner of dressing and the electronics wired into his clothing. "You've never been here before, have you," she said as a statement of fact rather than as a question.

Matt replied, "I came because I was unable to buy basic ingredients for making a salad at the WFMD. I met a young woman who gave me directions to come here. She said I might find what I was looking for."

"She didn't tell you how to pay?"

"No, we didn't get that far in the conversation." Matt began to feel uncomfortable.

"Well, I'll fill you in." she said without warmth or kindness in her voice. She had sized up Matt as a young wealthy geek. He was no more welcome here than she would have been in the House of Governors. "This is an Exchange," she said. "If you have some dried peas or beans or other commodity that I want, I'll give you your flowers. But I see you have nothing, nothing at all I need, only plastic, and I cannot eat plastic. Good day!" She stood up, dismissing Matt as she went about rearranging the vases of flowers.

Unused to such treatment, Matt moved away, bewildered. He wandered about taking in all he saw. When the people didn't notice him, they were joyful, teasing, and friendly to each other. When his presence was apparent, they withdrew and became quiet. Matt used up 20 to 30 minutes of the time he had until he would have to board the T going north. He was shocked by the treatment he had received and unsuccessful in his goal to purchase lettuce for his salad. He wandered in and out of the sheds. He was about to leave when he caught the eye of a bearded old man gazing at him. The sign on his table said 'Mushrooms' and a broken basket held his wares.

"So, what do you think of all this? We are the bottom of the heap, but a happy heap for the most part." the old man called out. This was the friendliest overture Matt had experienced. He walked over to the old man. The man held out his hand for a welcoming handshake. Matt felt a lump come into his throat from this first kindness. The hand was tan, with dirt embedded into the crevices and under the nails. It was warm and when Matt looked into the eyes of the old man, they sparkled with enjoyment. "I'm Jim Kranz," he stated, "nice to have a visitor in my domain."

Matt responded in kind, "I'm Matt Bordeau. I'm a student on a mission to buy some lettuce to make a homemade salad to impress a young woman."

"Impressing young women is way out of my league," Jim teased, "but I remember how urgent such a mission can be."

Both men laughed, brought together by the knowledge of the universal striving of youth. Matt came back to the errand he was on and asked, "Is it possible to find lettuce and other raw vegetables around here?"

"Oh yes, it is possible," Jim answered, "However I don't think you have any bargaining power."

Puzzled again by his answer and the workings of this place, Matt innocently brought out his pass card. "I thought I would buy some."

"Hmmm," the old man mused, "you are light years away from how we operate here. Don't you know that the buying and selling of food, the real, unprocessed, and homegrown food, is strictly illegal. Other commodities as well are taxed to such an extreme by the Governors that no one here would ever trade goods for money such as you have in your hand."

"Then what are you doing here with your baskets of mushrooms?"

"Oh, I am the Mushroom Man, the Mushroom Man, the Mushroom man!" Jim sang. He was teasing again and Matt felt more confused than before. He checked the time and saw that the next transport would leave in ten minutes.

"Well Jim, it was nice to meet someone who would talk to me. I have to catch the next transport in a few minutes. I guess I've failed the lettuce test."

"If you are serious in learning about how we manage here, I would be glad to talk with you again. I do appreciate the company." Jim had stopped singing and was more serious. "You have done nothing to deserve such bad treatment from me and others I would guess. Please come again."

Matt was thinking he would never set foot in this area again, but out of respect for the old gentleman he thanked him graciously and left the possibility of a return visit open. Matt turned and walked toward the station. Jim Kranz watched him leave. Suddenly he called out, "Say, Matt. When you come back, bring something to barter. I would trade you some mushrooms for an old jacket!"

Matt thought the guy was looped but he answered, "Sure thing Jim. See ya!" He sprinted up the hill and away from this world to the Rapid T Station.

Amy's day had gone much better than Matt's. In her own disciplined style, she obtained the can of well water early in the day, studied, went to class, did some research, ate lunch, straightened up her study, and checked her mail. She went for a long run in the early afternoon, taking her run-about south to a wayside along the Chippewa River and parking there. She ran along a section of old trail where she could enjoy the beauty of the river.

The trail upon which Amy ran was an extension of an old Indian Trail from the eighteenth century. The Old Abe Trail ran from Chippewa Falls to a park near Cornell. Extensions of the trail ran from the winter residence of the Native American Indians, the Ojibwe, near the banks of the Chippewa River north to the summer residence near Lac Court Oreilles. From there it followed the banks of the Namekagon River and eventually ended in the community of La Pointe on Madeline Island in Lake Superior.

The community of La Pointe was home to the Ojibwe Native Americans. According to Ojibwe prophecy, the Great Spirit told the Anishinaabe band of Ojibwe to move west from the Atlantic coast until they found the "food that grows on water." They found the wild rice on Lake Superior's Chequamegon Bay and settled.

When Amy returned home she took a long shower, setting the soap and shampoo cycle at six minutes. The misting soap and shampoo spray enveloped her from all directions, taking the soreness out of her. She set a cooler than usual rinse temperature and a cool dry without a normalizer.

Now she prepared her salad from the bartered goods at the farmer's market in town. Amy learned in the three years she had lived in the outskirts of Flambeau that she could buy prepackaged, processed commodities from the local food distribution center and then use these to barter with the farmers in the area who grew the vegetables she desired. She submerged the lettuce and spinach in separate bowls and washed a tomato and a pepper. It was mid-June and only a small amount of broccoli was available for a premium barter. She washed the broccoli and upon seeing a cabbage worm, she took another bowl out, filled it with water and stirred in a spoonful of salt. She let the broccoli and its hidden inhabitants sit in the briny bath. She turned back to the lettuce.

As time consuming as the process was, Amy enjoyed the art of preparing real food. When she and her mom purchased the property, the old house contained antique food preparation equipment. Amy begged her mom to keep it in storage for her. Now she used some of it. As she cooked she let her mind wander to the bygone era of a hundred years ago.

She imagined a history of this one property and the people who lived on this land before her. It was a shame to have the house sold for salvage and then destroyed, but it was not habitable. Rodents had taken over, enlarged their doorways and their families. Even for someone like Amy, always interested in the natural world, this was a bit much to deal with. So they salvaged and stored some interesting antiques.

One was a white appliance that came with a box of circular blades and other gizmos. There was a box shaped appliance that said, "Food Dehydrator"; some knives, heavy in weight with black handles; an assortment of stainless steel bowls, pots, utensils; and a heating device. There was also a heavy motorized machine with lots of parts. A silver band near the top of the machine said, "K5A". They found little documentation on these things and the salvage worker shook his head, saying it was worth more by weight of the copper windings than by its antique or functional value. But Amy insisted, and these things were cleaned and placed in a storage locker in Flambeau.

Amy was mesmerized by some of the pictures on the walls, most were in broken frames and the paper was brittle and yellowed. She did save one small one that she found in a drawer. It was a picture of a young couple and two little children with a dog. Amy was drawn to the photo of the woman. There was sadness deep inside this woman. Amy wondered about her story, the woman with the handsome young husband. The little boy looked to be about four and then there was the baby swaddled in a pastel pink blanket. The mother did not try to show the baby's face. That seemed a little strange. Maybe the sadness came from something about the baby. Amy wondered what had become of the young family. The county records showed that this building had been empty for over seventy years. The names Amy and her mother found on records meant nothing to them, but Amy collected some scraps of paper with names and dates which had not been destroyed by the elements and placed them with the aging photo. It seemed such a loss. The history of these people who once lived in a home on the banks of the Chippewa River--gone forever--as the salvage company picked apart the worthy goods and loaded the rest into the waiting dumpster.

With the lettuce washed and gently torn into bits, Amy looked at the broccoli floating in the water. Two little pale green caterpillar worms had succumbed to the salt. Amy peered at them, taking a spoon and lifting them out of the water onto the counter. The biologist poked about the multiple feet and the large head of one of the critters. Amy wondered about the potential food value and then considered the possible toxicity. She thought she remembered from her readings that silk worm larvae in China were eaten as a delicacy. Delicacy or not, food or poison, the worms were dumped into a small trash container and forgotten as Amy arranged the lettuce on her plate. She broke the broccoli into small bits, sliced a little tofu, and sprinkled some dried tomatoes on the salad. Amy was nurturing a tomato plant outside the window of her abode. It had flowers but no tomatoes yet. It was her first attempt at gardening. She had saved seeds from the tomatoes from last year. She bought a great many tomatoes and tried to preserve them. She took the dehydrator out of storage for the first time. Much of her effort was trial and error; some of the tomatoes had turned dark after drying and some were not dried enough for her taste. She dreamed of more success this year. She had found information also on the K5A machine. It turned out to be an 'aide' to kitchen work, the name she found was 'Kitchen-Aide'. It was a multi-use mixer. She learned she could make bread with it if she could find a source for the ingredients. It was the heaviest appliance she had saved other than the boxy electric contraption for the old-fashioned style cooking and baking. A dollop of yogurt, some salt and pepper, and a splash of vinegar finished off her work. She nibbled on the unused pieces as she cleaned up her kitchen.

Even the cleaning up of this small food preparation space was enjoyable. There was little room so the ancient equipment she had saved from salvage had to be reboxed and stacked. She put a bright colored piece of fabric over the stack of boxes and used the top as a place to put a vase (another salvage piece) with flowers she picked from the outside. Today she carried the vase and her salad plate to the study. Amy surveyed the scene critically. She made sure that the details of the salad and the vase with the flowers would be visible from Matt's stationary hologram eye. She stacked the papers and books behind her and left the clutter on the floor. A smile began to turn the corner of her mouth upward and broke into a full grin. "I'm really getting ready for a date!" she said aloud to no one but herself.

Matt closed off the noisy city sounds when he shut the door to his pod. He was not in a good mood. And he was exhausted. For the first time he was not looking forward to the coming encounter with the girl with the energetic ponytail. He consumed a bottle of water—Thundering Water—he noted and flopped his sweaty body onto the floor. Within minutes he was asleep. His dream was of a dark tunnel that was running down, down toward a pinpoint of light. The longer he ran, the farther away the light seemed and when he glanced backward, it was only dark. In his dream he turned around and ran backward, stumbling over rocks and unseen objects in his path, lit only by the light behind him. He came to a place where the tunnel ended; he was confused by this and felt the walls all around with his hands to find the opening that must be there. The walls were wet and cold like a cave and Matt's hands were wet and cold with a tingling sensation. He put his face to the wet wall; his hair and cheek quickly soaked up the water that must have been trickling in from somewhere. Matt felt thirsty and stuck his tongue out onto the wall. The bitter, acrid taste jolted him awake. He turned over slowly, painfully aware that his head had been cushioned by his hands on the cool, hard floor.

Matt shuddered as if to shake off the memory of the dream. It was still with him as he looked at the time, groaning as he shifted into high gear to shower before his dinner date with Amy. He selected a short sequence and while inside, switched it to a longer sequence. As he stepped out and dressed he realized he was famished. Matt did not typically wait to eat and was burdened by his gnawing hunger and his promise to Amy. Giving in to hunger he quickly chose a meal packet, placing it in the food preparer. He dug in, not enjoying it in the least but at any rate it satisfied his hunger. He drank more water and chose a bottled, fermented ale to sip during his conversation with Amy. He was now a little more relaxed and, with ten minutes to go, he carried snacks and the ale to the den. There was nothing to tidy up. Matt switched on the console, sighing over his failure to bring real food to the table.

When Matt called up Amy's code, he saw her empty den with her salad, flower vase, and glass of water. He was early; she wasn't late. Taking a sip of ale, he took time to really look at her addition to the standard pod. It was a small room with light streaming in from a westerly direction. There were books from floor to ceiling and a step stool leaning against one bookshelf. Matt thought about the stool and Amy's height. He hadn't considered this before. She would have to be rather short, maybe up to his shoulder. He saw trinkets, stones, and a photo of Amy with an older woman--her mother he guessed. There was also a photo of two young children with parents and a dog. He would ask Amy about those photos when it was the right time.

Amy had left her den to check on her appearance, something she never took time to think about. She scrutinized her reflection in the full-length mirror. Her mouth and nose were her mom's. She also inherited her mother's gene for being short. Her dark eyes and brown hair were more from her dad's side of the family. It would have been silly to dress up for this dinner date she thought. Then the corner of her mouth pulled upward into a smile as she thought about Matt and knew he would be waiting.

As Amy entered her study she could see Matt's hologram and she could tell something was wrong. Her inward smile disappeared. She looked at him before the cam brought her into his room, trying to discern what was wrong from the look on his face and his mood. Then she saw the glass of ale and cello bags of snack foods. Was this it? Was he ruminating over the food issue? She resolved not to tease him as she entered, "Hi Matt!"

"Oh, hi Amy." Matt's voice was subdued.

Amy considered her options and true to her nature she approached him head on. "Matt, something appears to be bothering you. Is this not a good time for us to meet?" and then the doctor in her added, "Can you tell me what is wrong?"

Matt's face broke into the big, warm smile Amy loved. "Well doc," he teased, "as you might have noticed, I've failed in my promise to bring a healthy, from scratch salad for dinner."

Relieved at his reply and even more relieved to see his smile she said, "I have a hunch you've never participated in the bartering for food system. I didn't think to tell you about it, I sort of assumed it was something you'd know about. Is that all you are eating?"

"This time it is my turn for a long story, as long as you have time for it," he joked. "I've eaten my regular fare already, foraging for food in the woods and prairies of South St. Paul has taken its toll. I was famished and couldn't help but eat when I got home. Sorry. Please, you eat, I'll watch and drool."

Amy laughed and picked up her fork. She was very hungry. "So tell all."

"Well I located a WFM—and planned the trip to get lettuces

and other things I might buy to coincide with my run today. They would only allow me to buy processed food. Then I met a person who told me about a gathering place for people who might have what I needed. I took the Rapid T there and tried to buy something—actually," Matt looked at the lovely bouquet of flowers on Amy's desk and hesitated before deciding to divulge more of his feelings for Amy, "actually it was flowers. I tried to buy a bunch of flowers from a woman at this place." Matt stopped, wondering what Amy thought and unsure if he should look at her face.

Amy, for her part, felt a warm flush come into her face when Matt talked about the flowers. She tried not to show the significance of what Matt had just said. "What happened?"

"She was very haughty, gave me a hard time, and made me feel very foolish. As you can see, she didn't let me buy flowers."

Amy noticed his second use of the word, 'flowers'. "Did she tell you about the bartering system?"

"Not really, she alluded to it. I still don't really get it. Later I met this old guy with mushrooms on his table."

"Mushrooms, wow!"

"Do you like mushrooms?

"Fresh mushrooms are something very, very hard to come by. I wonder how he came to have them? They are worth a lot and the bartering of mushrooms is looked upon by the government as highly suspect. That old man was taking a risk."

Matt whistled. "Well he wouldn't sell any mushrooms to me, but he was the only one who was nice enough to have a conversation with me. He actually apologized for the behavior of the people there. Then he got a little goofy and started singing some silly song about being the mushroom man. When I started to leave he sort of gave me an insight into the system when he told me to bring a jacket for him and he would give me mushrooms."

"Do you have a jacket you could do without?"

"You really are interested in those mushrooms," Matt joked, then he added, "Do you think I would really get some mushrooms for an old jacket?"

"Well, that depends on whether the jacket has value for the old man. If he is about your size and could wear the jacket, needs a jacket, then he will give you a fair amount of mushrooms for it. However, mushrooms are very perishable. He might not have any in the next few days. I still wonder where he gets his mushrooms."

"Would I be able to use some or all of the mushrooms to get fresh lettuce and other vegetables like you have?"

"Very likely! These items are more common. Many people who make a living by trading commodities in the people's market will have these vegetables. But you need to bring containers of your own to put them in."

"Whew! More and more complicated! I can see why the Governors let us buy our processed foods—but why the problem with using my pass card for the purchase of fresh food?"

"Selling unprocessed vegetables and fruits is strictly prohibited. The Governors say the food is unsafe, and they tout the processed food as being more delicious and easier to prepare—which it is, at least easier to prepare. As far as being unsafe, I have my own opinions and theories about processed food and bottled water."

Matt and Amy were quiet, Amy thoughtfully poking at her broccoli and Matt sipping his ale.

Matt broke the silence. "Maybe I have to break another promise, this one to myself."

"What's that?"

"I vowed never to return to that place, but maybe I have to. Maybe I have to bring that old guy—Jim is his name—a jacket."

"Hmmm," commented Amy as she finished her dinner; she was thinking it would be fun to show Matt how to barter. Originally it had taken quite a bit of courage to approach a table at the farmers' market and open a conversation with people she had very little in common with. She was unsure of the value of the food and afraid of being scorned or laughed at so she wandered the aisles of tents and tables watching others do their shopping. The first time she bartered she gave a pound of sugar for just a few tomatoes, something she would never do now. As Matt chatted away about the jacket he had that might fit the old man, Amy only half listened, lost in her own thoughts.

"Say!" Matt startled her with his sudden declaration. "Would you consider coming here to help me barter my jacket for some mushrooms from Jim?"

Amy wondered if Matt had read her mind. She was suddenly glad the technology had not advanced in that direction. She looked at his face, boyishly excited about his idea. In some ways she wanted to go, to help him learn some of the strategies for bartering that she had figured out. However, a voice in the back of her mind cautioned her against it.

Amy smiled at Matt, carefully choosing her words, "Matt, this is something you can figure out on your own, without me. I think if Jim is there he will help you along with some sage advice." She noticed his smile becoming forced, but he did not look away from her eyes. She tried to explain, " The city is a place I'd rather not return to." Matt continued to watch her closely.

"I'll tell you what, if you do go back and get mushrooms tomorrow, you can bring them here, to Flambeau. There will be a huge celebration this week-end—at least huge for Flambeau," she added. "It is their centennial, a hundred years celebration. They have one like this every hundred years. This must be their fifth I guess or maybe their fourth. They will dig up a time capsule Friday night that was placed in the ground a hundred years ago. Over the weekend bits and pieces from the time capsule will be made public and some stuff will be on display. We can take some of your mushrooms to the farmers' market and barter them for the lettuces you couldn't get in St. Paul." Amy began to envision sharing the weekend activities with Matt and her imagination took hold of her. Then we will come back to my abode and prepare a meal..." Amy flushed with embarrassment as she realized how she was taking over.

"I'm game!" Matt cried out.

Amy wondered again where all her words came from and why she had invited Matt so easily. Her life was getting more and more complicated. Especially since Matt was going along with all her imaginings.

"I'll go back tomorrow to get those mushrooms before I lose Jim," and to himself he added, "and your invitation."

Amy stopped wondering why she had invited Matt. She had said the words and now worked on a plan of action. "And we can look now to see how close the mass transport comes to Flambeau. It's been a while since I've had to take it with my run-about. I think it will come to Chippewa Falls but no closer. I'll hike or jog in to Flambeau to meet you and we can use your run-about to tour the area around the two rivers before the grand opening of the time capsule."

"Let's see," Matt was ticking off the tasks he needed to complete to make this work, "I'll bring along some of the beer from the ancient brewery in St. Paul. They stopped making it before the year 1995 and then when they had all this excess mash from the production of ethanol, they started up again, in the same old brewery. When the production of ethanol stopped, they were going to close down, but the Minnesotans had become so enamored with the brew that they found another source for the mash and probably the water. You can still buy it today."

Amy laughed, "You don't need to bring anything but mushrooms!"

They spent the next fifteen minutes checking on the mass transport routes and schedules. It did indeed come as far as Chippewa Falls; the best option for Matt was the afternoon arrival a little after five. Matt would call Amy after his rendezvous with the mushroom man to confirm. It was 11:30 PM when they finished all the arrangements.

"Well, goodnight," said Amy.

"See you tomorrow," Matt answered.

Amy turned the console off, realizing how much she would like to do before Matt's arrival. She realized she had not considered that he would be staying with her in this small abode, crammed from top to bottom with her belongings. Amy carried her dishes to the kitchen and into the sink. She stood there with another realization: it was at least four years since she prepared food for anyone but herself. This visit was going to be a challenge in more ways than one. She stared out the open window at a rabbit nibbling on the grass. She was suddenly weak and nauseous, and extremely exhausted as she wondered what she would do about the water? Would she hide her precious water from Matt or would she tell all. Too tired now to clean up her supper dishes, Amy made her way to the lav and prepared for bed. There was so much to do, so much to carefully think through. She lay down upon her bed and fell into a restless sleep dreaming of Ned, her well, and Matt.

Matt was on cloud nine. He turned off his console and the holographic image of Amy, but he could not turn her image off in his mind. This day, although he failed in his attempts to impress Amy in one way, had turned into a big forward movement in the development of their relationship. Tomorrow, he would win over Jim's support, bring back mushrooms for Amy, and maybe even get flowers for her from that obnoxious woman. Matt couldn't contain his excitement. He located a duffel bag and packed his clothes and lav supplies. Then he located the jacket he planned to give Jim. Seeing two shirts that he didn't like wearing, he folded them and placed it all in a vacpac. Then he paced around his pod trying to find just the right item to barter for flowers. He checked the FSD. There, toward the back was a chocolate bar he had never opened. Grinning, he placed it atop the vacpac. Flowers for chocolate, he thought gleefully. It was 1:05 AM and Matt was still wired as he prepared for bed. Out of desperation he took a relaxant, a seven-hour dosage so that he would be able to get up early.

The next morning, moments before the relaxant disappeared from his blood stream, Matt opened his eyes. He couldn't move yet, but his mental faculties had returned. At 8:15 Matt's body cooperated and he bounded up from bed. He chose a high caloric energy drink for breakfast. As he gulped the orange, milky fluid he looked over the packing he had completed the night before. He pulled on his running clothes and stuffed his small running pac with the jacket, shirts, and chocolate bar. He tried to add a bottle of water, but it didn't fit so he decided he'd carry it as he ran. He was out the door by 8:40.

Matt was dripping with perspiration as he entered the 400 Rapid T. The immaculately dressed crowd, each sitting as though an invisible shield separated them from the rest of the humanity on the bus; wirelessly working, in deep concentration, didn't notice his arrival on the train. A few of the locals gave him a glance that said the expenditure of energy and subsequent loss of water from his system was stupid. Two teenage girls eyed him up and down, giggling to themselves. An old duffer in a blue suit, hanging on his frame, commented under his breath. Of these passengers and others, Matt was completely unaware. His focus was Jim, Amy, mushrooms, and flowers. His imagination was taking hold of his thoughts. Everything else faded from his consciousness.

As the Rapid T slowed, the doors opened and Matt was carried by the wave of people; the momentum of the crowd carried him, a surfer, out of the transport and deposited him a distance away. The wave receded, dispersing the individuals, as easily as grains of sand, to the series of semi-circular buildings. Here, the aggregate grew again, milling about as if with no purpose.

Matt had a purpose. He moved with great strides towards the place where he met Jim. He moved past the flower lady. She didn't make the effort of glancing his way. He wondered if Jim had bartered all the mushrooms, or worse, would not be there to offer friendly advice and ideas. He shouldn't have worried, mushrooms were too exotic for most of the locals and Jim had only traded a few measly bags. He was there, lounging in his old chair in the shade, a few mushrooms graced the folding table, proclaiming their availability.

As Matt came to the table, Jim smiled broadly. "Hey, I see you're back! What can I do for you today?" Jim eyed the pac on Matt's waist.

"I brought you a present, well, sort of," Matt said, "I need mushrooms and advice, and I would appreciate your friendship and help in learning the ropes around here."

"So, you're still after lettuces and a girl?" Jim teased. "You've come to the right place. I won't vie for the damsel's attentions, lettuces are far more interesting to a man of my years."

Matt smiled. He was beginning to be fond of this old guy. "I have a jacket for you, and also two shirts." He opened the vac pac, pulling out the shirts and shaking out the wrinkles. He handed them one at a time to Jim as he finished. Then he held up the jacket.

Jim's eyebrows went up and he eyed Matt. He would have, in his younger days, taken advantage of Matt's inexperience. Now, at his age, he needed more than clothing and shelter. He needed kindness and friendship.

"These are worth all the mushrooms I have." Jim lifted a cloth covering a cardboard box filled with mushrooms.

Matt smiled. "I could never use or carry all of this, I'm trading for mushrooms and intelligence. Would you help me with some other things here?"

Jim looked at Matt. If he could have had a son, he would have traded everything he owned. But he kept his emotions to himself and said, "I'll help you in any way I can."

Matt reached across the table to shake Jim's hand. It was dry, warm, and surprisingly strong for an older man. The two men, separated by class, advantage, and age smiled upon each other.

Matt explained his wish to bring Amy flowers. He showed Jim the chocolate bar in the bottom of his pac that he intended to barter for flowers. It was a little soft from being out of the FSD. Jim eyed the candy bar and his mouth watered. Then Jim asked what size bag Matt had to carry the mushrooms. Matt had forgotten he would need to bring something to carry his bartered goods.

"Here's what I propose," Jim leaned back in his chair, "I will keep one shirt, the jacket, and the candy bar. Rita, the obnoxious gal over there with the flowers has two grown boys. She will value the shirt above the candy bar. Her flowers aren't worth much, but she just bartered a bowl of tomatoes and peppers and she has some bags that she uses around here. You need a way to keep the flowers cool and fresh for your trip. I say we give her a shirt for a bouquet of posies, 2 tomatoes, two peppers, and two of her bags."

"You think she'll go for it?" He gazed over at Rita.

"Now don't blow it by staring at her!" Jim reprimanded Matt and then added more gently, "You see, Matt, everyone here is so tuned into the behavior of people around them. If you, an outsider to our community, stare at her, she will know you want something and the stakes will be higher."

"See Jim, you are worth your weight in mushrooms and intelligence!"

Jim smiled and got up from his chair. "Let's mosey on over the other way so she forgets about you for a while." Jim and Matt meandered around the tables of the vendors, with Jim telling stories about the people; their lives and their troubles. Matt was fascinated by Jim's stories. Most of the people looked older than Jim's estimate of their ages. Matt attributed this to their hard life. He thought about how easy his life was in comparison and he thought about how his parents used their lives to give him everything necessary to achieve his dreams. He imagined himself in the bio-chem industry, helping the common man have an easier life.

After almost an hour Jim's pace slowed and his left leg dragged a little in the soft dirt. Matt said, "You know, Jim, I want to come back and learn more from you. But could we finish our trading now so I can catch the transport to Chippewa Falls?"

Jim regarded Matt, a young man with dreams and the means of achieving them. He thought about the girl of Matt's dreams and picture of his own wife, dead now for many years came into his mind. In his memory she was toiling in the garden, pregnant and happy. His heart caught in his throat. He didn't want to remember more, more of the miscarriage, sadness, and pain in their lives.

Many people living in the housing complex with Jim and his wife suffered the loss of infants and young children. If these people would have access to the statistics, they would have learned that the mortality rate for the young and old in this socio-economic class was very high. But of course no one in Jim's social class would have the means to search a database with this kind of classified information. He came back to the present and grinned at Matt, "Well, young sir, we are right here!"

Indeed, they had made a complete circuit of the market; coming up on their left was the ominous flower lady. "Hi ya, Rita!" Jim called out.

"Well, looky here, an old duffer with a young gentleman." Rita was more friendly with Jim than she had been yesterday with Matt. "Ya know I'm not fancy enough to cook mushrooms and serve them on a platter with a silver spoon. So what are you wasting my time for?" Rita was teasing Jim with a dig at Matt.

"Whoa, girl, I'm not here to sell you any of my special mushrooms. My friend here has a trade he'd like to make with you."

Rita frowned slightly, remembering yesterday's encounter with Matt. "Well now, what do you have for me?"

"Hello Rita. I would like to give you a shirt for your son if you would give me a bunch of your pretty flowers, two tomatoes, and two peppers." Matt pulled out the shirt from his pack.

"And," Jim interjected, "The young man needs two of your shopping bags."

"What?" Rita was not pleased that Jim was helping Matt. She was sweet on the old man, but distrusting of the young one.

"I need the bags to carry your things and mushrooms from Jim." Matt explained.

"Well, I'll give you the flowers and two bags, but no veggies in trade for the shirt." Rita sounded unconcerned with Matt's plight, however, she had noticed his waist pack and was calculating whether Matt would part with such an expensive item.

"Come on Rita, give the young fella what he's after. Have a heart." Jim cajoled.

"Listen here, Matt. I have two sons and you have only one shirt. If you were, say to give me also that silly pac on your waist, I'd trade you a big bunch of flowers, the two tomatoes and one pepper."

Jim smiled and winked at Rita. She was one of his favorites, often plucking a flower from her bouquets and putting it in his button hole. Rita saw the wink but her countenance toward Matt did not change.

Matt kicked at the dirt with his toe. "<u>Two</u> peppers," he countered.

Rita smiled broadly. She won. "You drive a hard bargain, young sir," she stated as she put the tomatoes, peppers, and bunch of flowers into one of her cloth bags. Matt undid his waist pac, removing his pass card. "I thought I got what was in the bag too," she teased.

Matt realized it was a tease and he smiled genuinely at Rita, "Thank-you, kind lady. I hope I can come back and do business with you again."

Rita reached out to shake hands. Her hand was large, rough, and dry. It held his hand, smooth, muscled, and strong. Rita looked at this man-boy, only a few years older than her son with such a different life ahead of him. His handshake had given her an insight into Matt's character. As they parted and he turned to walk away she smiled to herself. He was heading in a new direction from others in his class; she could feel it.

FLAMBEAU 2187

A mechanical voice announced, "Rural Transport arrival one minute, Chippewa Falls. You will be exited at ramps A & B. Your support of Mass T supports a cleaner environment." Matt disengaged the parking brake of his run-about. He was surrounded by his backpack and the two grocery bags from Rita. Her flowers looked a little less perky than when he bartered for them. The mushrooms gave off a pungent smell. The tomatoes and peppers were probably fine, he had wrapped them in some paper to try to protect the ripe vegetables from being bruised.

Automatically his run-about began its downward descent to the ramp. When it arrived at the bottom, he engaged the clutch and it was on its own power. He was near the large power generating plant of the city, located in the same place as the electric turbo plant of long ago. It still boasted the name NSP, but this time the river water served another purpose in producing electricity.

He parked his run-about, getting out for a brief stretch and to program his GPS to find the road to Flambeau.

Unknown to Matt, the road he was about to take had a very long and rich history. Part of the road included Amy's favorite trail along the banks of the Chippewa River. Part of the road was called Old County E and part of the road was designated a Rustic Road. It curved along the Chippewa River providing a view of the oldest mountain range in the United States, the Blue Hills. Geologists would tell you the Blue Hills and Flambeau Mountain where Amy ran were of the same vintage. The exposed rocks were the oldest rocks one could see in Wisconsin.

Amy made some preparations for Matt's visit during the morning and early afternoon. She was unaccountably nervous and felt the way she had felt when she made the decision to move to the little abode in Flambeau. By 2:00 she was ready for a shower and eager to leave her abode, an unusual feeling for Amy. She dressed for her run, but took a small backpack with a tunic to wear later on when she met up with Matt. She felt a premonition. Something was about to happen that she couldn't grasp.

She left at a little after 3:00, way too early she told herself. She had tried to do some reading, tried to work on the writing for her research. Her typical disciplined style was gone. "Oh well", she thought, "I'll look around at the festival and see if there is anything Matt might enjoy. Maybe check out the farmer's market to see what's available". She did not know how she would keep busy, but anything was better than being alone.

The time went slowly for Amy. She wandered aimlessly around as she cooled down after her run. Matt had called to say he would get there closer to 4:45. There was still a lot of time to kill. She meandered down the main street, really the only street of Flambeau. She saw Ned and would have gone over to talk with him except that her instincts told her that it would not be wise considering Matt's pending arrival. It was lucky Ned hadn't noticed her. She came to the center of the town. The left and right side of the street parted around a small flower garden and statue of a Native American, caste in bronze. He was drinking from what would have been a leather pouch. The inscription indicated the confluence of the Flambeau and the Chippewa and was meant to show the significance and strength of the Ojibwe nation, nourished by the waters of the two rivers. Amy had always enjoyed looking at the statue, even as stereotyped as it was. She enjoyed trying to understand the history of the Lac Du Flambeau tribe of the Ojibwe. It was interesting to think about how they must have lived not far from her abode but separated from her by three or four hundred years.

Here, at the statue, was the place that the time capsule had been buried, exactly one hundred years ago. Amy found that to be very exciting and she hoped Matt would find it to be at least interesting enough to watch the ceremony of the unearthing of the vault and capsule. She wondered what information people from a hundred years ago would feel was important for the future. She read the poster describing the ceremony and learned that along with the Flambeau community time capsule, there would be other capsules that were purchased by individuals who lived in 2087—people who wanted to share their own stories with relatives in the future. The festival organizers were taking this opportunity to raise much-needed funds for the children in the community by offering to match the DNA of today's citizens with the DNA of people who purchased time capsules back in 2087. Funds were to go toward reducing the cost of health services. This was a mission near and dear to Amy's heart. She was torn between medical research and pediatrics. She made a mental note to purchase a ticket for the opportunity to see if her genetics were a match with any of the people who had individual time capsules. She was quite sure she wouldn't be a match but the money was for a cause she believed in and it would be fun to have the chance to submit her DNA. It was just a lot of hoopla she felt, but still good fun.

Smiling with this thought, she glanced at the time and decided Matt would be arriving soon. She began walking with a purpose, her heart beating more quickly in anticipation of seeing Matt, in the flesh. Arriving in the park she sat on an old wooden park bench and suddenly wondered if he was really coming or whether he encountered any unforeseen delays. She decided to call rather than wait and get more and more nervous, but before she could, she saw movement in the distance and within a few seconds, there he was.

Matt was smiling broadly, and to Amy's eyes he looked darker and more handsome than his hologram. She reached out to shake his hand wondering how she appeared to him. She felt Matt take her hand. He held it and didn't let go. When she started to giggle nervously, he brought her hand to his lips, giving it a gentle kiss. "Hello, Amy Anderson!" he said, letting go of her hand.

"Well, hi yourself, Matt Bordeau!" Her discomfort melted away. Not to be outdone and always a tease, she placed her hands upward to reach the sides of his face. "You are quite a bit taller than the holocam shows."

Matt opened his pack to show her the mushrooms, but he kept the sac with the flowers from her sight.

"You know, Matt, it is really quite early. Let's take your run-about to my abode and we can store the mushrooms for a meal tomorrow. Tonight I thought we'd sample some of the local festival cuisine. Then we can take the scenic drive back to Flambeau. We'll get here in time for the unearthing of the time capsule, we'll have dinner, and then go back home."

"Sounds good," Matt replied, "I could stand to wash up a little and get my bearings."

They wedged themselves into the run-about. Amy felt peculiar about all this touching but it did feel right. Sitting beside him she pointed out where to turn and chatted about some of the lore of the Flambeau community.

Matt tried to look at Amy from the side while listening to her talk and while trying to understand where they were going so he could seem more in charge on the way back. There were too many things to think about and he resigned himself to following her directions and looking at her when he could. She had him stop on a small hill to look back at the town. "There's the town park with the Native American statue I told you about. That's where the time capsule is."

"That should be interesting," he commented, though history was not on his mind. Matt had never been interested in history, probably because his family had never encouraged his curiosity about the past.

Amy sensed he was not interested and she tried to tell Matt what she found fascinating. After a few moments she could tell it was a lost cause. She directed him to the trail that lead to her home. Along the way Matt asked questions about the infrastructure of Flambeau, where the electricity was produced and where the drinking water came from. These were topics that he knew a lot about and could converse about easily. Now it was Amy's turn to say, "That's interesting."

Matt laughed. "No it isn't, it's just my all consuming interest. But I did think the topic of water would spark more enthusiasm".

Amy answered quietly, "Not enthusiasm. Remember, I am truly worried about the water."

"I apologize." Matt said, remembering how passionately she spoke that first day.

"I'll tell you more one day if you like—not today." They turned in the driveway, a driveway overhung with great limbs of leafy trees. Matt stopped the run-about between Amy's window and the well. Amy bit her lip. This was not important she told herself. Outwardly she smiled, "Home sweet home." They cautiously negotiated the space between them as they extracted themselves from the run-about. Matt pulled out the mushroom bag. Amy reached for them, intending to help Matt.

"Nope. I'll carry these." Putting the mushroom bag down on the ground, he reached for the other sack and carefully exposed the flowers. "These are for you to carry."

Amy blushed, a non-typical body response, she thought, but she said, "That is very sweet of you."

"Remember my story of Rita? These are from her table."

Matt reached for his duffel bag with his right hand and picked up the mushrooms with his left. "Ready," he said lightly.

Amy led the way to the door, hoping the smallness of the abode would not shock Matt. They stepped inside and Amy retrieved the vase from her study. She almost reached without thinking for the counter top water dispenser. She caught herself and turned the tap on filling the vase, placing the flowers into it. "Lovely, thanks," she said with a smile.

Matt was gazing around the kitchen, duffel in one hand and mushrooms in the other. "Well, now may I have the mushrooms?" she teased.

"Wow!" Matt said, handing her the mushrooms. "This place has a lot more personality than my hut."

Amy laughed. "My mom and I set up sort of a play housekeeping years ago. I've never gotten around to really change it. I just add more stuff." Amy had put the mushrooms away. She was now feeling uncomfortable. It was time to show Matt her room. She planned to sleep in the study. "You can leave your bag here where you will sleep." she said carelessly.

Matt quickly sized up her offer. "I'll be happier in your study, remember I've been there a lot. It's almost like home." Matt looked down at her knowing how hard this was, having him stay with her. She was about to say something, to tell him that she wished him to sleep in the nicer space. "Please?" Matt asked.

Amy sighed, "You win." and it was settled.

While Matt used the lav, Amy quickly poured water from the dispenser into two glasses. When he returned, she handed him a glass, "Cheers!" she said.

They each took a drink, Matt studying her. "You know Amy, I don't think I buy your theory that this water is bad. Amy smiled.

They finished their drinks. Amy went to the lav, leaving Matt alone. He looked around the kitchen, and wondered about the dispenser on the counter. Amy caught him contemplating it. She patted it, and said, "Lots of history here. But then history doesn't interest you,"

Matt found he had nothing to say.

After Amy and Matt made up the sofa in the study into a bed, they went outdoors. Amy suggested taking her run-about so Matt could look out around the countryside and not have to concentrate so much. In truth, her run-about was a little wider and she hoped to feel more at ease in this way, next to Matt's body. It still was close quarters for someone who had had no contact with a man her age.

Matt noticed the coneflowers in the sun and the bench in the shade where her run-about was parked. "Looks like you sit here often," he said.

Without looking directly at Matt, Amy said, "It is one of my favorite spots. From here you can't see the river but you can imagine it, where it is, a half mile down the trail that the deer use, beyond the tree line. The trail the deer take eventually hooks up with the Old Abe trail--the one I was on at the top of Flambeau mountain when that doe crossed my path."

"Can we go there?" Matt asked.

Amy looked at Matt, wondering why this city boy might be interested in the river or the trail. "Well sure. But not this evening. It is not an easy walk. The deer seem to slip through places you and I would have trouble with."

Matt was silent as they climbed in Amy's run-about. They were comfortably close. He would have liked to put his arm around her; it would have been nice, but he didn't want to make an error in judgment. After all, they would be in public and he didn't want to do anything that would push Amy too fast, although he felt he had known her for years.

Amy drove slowly, pointing out things in the natural world that she knew. When they arrived in Flambeau she drove slowly around wondering what to do next. With sudden inspiration she drove to the statue of the Ojibwe man drinking water and paused. She turned to Matt and teased, "You look a little bit like him."

It was Matt's turn to be uncomfortable. The statue wore only a loin cloth and had a very muscular build. Was that what Amy was referring to; their bodies were alike? He could only smile and say, "Hmmm."

Amy then drove to the other side of town. The roar of the river over the broken concrete of the aging dam prevented much conversation. Amy did have a chance to say that this was the site which was under consideration for the carbon scrubbing plant. It was too noisy to say much more. They parked the run-about and walked toward the center square slowly. Again Matt felt the urge to reach for her hand as they walked and he continued to remind himself that they had met only two hours ago. Instead he tried to divert his own focus to the topic of the carbon scrubber. Amy had not kept up on the status of it so she could add little to his knowledge.

They approached the gathering of people at the statue. Amy changed the subject and began to tell Matt what was about to happen. He could see that she was extremely fascinated by the time capsule event.

"Matt, I'm going to do a donation to the Flambeau children's health fund by purchasing a ticket to check my DNA against the DNA of the individuals who put in their own time capsules. I know a lot about my family history, and I know I won't be a match, but it is for a good cause." Amy pointed out the inscription on the rock that she had read earlier in the day.

Matt looked at the cost of the donation and thought to himself that if Amy valued this cause so much, he could make a contribution also. He followed her into the small line. She paid and plucked a hair from her pony tail, placing it herself into the labeled container. She turned to go and found Matt holding his pass card out to the volunteer lab technician. She reached for his arm and on tiptoe whispered in his ear, "Matt, you don't have to do this." Matt smiled. His gesture was having the right effect.

Matt joked with the lab technician about losing one more hair as he filled out the label for his strand of DNA. He asked when he would know the results. "We will run tests tomorrow and will notify you whether or not you are a match by text message as the results come in. Then, when all tests are finished, we will call in the matches to pick up their capsules –I would guess it would be Tuesday."

Amy and Matt didn't say anything else about it. After buying sandwiches from a vendor, they sat on the lawn, talking about the community and their own goals as they waited for the unearthing of the big time capsule to begin. Precisely at 8:00 PM there was a loud boom and the community band marched up the street. Seeing an amateur group in old-style uniforms marching up the street almost in step had a strange effect on the two young upward bound geeks. Amy felt a lump in her throat; sadness for everything lost that she would never experience. Matt's experience was one almost of fear, an overwhelming desire to flee this town and the secrets it held. Of course he didn't act on his fear; he sat there on the ground with his unfinished sandwich and glanced at Amy. He couldn't imagine her being afraid. He guessed that it was his limited experience of these backward communities, a fear coming from the unknown. If Matt could have been less naive and more in touch with his own psyche he would have identified the fear as coming from within, within the vast amount of family history of which he was unaware.

When the band finished their promenade around the city center, they stood at attention while the next parade unit came through. These people danced, moving up the street to the sound of a primal drum. Amy reached over, putting her hand on Matt's, if somehow sensing his discomfort. These people, Native Americans, descendants of the ancient Ojibwe, danced around the statue, chanting deep, unfamiliar words and melodies to the beating of the drum. They had jet-black hair; some men even had long braided hair. The children were moving among the adults, accepted and contributing. In the middle of the gathering of dancers was an old man with white thinning hair. Matt whispered to Amy, "He must be almost seventy."

Amy turned and looked at Matt, "I read that this is Chief Flowing Waters; he is over one hundred years old. He's considered one of the wisest of the Ojibwe elders. He will be giving the blessing."

Matt sucked in a breath; to have lived a century! In Matt's experience, that was not possible without extended life support systems and replacement surgeries. Only the wealthiest of the Governors of the Earth were able to achieve the century mark. The commoners were given little information about this kind of longevity.

The Chief gave a blessing in the native language. He had a musical deep voice and when he spoke he used few words, pausing for many seconds between sentences, looking out at individual people with a slow steady gaze. The blessing was not interpreted but the crowd seemed to know what the blessing was. As he finished he gazed again over the crowd, this time Matt distinctly felt the depth of the piercing gray eyes looking through him to his core.

The third and last parade unit followed the blessing. It was a transport that held the Flambeau Council of Government. The transport stopped and the council members, three men and three women, disembarked, each one carrying a small new shovel. Again there was a short speech. It was about the importance of community and carrying on the history of the town. Then the seven council members gathered around a plaque and placed their shovels ceremoniously around the perimeter. The community band sprang to life. With great fanfare and drum roll, the plaque was lifted out of the earth, exposing a vault like structure below.

Of course, the onlookers could not see everything that was happening. In fact, the plaque had been loosened weeks before in the dark of the night. A sand and peat mixture replaced the hard clay around the vault and the vault lock had been primed for easy release during the ceremony.

The council moved aside to allow a large mechanical lifter move into place. The operators placed chains onto the vault attachments and upon a nod from the head councilman, lifted the three-foot diameter cylinder to a prepared place on the ground in front of the statue. The band muddled through a rendition of the Song of the Earth, finishing almost precisely at 10:00 PM. Another large boom startled the crowd before they were treated to a light show in the sky. Spotlights were focused on the cylinder and it was ceremoniously opened. The honor of removing the first document was given to Chief Flowing Water. He handed a letter from a sealed container to the head councilman. The crowd was silent as they heard the first words from one hundred years ago. Other items were removed and the dancers held them high overhead so all could see as they walked around the statue. Last to be removed were ten locked capsules which were the ones purchased and placed by individuals to be given to their identified descendants. Closing remarks were brief and the show was quickly over. It would be a few days before the contents of the main capsule would be on display for the general public.

Amy looked at Matt and smiled, "Thanks for coming to this with me. It meant a lot."

"You're welcome," Matt said and as they got up to leave he continued, " You know, seeing this small community, with its pride in its history, makes me realize how shallow our lives are. We are just a bunch of worker bees. Granted, our work requires education. It's dependent upon the knowledge we gain in our college programs, but more importantly how we apply it to our professions. But these people—they have a reason for life that seems to me to be more significant. I feel that getting to know you has broadened my outlook and yet made me more focused on what I can do for the world, for people. I mean, beyond myself and my own little sphere of happiness."

Amy didn't say anything. She was tired, overwhelmed by the power of the community she was not really a part of, overwhelmed by the personal and professional responsibility she saw herself taking, overwhelmed by the ongoing challenge of protecting the water in her forbidden well, and overwhelmed by how insignificant she was in the larger scheme of things. Matt was in a different place. He was at the beginning of this ever intensifying spiral of awareness. Right now she was too tired to respond to his passionate comments. She nodded her head but was quiet as they climbed aboard the run-about and made their way home.

The next morning Amy awoke with a start, remembering she had a guest in the study. She waited quietly to hear if Matt was awake. When she heard no sound, she dressed quickly and cracked open her door. From the next room she could hear Matt's even breathing. Amy was in a quandary. She was out of drinking water from the well and she did not want to bring Matt into her forbidden activity, not yet. She could not bear to drink the tap water from the tank Ned connected. Driven by her need for real water, she took her watering can, opening and closing the door to her abode as quietly as she could. She trotted over to the flowers near the tree and giving them the last drops of water sat on the bench under cover of the tree. It was very quiet this early in the morning with the dew on the grass and the birds beginning their day. Amy did not take time to enjoy this peaceful start to the day, but parted the bushes with the can and crawled through the bushes. However, this time her activity did not go unnoticed.

Matt had heard her but feigned sleep. He had been up earlier and had stood at the window of the study which looked out toward the tree, the flowers, and the bench. He could see little in the dim light so he returned to the sofa. It was this noise, a strange sound in her space, that jolted Amy awake. When he heard the outside door open and close, he again stood up and looked again out the window. There she was, dressed in her clothes from yesterday with a ponytail askew, watering the flowers. He watched the entire proceedings, the bench and the disappearance into the undergrowth. Matt grinned to himself, feeling sneaky and inclined to surprise her. He left the house as quietly as she had, came to the bench and sat down. He peered into the underbrush where she had disappeared but could not see her. Instead, he heard a creaking sound, metal against metal, and he heard the rush of water. Puzzling over this, Matt sensed his presence was violating Amy's privacy. He considered going back to the abode, but before he could make up his mind, the sounds changed and the brush moved as Amy pushed the watering can through the hole.

He watched as Amy came through and took in his presence. Her eyes looked like the eyes of a scared little animal caught in a trap. He both wanted to laugh at the humor of her escapade and wanted to take her in his arms. He did neither, "Good morning sunshine." he said, smiling down at her, "Can I help?"

"No, no, I've got it. Did I wake you? Sorry." Amy couldn't bear to look at Matt. Out of habit, she sat on the bench with the watering can full of ice cold well water beside her. She said nothing more, but stared at the flowers. Matt realized he was the trespasser and he found no words. Uncalled for, a lump rose in her throat and her throat and nose plugged with the effort of keeping the tears out of her eyes. The two young people sat for many moments unable to bridge their feelings. Then Matt took the initiative. He gingerly put his arm around Amy and with out saying a word began to stroke her shoulder. Amy moved her mouth in vain, her last attempt to withhold the tears. They dripped down her cheeks and her nose was wet. To keep her nose from dripping, she sniffed. The sniff turned to a sob. Matt no longer had to think about what to do or what effect it would have. He pulled Amy toward himself and onto his lap. Like a small frightened child, she buried her tears in the shirt on his chest.

What more can be said about what happened next? Anyone who has experienced the depth of feelings of love and acceptance will know without being told.

By mid-afternoon Matt and Amy, driven only by hunger, ventured out to the run-about and into Flambeau. Their goal was the farmer's market. The insecurity of first meeting each other and the town pageantry of the night before was no longer important. They came to Flambeau as a couple. Anyone walking along, visiting the farmer's market that day and seeing them would smile, and think of the one person in their own life they loved and would die for.

Much to Amy's surprise, Matt had listened to her story of the water, the well, and her fears about the artificially produced water with great seriousness. Matt was embarking on a new path, not only because of his relationship with Amy, but also because he was beginning to believe that the people, the authentic, real people as he thought of them, were at risk from the governing body of the world. He came to this understanding in a flash of intuition, synthesizing the events of his childhood, the early death of both his parents, Amy's life, Jim's life, and that single gray hair on his own head. This was very different from how his engineering brain usually worked: methodically sorting and categorizing facts, analyzing their validity, and arriving at a conclusion.

Laden with produce after the farmer's market, Amy taught

Matt about food. Amy taught him how to wash and trim the vegetables, shred cheese, stir-fry sliced and marinated tofu, cook potatoes not in a food preparer but in real water on a old-fashioned cooking contraption called 'Hotpoint.' In some ways this was playing house, in other ways it was working at learning skills lost to others in his generation--life skills. As he peeled potatoes, Amy slipped her arms around his waist and rested her head on his back. "Matt Bordeau, I don't know why you have come into my life at this point in time. But it feels like you have always been here, like a ghost following me around, suddenly becoming visible and present in my little world."

"No Amy," Matt said, wiping his wet hands on a kitchen towel, an object he had only heard about by listening to his mother read the fairy tales of his childhood. "I am no ghost, just a man made real by the love of a beautiful woman." He turned and they kissed, a kiss that would have lasted longer except that Amy's stomach growled. They both giggled and Matt acknowledged, "I have never been so hungry! If we don't finish this soon, I will dissolve like your ghost into thin air!"

As the potatoes boiled, Amy turned off the electric heating element for the tofu and set it in the large heating cavity to keep warm. They sat outdoors under the oak and ate their bowls of salad with gusto. When the intensity of hunger was abated, Amy mused that she would like to learn to make bread. She had read about it, but had not figured out how to come by all the ingredients. They talked about what they knew about bread, stories mostly, again stories from childhood. "It is so strange how much society, at least the society you and I are familiar with has actually deteriorated," Amy said. They walked back inside and finished, dressing the potatoes with a little salt, butter, dill, and pepper. Amy portioned out the tofu and potatoes on their plates and the few green beans that they had decided to try from the farmer's market. Not knowing how to eat the beans, they had cut some onto the salad and cooked the rest in water after the potatoes finished cooking. The woman from the market had told them to blanch the beans for 3-5 minutes. They were too embarrassed to ask what blanching meant.

Before they could sit down with their plates, Amy heard a faint beep alerting her to an incoming voice call. Being programmed to respond to incoming mail, she found it impossible to ignore. Excusing herself, she pulled out her passcard. It automatically opened to allow her to answer the call. She listened briefly and responded, "Thank-you for calling. I hope the donation will help our children." The passcard closed when the call ended.

Everyone born after 2145 has a tiny chip embedded in the left hand between the thumb and forefinger at birth. The chip is programmed at a regional central office at age thirteen; it is like a rite of passage in many world religions. For those destined to become highly educated, the chip will be reprogrammed to upgrade their status and access to education and wealth. This occurs when they are accepted into elitist programs of higher education. The chip recognizes who they are and allows any console or passcard to work for them, documenting use to a central off site server and data storage. If they lose their personal pass card, it is of no consequence other than the irritation of card replacement. When they sit in front of a console which is turned on, it automatically recognizes them and can retrieve working documents, class schedules, dinner menus, food orders, --anything that they need in order to function. In this way, Matt and Amy could use each other's console and if necessary, each other's passcard. Persons of lower social status will have access to only a limited number of features.

Data communication, including voice, text, and visuals (known collectively as VTV), is all satellite based in the twenty-second century. Tall transmission towers no longer violate the land. Everything is wireless.

The newest technology is the third generation of holigraphic imagery for VTV communication. It took two hundred years to bring this technology to the industry standard now enjoyed by Matt and Amy. As with other technologies, holigraphic imagery in daily life can only be used by those with appropriate chip programing.

Like all great inventions, holigraphy, developed slowly, beginning in the late twentieth century. The equipment needed to produce and project these three dimensional images filled an entire building. These images of beautiful color but of low resolution were possible using laser technology. The light shows featured ever-changing shapes and colors and dominated the outdoor night scene entertainment industry in the early twenty-first century capturing the imagination of the populace in the same way that a simple sparkler entertains a young child. There was very little functional use for holigraphic technology.

It might have been the magical memories of long ago celebrations with fireworks that sparked the next generation of holigraphy. One can almost picture the two little boys, brothers, gazing with wonder at the night sky over Disneyland, the light shows engaging their imagination.

The two brothers grew up to be computer engineers. After retiring. they found themselves once more as fascinated by the sparkling suspended light, as did their grandchildren around them.

Working alone and together, these brothers, two old computer geeks, played with the concept of projecting light and color on the subatomic particles in air. This discovery, in their retirement years, advanced the field of digital communication and began as many significant discoveries begin-- with a mishap. They were each using projection screen airmacs, a miniature lazer technology that had greatly advanced the old liquid crystal display systems. One brother was attempting to baby-sit for his grandson while using his computer. The active baby reached for his grandfather's cup of coffee. The grandparent reacted and spilled some of his coffee into the projection module rendering it useless.

"This is all a piece of crap," he later relayed in frustration to his wife and then to his brother. "A machine shouldn't become trash just because of a little spilt coffee." His wife raised her eyebrows at his outrage and maybe at his inattentiveness to his grandson but said nothing.

His brother said very little but by morning had sent him some programming related to projecting light onto subatomic particles. Energized by an intriguing possibility, they began to experiment in earnest, ionizing air molecules with electromagnetic waves. They found that they could phase shift specific ions in a manner that would cause them to resonate in the light spectrum, the photons reflecting the full color spectrum, hovering just above a touch control device positioned on the lap or on a table.

Thus in 2042, the Nobel Prize in Physics was awarded to these two old men for their contribution to the second generation, two-dimensional holigrams. The invention of this technology was a big step forward because it eliminated the need for the projection screen of the old airmacs. By eliminating the screen, one could fully utilize the miniaturization technology for the processors, giving the user a powerful and extremely portable machine.

It would still be another one hundred years before the development in holigraphic technology would provide the clarity of resolution in life size, three-dimensional images that Matt and Amy use everyday of their lives.

Amy declared the green beans to be the best part of the meal. She had looked up 'blanch' as they prepared the food. Matt couldn't get enough of the potatoes. "Fruits of the earth!" He inhaled deeply, closing his eyes. "I have never had such an experience with food," he declared. "I've always seen eating as something one must do in order to live, like drinking water, sleeping, or brushing your teeth. This experience was more like..." Here he paused, unsure of how to say it, not wanting to offend Amy. "More like being deeply in love, and having your love returned fully."

Amy looked at Matt and nodded. She was thinking how she loved Matt but also loved this place, this life she had made for herself. She was thinking about the picture of the woman and her family. Secretly she had hoped that she would be genetically connected to her. She felt she was connected and was sad that the connection wasn't genetic.

As she was musing, Matt's card beeped. "Yes." she heard him say. She guessed it was the same call she had received before they ate. "Okay." and then "I think tomorrow at 10:00 would be fine. Could I call you back if there is a problem?" After a moment of silence he said, "Well, thank-you for the call." His passcard closed and Matt stared down at the ground, not moving. Matt was in a different place as the call ended and Amy chose to remain quiet and wait for his return. She analyzed the side of the call she had heard and guessed it was not the same call she had received earlier, but something serious about his program at school and assumed he would have to leave early or at least connect with her console to his program chair. She was not prepared for what Matt said next.

"Amy," Matt turned toward her and took her hands in his, "Do you believe in fate?"

Amy laughed, "Matt, you are acting pretty scary!"

"I'm not trying to be scary. That was a call from the people about the time capsule. I am a match."

The blood in Amy's face drained. She couldn't speak.

Always the practical engineer, he added, "It doesn't change any rights of ownership; you still have complete ownership."

"What?" Amy began to understand some of what Matt had said.

"I am a genetic match to the person from this property who placed a time capsule in with the others a hundred years ago." It was Matt's turn to fade away as he assimilated the few pieces of knowledge he had been given in that very strange call. He put his plate down on the ground and picked up his glass of water. He held the glass up to the light of the sky, looking through the clear glass as if trying to see into the molecules of water. Closing his eyes he took tremendous gulps, draining the glass. They sat silently, each with their own thoughts for a long while.

That night neither could sleep. Eventually, Matt slipped out of the bed they now shared, trying not to disturb Amy. First he sat in the study. Then he put on his shoes and walked outside. He sat on the bench under the tree by the well and thought. He was a logical thinker but at the same time a romantic. He knew he was in love with Amy but he couldn't understand his connection to this place. It made no sense to him that out of the tens of thousands of people who could be descendants of Amy's land that he would be the one who submitted his DNA, submitted it only to impress Amy. He went over this again and again, trying to find anything from his childhood that would have pointed to a connection to Flambeau. There seemed to be nothing until a faint memory of a doll came to him. It was an Indian doll that his parents kept as a decoration in their room. Once, as a six year old, he had taken the doll off the cabinet to play with. His mother took it away, saying something he didn't understand. Something about it being the only thing his dad had left. Intuitively he knew this was the connection. He tried to remember what became of the doll after the apartment was closed.

Matt began to think about his own looks and how he resembled his father. He was tall, like his dad. He remembered his father with very black straight hair before he got old, the same hair he had. His father also had a lean, muscular build and high cheek bones. Matt shared these also. Matt had more of his mother's eyebrows and eyes. He also inherited her musical voice. Matt's thoughts wandered to the statute in the square where he and Amy had sat. It was really only less than two days ago and yet it seemed a lifetime away. The lean, muscular bronzed man upon a horse; was this part of the history his parents hid from him?

Amy peered out of the window at Matt. In her own struggles she came to the conclusion that her relationship with Matt was a deeper cosmic phenomenon. As a medical student, she had been taught that this kind of thing was not real, simply something made up by uneducated people dealing with deeper questions of life and death. However, Amy was convinced, even before becoming acquainted with Matt, that these phenomena did exist and were real. Her concern was whether Matt needed to struggle alone or whether she could be there for him. She really didn't know him well enough and she feared she might push him away at this time when he was surrounded by events and emotions that he had not looked for.

The full moon gave a faint light and created a shadow of all that came between the light and the earth. A slight breeze moved the shadows upon the ground and the abode. Matt watched the shadows. His eyes followed the movement to the window of the abode where Amy stood watching him. He saw her there and smiled to himself as he waved. Amy put her fingers to her lips and pressed them to the glass momentarily before coming out to join him. Amy and Matt spent most of the night there by the well and the old oak, returning to the abode only when the cool and damp of the night became uncomfortable and in the morning hours the ghosts of generations past watched over them as they slept in each other's arms upon Amy's bed.

Hand in hand they walked into the council office together a few moments before 10:00. They were seated together in the council chambers and Matt was verified as the rightful owner of the time capsule placed by an unknown relative of the past, Callie Nelson. He signed for the capsule and listened to the head councilman's request that he come forward with any information pertinent to the community of Flambeau. Matt felt Amy squeezing his hand. So he made some non-committal remarks and stated that if there was anything of interest outside of personal family information that he would contact the council. The capsule, a titanium alloy metal box nine inches wide by 12 inches long and two inches deep was sealed in a translucent plastic together with a key. Matt let go of Amy's hand as the head councilman solemnly placed the box in Matt's outstretched hands. It was surprisingly light in weight. The plastic outer coating had been recently been wiped clean of 100 years of accumulated mildew.

Amy couldn't resist asking, "How many capsules have been found to have a match?"

The councilman shook his head. "Well, your friend and another person who is from Flambeau are the only ones who paid to have the match genetically verified. However, we feel there are a few more matches of members of our community, simply by the names on the containers and in the Flambeau writings. We will need to decide what to do with these and two others that seem to have no current connection to Flambeau. It will come before the council for a vote at the next meeting."

"Is the meeting open to the public?"

"Yes, of course," the councilman replied. "It will be the last Friday in July, if you are interested, at seven."

Amy had another question. "Do you have any idea when all the information from the main capsule will be available?"

"We plan to have an open meeting to summarize the information from the time capsule at that time also."

Matt shook hands with the members of the council as he and Amy stood up to leave. The councilman reiterated his request to Matt, adding that there may be information in the capsule that would help identify other owners or information that would be helpful to Flambeau. Matt assured him that he would be in touch.

Matt held the capsule close as he reached for Amy's hand. The warmth of her hand reassured Matt that whatever he would learn about himself in the time capsule would be okay. "Where do you think we could go to learn about my ancestors?"

Amy squeezed his hand and grinned, "I've got just the place," she said, but she didn't tell Matt where they were going. They hopped into her run-about and Amy drove slowly out of town. Then, changing her mind, she turned back, "I think we may need some refreshment for this." Amy stopped at the food store, leaving Matt for a few moments. She picked out veggie crackers, a wedge of cheese, two apples, a bar of dark chocolate, and feeling impetuous, she added a bottle of wine, not realizing she would need glasses and a way to open the wine not to mention a knife to cut the cheese.

Amy drove Matt to an abandoned Indian cemetery a little ways from Flambeau. Matt rolled his eyes at Amy when he realized where she had taken him. They spread a ground cloth over the grass and set the snack aside. Matt lay back, his eyes closed and his head resting upon his arms. Amy sat cross-legged, looking out over the river and then to the south and east, to the hills that the natives called Flambeau Mountain.

After a moment of quiet, Matt sat up taking the time capsule into his hands. "Wait!" Amy said, "We should have some wine to toast the opening." As she said this she realized her dilemma with opening the wine and the lack of wineglasses. "Well, it was a good thought," she added, "I didn't consider how to open or drink it." Amy shrugged. Matt's engineering brain came to the rescue of the problem of the wine cork. He fashioned a tool with a piece of stone and a small red folding knife he never used, a keepsake from his parents. After a few tries, the cork was out, albeit in a few pieces.

"Dr. Amy, would we die of germs if we drank from the same bottle?"

Laughing, Amy replied, "I don't think germ transmission should be our concern at this juncture. However, we should really finish the bottle once we have contaminated it by drinking from it."

Matt held the bottle out to Amy. "To your past and to your future," she toasted, taking a sip of the red wine. She handed the bottle to Matt.

"To the past, and our future," he replied. He took a few swallows of the red wine without taking his eyes off of Amy. His eyes were serious and piercing. Amy felt a rush of heat come up to her face but she didn't look away from Matt. He wrapped his arms around her and they kissed long and warm, the taste of wine shared in the kiss.

"What did we come here for?" Amy teased. Matt kissed her upon the forehead. Then taking another few swallows of wine, he handed her the bottle and reached for the time capsule. Amy watched him as he opened the box. Their eyes were now focused on the contents.

Under the cover was a one-page hand written letter.

August 14, 2087

To my people of the future,

I hope this time capsule finds you in good health and in relative happiness. My reasons for participating in the time capsule project of Flambeau is to share the little knowledge

I hold concerning the history of this land you live on and the legacy that is hidden in the depths of the earth upon which I now stand. It is a treasure more valuable than the genetic line that connects me to you, my unborn ancestors, and more valuable than the wealth of the wealthiest individuals on the earth.

The treasure I speak of is the water that flows thirty feet below, which I currently access by a simple mechanical hand pump connected to an ancient well. The well and the pump are now housed in a small stone building on this land that I love. The pump and the building are temporal, I hope the water and the well remain for as long as the stars shine upon this earth.

The first generation of the Bordeau family living upon this land created the well and generations after the first generation have protected it as I do now. I do not know whether my son or my grandchildren will ever return to this land when I am gone. Therefore, I am undertaking this writing out of honor to the first generation of Bordeau's and their part in the creation of the well and out of my contribution to the safe keeping of the well.

This water is life. I have come to believe, from my direct experience, that the bottled water provided by the government shortens one's life, produces birth defects, and even kills. I have experienced great sorrow in my lifetime from this contrived water.

I am now closer to the end of my life and my last important task is to pass on *what I know to the future generations of Bordeaus. In this capsule are the stories and pictures of our ancestors and events that have shaped my life and now are shaping yours. If you are in possession of this time capsule and are able to locate the well, you may find additional updated information that I hope to add before I leave. If I am able to follow through on my plan, this information will update you on events after today, August 14, 2087. I will do my best to seal the information from the effects of moisture and time. It will be placed in the soil on the north side of the casing of the well, approximately one-foot from the center point of the casing and about six inches down. On top of the soil I will place a large flat piece of slate as a marker.*

I have made my preparations and am now at peace with the ancestors and myself. I pass on to you the responsibility for this legacy.

All my love,
Callie Ann (Bordeau) Hanover-Nelson

Matt finished reading. He found he was deeply affected by the words of this woman he did not know. He composed himself and turned to Amy, "I'm not sure if I can handle learning anything more just yet. Do you mind if I just let this much sink in?"

Amy laid her head upon his arm. "I think that is what Callie would want, that you take your time in learning this history. The stories of your ancestors have been waiting a hundred years to be told; they will be patient." Matt was comforted by Amy's words and he thought about how she had referred to his ancestor, Callie, as if she were present, real. As much as he both wanted and feared to learn more, he was grateful for Amy's patience.

They opened the cheese and the crackers, rubbed the apples

shiny red, and retrieved a bottle of Callie's precious well water from the run-about. They ate slowly, re-reading and mulling over Callie's words. Amy had a sudden awareness concerning a picture she and her mother salvaged before they built the abode. "I think I have a picture of Callie when she was younger, a picture from the old house. I have it on the bookshelf in the study, I think it may be Callie and her family." Amy was now eager to have Matt look further into the box. He, however, was troubled by the reference to the danger of the bottled water. The scientist in him was analyzing the process for making water, the carbon scrubbers that halted global warming, and the differences in the haves and the have-nots he recently learned about. A chill came over him when he remembered what Amy said about the age of the noted chief who gave the blessing at the time capsule ceremony.

Amy picked up the letter again. She was thinking about the great effort and probably great cost Callie had undertaken and because of it, the turn of events in her own personal life, Matt's life, and even in both their professional careers. "It's our turn now," she murmured, with the realization that she must, with or without Matt's support, extend Callie's gift to the people of 2287 by adding 100 years to Callie's information.

"Would you like to learn more now?" Matt asked. It was really a statement of fact. He knew he was holding back, almost unwilling to take the next step.

"Only when you are ready," she quietly replied.

"Let's look at the next item in Callie's box here and then go back to your place where we can organize the information and keep it safe."

"That makes sense. I was just thinking that it is our turn now to create a time capsule for the future and add information about your family. How do you feel about that?" Amy looked sideways at Matt, again thinking that she should not assume anything about him at this point. Matt's eyes looked out over the river and to the top of the mountain.

"You are way ahead of me, I hadn't even considered the future. I seem to be stuck in this void in time between myself and Callie.

It doesn't seem as though she were my direct ancestor, just because her last name is not the same as mine. Though I suppose she could have changed her name."

"Well, in terms of the time capsule, I remember hearing that the council will be taking a whole year to consider the information in the city capsule and possibly the individual capsules like yours before actually entombing the next one hundred year capsule." Then she added, "So we have time. You would feel better about sharing your information for the future if you could know your past. If it is okay with you, I will let the council know that we are considering contributing to the new capsule."

"That would be fine. I can't really go there right now. I have too many questions about my past."

Matt reached in the box for the next package. It contained a few pictures with a little identifying information hand-written on each. One of the pictures was a copy of the small framed photo Amy had. "It is Callie! I was right! Don't you think she looks sad here? This is her little boy and here is the baby, her daughter."

Matt scratched his head. "That still doesn't tell me more about myself. Am I the grandson of the little boy, the one that evidently did not come back to Flambeau? It says 'Jordan, Callie, Sam, Marta, and Mutsy. What a name for a dog!'"

They studied each photo in the package, unable to unravel any more of Matt's history. Callie's hand-written letter referenced the next package with a memory card. Matt said neither his console nor Amy's would have a port for a memory card. Feeling a little discouraged, the two packed up and headed back home.

Amy cleared off a narrow table, that had been the place for her many unfinished ideas and projects. It was upon this table that Matt carefully placed the sealed bags from the time capsule in the order in which they came out of the titanium box. And on this table, at the very end was another unopened, well-sealed plastic bag the pair had now retrieved from its long ago entombment near Amy's well. Amy carefully washed away the grime of what could be almost one-hundred years. The plastic was cloudy, not clear, but had not disintegrated over the years that it had been buried in the earth. Amy thought about how she had observed massive landfills and people in poverty picking through the smelly, disease ridden plastics and metal for things they could salvage to use or sell. Looking at the package Callie had placed for them, Amy could understand first-hand how any piece of plastic one might drop onto the ground would last and affect the quality of life on this earth. When they had time, she would share these thoughts with Matt, but now the two of them were fully engaged in sorting out the objects in the capsule so they could begin to understand Callie Nelson and her life in the 21st century.

As promised in the opening handwritten letter, Callie had attached her own comments to many of the photos. Some of her comments were a few pages long and appeared to be transcribed material from old diaries or journals or childhood memories. Other writings were more brief: simple descriptions of the hundreds of photos in the time capsule. Many of the photos were too faded to see. They could not access the data on the memory card with the technology they owned but that didn't stop them from wondering what Callie had stored in this ancient digital format.

FLAMBEAU 1919

The two workhorses plodded along the narrow roadway. Wooden wheels with steel rims cut into the soft snow behind the horses. It was a bumpy ride; the softness of the snow did not provide a cushion to the potholes and stones on the roadbed. Even so, the two little boys slept on. They were wedged between chairs and a dresser and they lay atop all the clothing the family owned that they were not wearing. On top of them, two down-filled quilts, two cotton quilts and a piece of canvas tarp tied to the wagon and the legs of the chairs. The tarp did little to keep the wind out but did provide some measure of protection from the falling snow.

"Bess, lay down with the youngins and git yer rest," commanded Joshua Bordeau to his plump little wife.

"What? And let you nod off? The horses will stop and we will all freeze to death before morning."

Josh felt glad for her company in spite of himself--however he needed to have the last word, "Well, you just don't take nuthin from no one. Well, suit yourself." They were quiet and the horses plodded along for another 10 minutes or maybe a half mile.

Bess' ruffled feathers relaxed and she snuggled into Josh for a few moments. "The blanket needs fixin'," she complained but before adjusting the blanket around them both she turned to size up Josh's appearance. Then she tugged the ear flaps down further on his wool cap pulled the hood tighter and planted a juicy kiss on his whiskery mouth. She finished her kiss and teased, "Warm now?"

Josh took his eyes off the horses' rumps and contemplated Bess. "You're still just as sassy as before we tied the knot."

"And you're still the liar I married," she replied.

Bess was barely 17 when she met Josh at a barn dance in Haugen. He was almost 10 years her senior. The fireworks between them could have burnt the barn to the ground. He came to visit her brothers every day he could after that eventful night and in two months there was a shotgun wedding. Married life did nothing to snuff out the fire between them. Their arguments by day were loud and emotional matched only by their passion at night. Eight months after the wedding Weldon was born and 10 months later Edward. Josh helped deliver both boys as he had delivered dozens of calves. The difference was that at these births he felt fear, fear of losing the love of his life. He almost did lose her when Edward was born. The baby was breech and Bess almost passed out from his efforts to do the only thing he knew for certain would turn the baby. When he couldn't, he left Bess and baby Weldon alone as he ran after midnight, a mile to the neighbor woman's home. Her husband met him with a shotgun pointed at Josh's face, almost pulling the trigger before he awoke enough to comprehend that this wild man was his neighbor. Joshua ran back home to Bess as the neighbor's wife gathered some paraphernalia and and a flask of whiskey. The neighbor hitched up the wagon and drove his wife to Josh's farm, cracking the whip to urge the horse to greater speed. Nellie held onto her shawl and basket. When they arrived Nell gave her husband a look. "You take a swallow; make Josh take one, and leave the bottle here. Bess will need it."

Josh was back at Bess' bed. He saw that she was breathing hard but not having a contraction. He turned to the squalling baby. "Shhh! Welly, can't ya see your momma needs you to be quiet," he hissed. Bess shook her head and groaned.

Nellie opened the door to the Bordeau home and took in the scene. "You go have a swallow of the jug my man has. Now mind you, take that baby with you and don't you kill him." She threatened him briefly with her fist. Her fist opened and she stroked the wet hair out of the eyes of her patient. She smiled gently at Bess. Bess regarded her savior briefly before the next wave took her over. Once over, Nell tidied the space around Bess, pulled the curtain to give privacy from the men's fear-filled eyes. "You'll get through this Bessie girl, you're a strong one. Now you just do as I say and don't mind calling out fer yer God. He's gotta hear ya if ya wants his help."

Twelve feet away, the men poked around with the fire and put a pot of water on the stove as per Nell's direction. In his basket, Baby Weldon sucked on a piece of rag soaked with diluted whiskey and sugar. When the contractions came, Bess did her part calling on God and damning Josh for her predicament.

That was over seven years ago. Now they were all packed up with the little boys, moving the seventy some miles from Haugen to a small village called Flambeau. They were told the house wasn't finished but there was wood ready to heat the house for winter and five acres cleared. They were told the dug well next to the house had good water. They were told there were trout in cold streams, rabbits in the meadows, and deer in the woods. And they were told about the land. Land ready to be cleared and plowed and cultivated for crops and cattle feed. It was the land of plenty. They would buy a couple of cows once they raised the barn. It was in Joshua's head to start farming in the spring once they were established.

******

Weldon and Eddie grabbed fish poles after school and after stuffing their mouths with leftover cake they raced to the little stream. They were seven and eight years old, too little to help Josh with the heavy work but old enough to contribute to the family's well being by doing chores, hunting rabbits with snares, and their favorite—catching trout and other fish for their mother to cook for supper. Although Bess had forbidden it, they also often amused themselves in the hottest days by jumping in the small pool created by a bend in the stream. Nearby they could hear the sound of axes dropping the last of the timber on a neighbor's farm. The neighbor would use dynamite the following year to get rid of the stumps before plowing and planting.

Before Eddie could toss in his line he noticed a foul smell. He followed the smell up the stream a ways and there he saw the remains of a small trout. The flesh on the bones was almost gone and the flies were crawling over the carcass. Skunks had likely eaten their fill a few days before. Weldon and Eddie often saw a dead fish in the tall grass next to the stream. They thought nothing of it . They didn't know that the stream and the fish were dying, dying because thirty years earlier the last of the virgin white pine had been logged off the land and now even the smaller trees were being cut to make room for more farming. The massive trees had provided shade for the many streams and the icy water of the small streams was home to trout, trout that were occasionally harvested by the Ojibwe in the 1800's as they passed through the land. These trout were not the size of the ones Eddie and Weldon now caught. They were sometimes almost a foot and a half long. The trout the boys caught were little more than pan-fish size. By the time Eddie would marry and come back to the land, they would be no more. Indeed the icy streams would be no more, just ditches of spring runoff, muddied by the hoofs of the ever growing herds of cattle seeking water.

FLAMBEAU 2187

Matt and Amy curled up together with one photo and a few pages of Callie's writing. They had decided the day before that they would be disciplined about this, using the daytime hours to study and the evening hours to continue to read and piece together family history from Callie's writings.

Matt held a yellowed photo that showed the outlines of having been in a frame for many years. Like all the other photos it was encased in plastic and had a number that corresponded to the page or pages in the binder that held all of Callie's information.

"I think I can make out a man sitting in a chair and two children, one a little taller than the other. There is a person at the back but very faded.

Amy bent down to look closely. "I can't tell, but I can guess. It could easily be a family portrait. The children are probably boys. And the figure at the back is the mother. This must be the first family who lived here. We'll have to figure out how many generations back the man would be from you."

Matt started to do the math. "Let's see. Callie would have been in her 70's or 80's in 2087. So there probably was a teenager or young adult somewhere who might have had a child within a few years, who might have had a child twenty-five to thirty five years later who might have a child in the 40's or 50's that could be our generation or our parents."

Elly counted on her fingers. "I think that makes us—you—five or six generations from Callie. Now how many generations from the first is Callie?"

"Oh God, about five, just read—we'll do the math later."

"No, no. Let's just assume 25 years per generation. The way I figure is that Callie would have been born between 2010 and 2020. If she were directly related to you she would be your great, great, great grandmother. Isn't that about six generations?

"Let's just say I am 10 generations removed from the father in the picture. Let's see what Callie has to say about the picture."

I believe the photo of Josh and Bess Bordeau with their two older sons, Weldon and Edward, is the oldest that I found after my grandmother's death. It was taken either before the Bordeaus left Haugen or after they arrived in Flambeau. Other family portraits seem to have been taken as families prepared for major changes in their lives. My guess is that this photo was before they left Haugen.

Edward is the younger child in the picture. The older boy is Weldon. My grandmother was

Edward Bordeau's only child. Her name was Elly. From what she had told me before she died, there were three more children born to Bess and Josh after they moved to Flambeau. There was a set of twins, Ella and Anna, and then a little boy, John. I found no pictures of these three, perhaps because of the hardships the family endured at Flambeau.

According to Elly, the family lost the first well that was on the property. It went dry in the late twenties when her father was a teenager. He helped dig a new well and when Elly was a child he told her stories of the well, impressing upon her the value of water.

The other major hardship was the death of Anna, one of the twins. Elly didn't tell me a lot about this, only that Weldon left home after that.

"Hmmm," Matt said. "Elly was an only child and Weldon left home. We don't know about John. I've got to be a descendent of either Weldon or John. Unless there is someone else in the family that connects Callie to me, I am probably not directly related to Callie.

"This is rather strange." Amy picked up another sealed plastic encasing a lock of dark hair. Around the hair was a metal band. "Whose hair do you think this is? There is no information from Callie on this. I wonder whether she knew anything about it."

Matt took the sealed plastic from Amy, holding it up to the light. "I don't know much about children, but this doesn't look like the hair from a very young child, though I would have guessed if it was Bess who saved the hair, it would have been from the child who died."

"Or from the child she lost..."

"Weldon! Wouldn't you keep a lock of hair to remind you of your first born?"

Amy looked at the picture of the young family again. "I agree, it's probably Weldon."

FLAMBEAU 1927 - 1929

Edward woke with a sense of purpose and direction. He was eager to begin the task with the optimism and self-confidence born of youthful inexperience. For the past months he had dragged himself out of bed before daylight taking a swig of stale water to rinse his mouth and drinking a cup of cooked milk to tide him over.

"You're a good boy Eddie," Ma said as she handed her growing son a warm slab of baked cereal cake. Ma looked as she always did these days, tired and with an inner anxiety that stayed hidden from the boys but was unleashed upon her husband when she perceived the children were out of earshot. Edward didn't think or wonder how long she had been moving about the kitchen, preparing coffee, hot milk, and baking the cereal cake, one of the staples of the first breakfast for her family. This was how it always had been as far back as he could remember. Two breakfasts, one in the early morning before chores and one after chores before school. In the summer months when there was no school, the second breakfast was more relaxed. Bess created a warm, loving environment in the sparse farm kitchen with the little girls, the twins, toddling behind creating havoc and entertainment for Weldon, Pa, and Eddie.

"Pa up?" Eddie asked, already knowing the answer.

"Yah and Weldon too. Those cattle are having an early milking today. You'd better hustle and get water." Eddie nodded and headed out the door, but not before grabbing another slab of cereal cake. Ma pretended to slap his hand, but he knew it was in jest. Ma always made sure they had as much to eat as they could hold. The food she prepared was dependable, hardy, and tasty to their palates. She made do with what she could by preserving the fruits of her labor, her vegetable garden. She had lard from the butchering of the pigs and meat from the pig, cow, chickens, and rabbits. Fresh apples kept in the root cellar through December when they went soft and had to be baked or stewed. Potatoes were stored to the ceiling, filling the cellar. They sold the best and Bess prepared mountains of the littler ones into bowls of mashed, boiled, or fried delights. The shelves in the basement held jars of canned apples mixed with raisins. They also held smaller jars of raspberry, blackberry, and strawberry jams. The berries had all been picked in the woods and meadows around their farm. Two large jars held pickled cucumbers. Two small pails stood in the corner near the opening to the cellar. They held recently gathered eggs. Bess rotated the pails to use up the oldest eggs first. They would keep for three weeks or more if she could keep them cool. If she had too many eggs she took them to town and traded at the store for groceries. The onions hung, braided between the rafters in the attic along with the garlic. Bunches of dill weed, parsley, and mint were tied and hung there also. She had not yet harvested the cabbage that would be made into kraut, nor the carrots or parsnips. Bess prided herself on her well-stocked and organized larder, but this summer was not a productive summer. It had been dry, very dry, and when the well went dry and the creek bed cracked from the hot sun, Bess went into a different mode, a survival mode. She drew water from the bog for washing and boiling, reused the water from the canning pot for dishes and bathing. She collected old containers and pots that could be pressed into service to hold this water for the day's use.

The well going dry was the severest hardship she had endured up to this point in her life.

Bess poured herself a cup of coffee and cut off a small piece of cereal cake. She helped herself to a large spoon of jam from the jar on the table. She sat alone at the kitchen table and allowed herself a brief respite; a moment to slowly eat, daydream, and plan the work of the day. First she would make the second breakfast, today it would be cracklings, the crisp, rendered pieces of pork fat. She would make her own version of baking powder biscuits with the soured milk, then a big fry pan of eggs stirred together with the cracklings. Bess closed her eyes as her mind continued the planning of her day.

A half-mile away, Edward pumped water into the two borrowed

milk cans. Still cool now, but the haze in the glowing sky predicted another very hot day. His youthful muscular body pulled the handle of the pump up and down, bringing the icy water from the depths of the well. Pa had paid the neighbor good money for this water, hoping for rain and the renewal of the old well. He could put it off no longer; he needed a new well before winter set in. He and Bess argued over the location. Pa was fearful of not finding water. Bess was adamant that the well be dug close to the house and barn. They finally agreed to bring in the expert; an old codger who it was said could witch water. Edward put the lids on the cans and hoisted them into his small cart. He began the walk home, pulling the heavy small wagon carefully over the bumpy dirt road, avoiding the worst ruts. Edward could have run this distance in three minutes, but he pulled his load slowly and methodically. It took him the better part of an hour. Yesterday, going too fast, he lost a third of his precious cargo when the wheel dropped into a rut in the road.

Edward was eager to see the water witching. He had heard his parents arguing over this. He had also heard his science teacher downplay the widely accepted belief in the power of a small fork of willow to find water in the ground. Before he turned off the dirt road into his yard, he saw the buggy of the man who would be their savior coming toward him. His whole body tingled with anticipation of what would happen on this day. He saw himself digging the well in a day. He saw his mothers eyes filled with pride when the well gushed water to the surface. Then Pa yelled for him to hurry himself up. The reverie was broken and he hauled the cans off of the cart and onto the porch of the house, standing one on a low bench and the other next to it.

Paul, known to everyone in these parts as 'Lemon Extract Paul', stood up from his wooden seat in the buggy and carefully let himself down the step and out of the buggy. He looked around, sizing up the job he had come to do. He had come for breakfast and with good luck he would get dinner here too, maybe for a few days. Without Pa telling them, the boys unhitched Paul's horse and tied him to the oak tree where he would be in the shade.

Weldon fetched the oat bag from the buggy and Eddie brought the buggy horse a bucket of water drawn from the river. They took the horse's harness off and stored it in Paul's buggy. Then the horse was turned out to pasture with the Bordeau workhorses.

The name 'Lemon Extract Paul' by which Paul was known came because he tried to drink anything with alcohol in it. If he wasn't working, doing odd jobs, digging wells or basements, he worked at getting drunk. Indeed, when the Bordeaus first moved to Flambeau, it was Paul who completed the half-finished basement under the house. When he found a jug labeled wood alcohol, it was all Josh could do to talk him out of trying that kind of brew. One swallow would have killed him. He only shrugged his shoulders when Pa told him this. "Nah, it only burns once going down," he answered, but he didn't challenge Josh's words with a foolhardy action.

Weldon scraped off the manure on his boots before he removed them. He washed his face, arms, and hands in the wash bucket outside the porch and left his boots next to the door before entering Ma's kitchen. Ma was fussy about those things. Pa didn't remove his boots today; Msa glared but didn't say a word in front of company. The odor of barn and fresh milk mingled with the enticing smells of fresh cracklings, biscuits, coffee, and fried eggs. The guest was seated, coffee poured and in the first five minutes of silence, hunger was abated. The twins toddled out of their bed in soggy diapers. Ma left to clean them up and the men were left to their coffee. The conversation began with broad topics about the weather and wound its way around the hardships, true and exaggerated. After these preliminaries, Paul settled into a discussion of water witching and told stories (whether true or fabricated) of the many underground rivers of water he had found in his lifetime.

It was forty-five minutes later when Pa pushed away from the table, gruffly calling out to Weldon and Edward, "Time is money. We ain't gonna find water a sittin' in the kitchen. You boys fetch the pick, shovels, some timbers, the wheelbarrow, pails, and rope." He pushed himself back from the table and made a beeline out the door to the outhouse. He would have used the gutter in the barn, but with company on his land, he preferred to appear more civilized.

Paul was left with the babies and Bess. He took a slow draught of cold coffee and started another story. Bess turned to the sink, appearing not to notice the beginning of a new tale. "AnnaElla, come here and let momma wipe you off." She spoke to the girls as if they were one child. They looked alike and it was often too much trouble to determine which was which. "Now today, momma's gonna pick them beans and needs your help." She went on and on, chatting to the girls and ignoring Paul.

Paul stood up, knowing he had been cut off. "Thank-you, missus, fer a mighty fine breakfast. Can't say when I et a better one. Now, I'll be gettin' that water found fer yah."

Bess murmured something but was careful not to turn around lest Paul start up again. Josh was right. Time was money and Paul's time was the Bordeau's money.

Eddie and Weldon stood in the background as Paul cut a forked willow branch from the tree near the bog. As Paul trimmed and whittled the branch to some unknown specifications, he spoke to Josh about the mysterious property of the forked willow, which caused it to seek water. Josh knew the story. Paul was really telling it for the benefit of the two boys who he knew with certainty were listening carefully The boys kept their distance lest they interfere with the miracle that was about to take place. The miracle was that the forked willow branch, held under tension by the skilled hands of Lemon Extract Paul, would search for a vein of water flowing under the ground. When it was above such a vein, the branch would twist in Paul's hands. Indeed it would be impossible for him to hold the main branch straight before the fork would pull downward toward the water. If the vein was a large vein of water it might even pull Paul to the ground.

Paul walked around the yard, knowing that a woman in a house would want the water close by. Bess peeked from her window as she cleared the breakfast dishes. Once or twice the branch seemed to quiver in Paul's hands. Edward hardly dared to breathe.

Weldon looked on. Being older and more educated, he was more skeptical. Paul looked sideways at the house to see if Bess was watching. When he saw her standing there, he walked away from the house, going south, with his back to her. Using a zigzagging path he turned north toward the house. The willow appeared to pull every so slightly midway. He turned back toward the barn. Nothing. He turned again toward the house. As he neared the half-way point, the willow took on a life of its own, twisting in Paul's strong grasp, the willow bent itself to the ground. As Paul passed the midpoint, the willow relaxed. When Paul retraced his steps, the willow repeated its magic. Now Paul did not have to look to the window, the boys, or Josh. He knew that he held their attention. Josh dropped his red kerchief on the ground to mark where the willow pull had been the strongest. Paul witched for water from the other direction zigzagging east to west. The pull was strongest at the red kerchief.

Ma was pleased with the place Paul had found water. She could look out to the well from her spot at the kitchen table or if she stood at the stove, she only had to turn hear head to the left to view the well. The location of the well would be halfway between the barn and the house. It was higher than the cow barn but a little lower than the house. If Lemon Extract Paul was as good at witching water as he said he was, Bess felt the money would be well spent. Everyone said Paul's word was good, so there it was. Nothing to worry about.

Pa was not so sure. He agreed with the location of the well because he had seen an outcropping of rock in that location, covered slightly by a few low bushes and grass. His instincts for geology of the land told him this was the spot to dig. But Josh was not given to trust his instincts. Perhaps his distrust came from years of being hen-pecked by Bess whenever he happened to be wrong. And of course there was the added benefit of Paul's experience in digging wells. He and the boys would be doing the first ten feet of the digging but it would be Paul who would take the risks as the work progressed. Basically the location of the well was irrelevant to Josh as long as it held enough water for the cows, for cooling the warm milk from the cows, and for household use. He was glad the well location would be acceptable to Bess. He did not want to fight that battle. He guessed Paul knew what he was doing after all.

Edward grabbed the shovel and ran to the red kerchief but he didn't start digging. The last part of the miracle was that the owner must break the ground for the well. Weldon sauntered up behind Edward, carting the pick, ropes, timbers and other necessary equipment in the wheelbarrow. Both boys stood and waited for their father and Paul. Weldon leaned against the back of the wheelbarrow. Edward kicked the dusty ground with the toe of his boot, every muscle in his body taut with anticipation.

"So you really think the water will be where you say it is?" Pa spoke in a challenging voice.

Lemon Extract Paul was not pleased with Josh's question. He believed in his own skill and the magic of the willow, but he had occasionally witched for water where the diggers had given up at forty or so feet, sometimes hitting bedrock. And once a man had died in the depths of an unfinished well. He felt that the willow would reroute the vein if it sensed non-believers. It was all tricky business, which is one of the reasons he now would only witch for water if the farmer paid him also for helping with the digging. The other reason was a few days of free room and board. "If ya don't trust the willow, ya kin find the water yerself." He spoke haughtily, glaring at Josh. Edward felt a pit in his stomach from this unexpected confrontation.

Before Josh could reply, the farmhouse door opened and Ma saved the day with the last slices of the cereal cake. There was just enough for each man and boy to have one. Pretending she had not heard the previous interchange and having silenced the men with her presence, she said, "Here's a little bite to get the digging started." She passed around the plate and then handed the empty plate to Edward, taking the shovel from him. "I will break ground for our new well." She placed the shovel next to Josh's red kerchief. Putting her right foot upon the shovel and with all the strength of her five-foot frame she thrust the shovel into the ground. She looked triumphantly at Josh. "There!" she cried victoriously, "Now get to work!" She took the plate from Edward, looking at him with knowing eyes. Paul watched her commanding presence make its way back to the house where the little girls were calling. He watched her as long as he dared.

The digging commenced with no other real confrontation between the men. Edward dug fast and furiously for the first fifteen minutes. Pa showed Weldon where he wanted the dirt from the digging and where to place the rocks that would be needed for back fill. When Edward's shovel did not penetrate the rocky earth, he grabbed the pick and wielding it high over head as he drove it into the earth with all the pent-up energy of his fourteen years. Again and again he held it high over his head and flung it into the ground. This time the pick struck a rock and the impact vibrated through his hands and arms. Edward didn't curse aloud, his ma would never have allowed it, but he learned by example a few choice words and those were expelled quietly with the next out breath. Throwing the pick aside he grasped one of the shovels. This time the energy went downward through his leg, his foot and finally pushed through a few inches of gravel before it met with the resistance of the rock.

Paul grabbed the pry bar, a hefty five-foot long steel bar. It was left over from Josh's days pulling ties for the railroad. It probably should have been left with the railroad company but by some unknown happenstance it found a home among Josh's tools and implements. Paul plunged the pry bar to the left of Edward's shovel. It went in a good 12 inches or more without striking the rock. He pried backward coming into contact with the submerged rock. Edward redoubled his efforts with the shovel and was able to penetrate the earth at the edge of the rock. Together they pried, Edward taking care that the wooden handle of the shovel would withstand the stress. As the rock moved unwillingly to the surface, Weldon dropped to his knees and lifted the small boulder from the earth. Edward paused, the sweat pouring from his hairline and streaking his fuzzy, yet unshaven face. Then Paul took the shovel from Edward before Edward was ready to give it up and began to enlarge the diameter of the hole to almost three feet. As Paul dug, Josh explained to the boys the reason for the larger hole and what they would be doing next. Weldon continued the wheelbarrow work and Edward went for a drink. He took the ladle from a nail in the porch wall and dipped a large dipper of cold water from the milk can, drinking deeply. He was hoping that today was the last day he would have to get up early for water. His ma read his thoughts.

"It will take a few days to dig, to set the bell, backfill and then wait for the water to clear." Ma said, "I guess you have a week left of trucking water from our neighbor." Edward must have looked disappointed for ma went up to him and kissed the top of his head. "A week is not a long time."

Edward sighed and turned to the porch door. Anna and Ella had started to follow him. He knelt down and clucked one of them under the chin. "You help our mama. Ella, you cook for your big brothers and your papa."

Anna grabbed the wooden spoon from her twin. "Me too!" she demanded.

"Yes, you too little Anna," Edward said and he open his mouth wide for the sister with the spoon as she pretended to feed him. "Mmmm good, you are a good cook."

This time it was Ella who was dismayed and she attempted to pull the spoon from her sister who screamed her protest. Both girls set up a howl and Edward left the house laughing, in better spirits than when he had come in.

Bess, as usual, was left to make peace in the family. Rather than taking a part in their little brawl, she quickly pulled out two small cooking pots and another wooden spoon. "We need some potatoes cooked and some carrots." The girls, distracted by the new set of implements and filled with self-importance, forgot their disagreement and set about cooking the imaginary potatoes and carrots. The toddlers were content for the time being, jabbering to each other as they went about their play cooking.

Bess took to scrubbing the new potatoes, the ones Edward had dug just yesterday. They were beauties despite the dry year, creamy white inside and a thin red skin with little or no blemishes. Potatoes grew well in the newly tilled soil. The virgin land had been a forest only a few years before and had only been pressed into agriculture in the last five years. Edward had brought in half a peck that he had dug from under only three plants. It would last them almost three days. Today she would make fried potatoes with onions and add the cracklings she held back when she served breakfast. She would serve green beans, the last of the fresh beans. The rest were already canned and stored in the basement. She would serve the last of the kraut from the previous year's garden. It was perhaps overly pungent, but hungry men wouldn't complain. There was some day old bread and plenty of pure white lard to spread on the bread from the rendering of the cracklings. For desert she baked a simple yellow cake that she served with the rhubarb sauce from this year's rhubarb. Of course there would be milk to drink, water from the neighbor's well, and another fresh pot of coffee.

Bess lived in her kitchen. Very few of her waking hours were spent anywhere else. Gardening, though extremely hard work, was her recreation. She tended the garden in the heat of the afternoon sun, plagued by the biting horseflies. She also tended it in the cool evenings swatting mosquitoes in rhythm with the swinging of her hoe. Bess was strong but she was also plump. She loved to eat. Providing delicious, healthy food for her family was her enduring mission in life.

Bess finished cutting up the last of the large bowl of potatoes from her place at the table. She had been monitoring the progress of the digging. Most recently both boys were taking turns digging and hauling the rocks and the soil. The two older men had been busy building a scaffold and setting up the windlass which would soon be placed over the hole. Paul shook it and inspected every nail as if his life depended on it. She realized his life would depend on the strength of this device and upon the skill, concentration, and strength of the men who remained above ground when he descended into the hole.

Ella crawled up into Bess's lap and pulled at the front of her blouse. "Nuss, Mama," she demanded. Upon hearing her, Anna came over and laid her head on Bess's knee.

"My two big helpers! Too big to nurse your mama." Ella whimpered as she was set into the makeshift highchair. But Anna grabbed her cup from off the table and spilled half upon the floor before Bess could intervene. "Anna!" Bess said sharply. She knew it wasn't the little one's fault, it was just that there was so much to do right this minute and now there was also a mess upon the floor to clean up. Anna had begun to cry. "There, there. Mama didn't mean anything." She helped Anna drink the rest of the milk while watching over Ella's skill with the cup. The girls were plainly pooped from all the pretend cooking they had done this morning. Bess scooped them up, one under each arm and after a wipe on each little mouth with the corner of her apron she lay them down together to nap. She paused for a moment to drink in the beauty of these two little dears as they curled up together on the bed they shared. She knew the diapers would be wet, but she would change them when they woke up. If she was lucky, that would be after she served the men their dinner.

Back in the kitchen she drained the water from the potatoes and heated the oil in the cast iron dutch oven. She estimated that it would take three to four batches to cook all the potatoes she had cut in the bowl. When each batch was finished it would be dumped into one of two stoneware bowls waiting in the oven--he oven that never cooled completely, not even on the hottest days of summer.

Bess gazed out of the window. The men had dug about five feet in the two hours they had been at it. They were working hard and would be hungry before she was done. She poured the first five cups of sliced potatoes into the sizzling oil of the cast iron dutch oven. All concentration now, the goal was to have a complete meal on the table cooked on a wood burning stove in an hour. She worked to clean and cook the beans, chop the onions, set the table, and boil up a fresh pot of coffee.

Outdoors, Pa sent Edward for a pail of drinking water. He knew without asking that Eddie would also check with Bess on how the dinner was coming. Eddie was the one who seemed to know when she needed help with more wood or needed more time. Eddie was ma's favorite though she would never say so. Only Weldon knew and he harassed his younger brother unkindly whenever he could. There was a funny streak in Weldon. Perhaps it was from the whiskey and sugar water he sucked as a babe.

Edward came back with the bucket and one ladle. He handed it to Pa and said in an off-hand sort of way, "Ma says about an hour." Pa didn't say anything or even acknowledge Eddie's words, but of course he heard and would pace the work accordingly.

Weldon came back with the empty wheelbarrow. He had just unloaded all of the biggest rocks for Ma's flower garden. He was hot, sweaty, and in a bad mood for having tripped and fallen on a jagged rock. It tore a hole in his overhauls, a hole his Ma would have to mend. When Eddie handed him the ladle of water he scowled at his brother. "Your turn with the rocks." he said.

Paul was given the ladle. After he drank deeply he leaned back on his shovel. "Time to put up that scaffolding and begin shoring up the edges of the hole."

He and Josh lifted the scaffolding into place. They argued briefly about its position. Paul had the last word. After all it was Paul who would be relying upon the safety of this, the winch, and the buckets. The two buckets Paul owned were his own design. He had the blacksmith weld them up so that they would fit between his knees as he crouched in the deep hole. One was smaller than the other; the smaller one was better for getting the dirt up and out of the well when the hole became very, very deep. Both buckets were sturdier built than any store-bought ones. The handles always stayed upright, never collapsing to the side. They were designed for safety. Should a bucket of rocks fall down a 20 foot hole and hit a man squarely on the head, it could kill him. Paul had a few close calls even with these special buckets.

The shoring up of the top edges of the hole and the securing of the scaffold took the better part of a half-hour. The boys did their other chores on the farm, cleaning the barn and gathering eggs and feeding the chickens. Everyone was tired and hungry.

Weldon looked longingly toward the house, hoping Ma would be almost finished with cooking. Ma, for her part, noticed the drop in energy once the scaffold was in place. Rather than have them stand around hungry, she called them in. She still had one pan of potatoes to cook. That would mean having them eat while she continued cooking. Then of course there would be the twins. As soon as they would hear the noise, they would be up and with their soaking wet diapers which would need to be changed before they ate.

The men sat down at the table and didn't wait on ceremony. They helped themselves to everything that was provided. They were quiet and surprisingly the twins did not wake up. Ma finished frying up the last of the potatoes, filling the empty stoneware bowl and setting it on the table. She checked on the water for the coffee and then sat down herself. After filling her plate, true to form, the twins toddled in, Ella grabbing the front of her diaper to keep it from falling down and tripping her. The sight made everyone laugh. Eddie pushed back from the table, "I got 'em Ma." He pretended to be a big bear and he swooped up the girls, hauling them to the bedroom, where he helped Anna off with her diaper and told Ella to step out of her diaper and get two clean ones. Luckily the diapers were only wet and not dirty. He quickly pinned the diapers on and took the wet ones outside to the pail Ma kept for that purpose. He washed his hands and gave each of the girls a small rag and watched as they earnestly attended to the washing.

Edward lifted Ella onto his knee and Weldon took Anna. Bess smiled at her sons. She was proud of them, their caring for their little sisters was evident in all they did, even when hungry and tired themselves.

The girls ate from their brothers' plates, sometime with their fingers and sometimes grabbing a fork or spoon. Bess finished her plate and cleared for herself, Pa, and Paul. She delayed serving the dessert, knowing that the little girls would eat more food if they didn't see the dessert.

The little that was left from the meal was consolidated into one bowl and the boys were encouraged to finish it so that Bess would not have to give it to the pig. They complied. They were bottomless pits of hunger. Pa would have liked his dessert immediately, but he was smart enough to know why Bess wasn't serving it. He sat, content with his coffee, like a king presiding over his people.

When the last plate was empty, the girls were set down upon the floor. The boys knew that when the dessert came around they would be up clamoring for some. Ma served more coffee and then the yellow cake--a substantial piece for everyone with the rhubarb sauce to sweeten and give it color and tang. There was more on the stove. Bess knew they would have second helpings. Anna and Ella came toddling in, pulling on the boys to lift them up to the table. They never missed a sweet.

Pa and Paul each lit a pipe and leaned back in their chairs. They rested after the satisfying meal, entertained by the twins.

The men gained another five feet of digging in the afternoon. Bess harvested tomatoes to cook and can. The twins busied themselves looking for bugs in the garden. Bread and cheese with mugs of steaming tomato soup were served for supper just before milking and Edward helped Paul finish some light work

The next day dawned hot and hazy. Paul had been given a place to sleep in the hay barn overnight and he was in the kitchen before breakfast waiting for his coffee much to Bess's dismay. Edward was out getting the water for the day and his brother and father were milking the cows. Today they would have to get the milk to town. Josh was hoping a neighbor would come by, knowing that they were digging the well and offer to take the milk into the creamery in town. If no one offered, he would send Weldon. It would take Weldon over two hours. This would cut down on the progress they could make on the well. After breakfast Frank and Rose stopped in on their way to town. After inspecting the progress on the well and offering unsolicited advice, they agreed to take the Bordeau's milk to town. Bess thanked them with a few pieces of yellow cake for their trip.

Relieved that he would have everyone to work on the well, Josh went to work. He took his turn down in the well. Before he went down, Paul pumped in air with weighted hay-filled gunnysacks. Weldon was trusted with the winching up of the bucket. Edward was in charge of the wheelbarrow and sorting the rocks for the backfilling. Life and death in digging a well depended not only on the safe handling of the loads being carried up the shaft, but also on knowing when the digger should come up for fresh air. This was because of the potential build up of methane gas and carbon dioxide in the depths of the well. The gases could cause the man in the well to become unconscious and die. This is one of the reasons Josh was glad to have Paul help with the digging of the well. He was the only one with experience.

Edward was eager to go down in the well. He had been assigned other tasks throughout the process and he desperately wanted to get in the hole and find water. After an hour his Pa called from the depths of the well to be pulled out. As Paul prepared to go in, Edward begged to have a turn. Josh agreed and one rope was tied to Eddie's chest to help lower him into the well. Down he went into the coolness of the well. Edward was surprised at the cold. In the first 15 minutes he dug furiously filling three small bucket loads in succession. At the top Josh took over from Weldon winching up the buckets and Paul stood by, ready to pump fresh air into the hole. As Eddie dug, he began to breathe heavily. He felt a head-ache coming on. His stomach churned but he didn't want to give up. Pa called down, "You doing okay, boy?" Bess, who was out in the garden, heard the uncertain tone in Josh's voice as he called to Eddie. She was furious that he, just a child, had been in the well. She came over quickly, sharply telling the twins to stay back.

"You pull him up right now!" she demanded. Edward was hoisted to the surface and helped out of the rope. He staggered for a moment on his feet and then fell a few feet away from the well. Bess was right there. After a few minutes it was clear that he would recover and Bess launched into a tirade at Josh and even at Paul. "That's it for Eddie today," Bess ruled. There would be no more work at the well for Edward that day.

The work slowed down as the men had to do without one set of hands. Nevertheless when milking time came, the well was at 18 feet with water slowly oozing through the hardpan. After supper, Weldon and Josh went to do chores. Paul, having fallen out of favor with Bess, worked to clean up the area around the well, readied the pipes. and dipped out pails of muddy water from the ever increasing depth of water. They would have to keep most of the water out of the well as they continued to dig on the third day. The pails of water lifted to the surface would allow them to gauge of how fast the water in the well would accumulate. It was the worst part of the digging. The man in the hole would be crouched perhaps ankle deep in icy water, reaching in with his small shovel between his legs in a space he shared with the bucket that hauled up the sloppy wet mud, rock, and sand. He would stay in the hole until his feet were numb with cold and he was near hypothermia, or until he began to feel the effects of the gases. His safety had to be carefully monitored by the men at the top who had little to do other than pump in fresh air, and hoist out the sloppy pails. It would be slow going tomorrow and Paul would be in the hole as much as his body could take. Paul finished his preparations and washed himself up as best he could.

Bess was over her anger at Josh and Paul. She was of the kind who quickly angered but never held a grudge. Edward was meekly sitting with the twins and encouraging them to finish eating. Edward knew that because of him the work had gone much slower this afternoon. Paul came in quietly and sat next to Eddie. "You doing okay, boy?" he asked softly. Edward nodded. The emotion of the day was deep inside and he didn't trust himself with words. Bess felt tears in her eyes. She had been frightened, and once the anger was gone the remaining emotion was very different. She reached over to the stove and poured a cup of coffee for Paul, setting the leftover coffeecake on the table for him to help himself. Paul ate in silence, finishing his coffee without asking for more. "Thank-you, ma'am. I'll be gittin' some rest now. It will be a long day tomorrow." Paul didn't expect a word from Bess and was surprised when she turned around to face him.

"Yes, tomorrow will be long. You git a good night's sleep. And thank-you for all your hard work." They looked at each other and Paul knew he was forgiven.

The next day dawned hot and with a dull, angry-looking sky. As the work progressed on the well, the men worked without talking, often glancing to the west at the gathering banks of clouds. Toward late afternoon, the storm was eminent. The well was at 24 feet. A heavy rain could falsify their estimate of the water capacity of the well. Paul was chilled to the bone so Josh went in the hole. He was careful not to work too hard and fast. He did not wish to increase his breathing and have to be pulled out unconscious. As he felt the consistency of the ground he was scraping, he sensed more sand. With each subsequent pail, there was more and more sand. He tried to stay and finish the job but the cold and the gas were affecting his actions and his judgment. He was pulled to the surface blue with the cold and dizzy.

Weldon had not been in the well and had not wished to go down there. After Edward's scare, it was never even suggested. As his Pa came to the surface, Weldon knew he had to offer to do it. The clouds were rumbling overhead and the sky was a greenish, yellow tinge. "Pa?" he said. Josh, shaking with cold, nodded. Bess, who had been monitoring the weather and status of the digging did not object. In went Weldon into the dark, dark hole. He felt the wet, clammy walls of clay and rock on the sides and looked up briefly upward. The light was obscured by the men watching him. He could hardly see anything and he felt great fear. His eyes adjusted to almost pure darkness as his feet hit the shock of ice water. It was almost up to his knees and he called up to the men to let them know. Paul called back to him that the pry bar was being lowered. He plunged the pry bar as deep as he had strength for and then rotated it much as Bess might stir a large thick pot, churning the sand and water between his legs. The water bubbled up from where he stood. It bubbled up so quickly it was all Weldon could do to collect his tools and his wits before being winched up to the surface. Toward the very last he had been chest deep in the icy water. He was shaking with cold as he was pulled out of the well.

There was no time to celebrate or to finish the well. The tension was as thick as the clouds rolling over head. Bess was employed to bring a canvas and stakes to help prevent water from going in the well. Suddenly a nearby flash of lightening and crack of thunder put everyone into high gear. Weldon and Josh were still shaking, from cold and from the experience of being far below the surface of the earth.. Bess herded the twins inside and the men prepared for the worst, anchoring the canvas with stakes pounded into the ground, boards, rocks, and dirt around all the edges. As the first few large drops fell, the men headed for the porch.

Josh cursed under his breath. Weldon stripped off the muddy clothes and rinsed his legs and arms before drying off and putting on dry clothes. Paul and Eddie stood apart from the others and looked at the sky. Eddie said hopefully, "This could blow over, ya know."

Paul considered Eddie's words. The rolling clouds were to the south. So far only large drops of rain had come down. Suddenly the wind on the edges of the storm picked up and the sky turned black. Josh screamed to Bess to get the twins to the basement which meant running through the rain to the back of the house and the entrance to the basement. The boys followed their mother and sisters down the stairs unwillingly. They sat themselves down on upturned buckets and wooden crates. Paul and Josh stood in the cellar stairwell as the masses of black, rolling clouds approached. Below they heard Bess singing to the girls. "Rain, rain, go away. Little Ella wants to play. Rain, rain, go away. Little Anna wants to play."

Eddie and Weldon knew better than to question Josh. They sat and picked at scabs and dirt under their nails. The damp cold in the cellar chilled their wet, steamy bodies. Eddie shivered. Weldon spat on the dirt floor. Both boys wanted to be in the stairwell with their father. Viewing the pending storm first hand was better than imagining the storm from their hole in the ground. Weldon cursed once under his breath, but then saw Ma's head turn slightly toward him.

Bess tried not to imagine what terror could descend within the next few minutes. She focused on the twins, on her song, and tried to put the chilling thoughts out of her mind. A tornado meant death and destruction. The house, stick-built with the cheapest supplies that could be purchased or re-used, would never withstand a direct hit. Bess tried to pray while she sang.

The wind howled outside the cellar, large droplets of rain spattered the dusty earth, and somewhere nearby a tornado touched down. Eddie's optimism about the storm blowing over them came to pass. When clouds began to part in the west, the sun streaked through creating rainbows of color in the eastern sky. Josh climbed down the stairs and looked at his family. He looked deeply into the eyes of each of his sons, patting them firmly on the shoulder, the greatest show of emotion he could offer. He turned squatting down to the level of the little girls, nuzzling kisses into their hair. He stood and faced Bess. He looked into the eyes and heart of his wife until he felt his own eyes swimming and he had to look away.

*****

In the years that followed the digging of the well, the Bordeau family, father and sons, purchased dynamite to clear a large field of the pine stumps left from the clear cutting of the virgin timber forty years before. The twins developed individual identities and were no longer known as EllaAnna. Ella had become the more docile twin, preferring to follow her mother about the kitchen and preferring Eddie to Weldon. Anna had become the tomboy. She would sneak off to the barn when the men were milking and ply her Pa with questions about the cows. She was curious about everything the men did from washing the teats and udders to feeding the cows and calves to the cleaning of the barn. She also liked to think that she had good ideas that her brothers and Pa had not thought of. She asked strings of 'why' questions and offered her own answers if the men didn't have answers for her. It was terribly good entertainment for the drudgery of the daily milking and barn cleaning. Ma didn't like Anna to be in the barn. She thought it too dangerous and unladylike. But Pa and the boys never objected with anything stronger than, "Anna, you do what your Mama says."

One particularly memorable event began innocently enough. "Pa, why do cows raise their tail to shit?" Weldon worked hard not to laugh aloud.

"Because."

"Because why?"

"Just because."

"But why?" Anna pursued this line of questioning as the cow in front of Anna raised her tail.

"Git back, Anna." Pa commanded.

"Why?"

"Cause I said so."

At that minute the answer became graphic as the cow raised her tail and the soft green manure from fresh spring pasture gushed from under the cow's tail into the gutter, splashing out of the gutter towards Anna.

Pa didn't know whether to laugh or cry. He picked Anna up by the least affected part while calling to Weldon to bring a pail of water. Once Anna was cleaned off enough to be given a real bath by her mother she demanded the answer to one more why question, "Pa, why don't you plug up that jeuda?" (Jeuda was a Bohemian word, left over from the generation of Bordeaus who immigrated to the United States in the late 1800s.) The story of "plugging up the jueda" became a beloved story about Anna in the Bordeau family oral history. It was a poignant story because of what happened later that year.

Dynamite was a powerful but extremely dangerous asset for the farmers clearing the huge pine stumps left after the loggers cleared the last of the virgin timber from the land. It was not difficult to obtain. The strategies for placing the dynamite, the mud caps on top the dynamite, the length of fuse—all of this life and death knowledge was handed down from one man to the other at the farm supply, from grown man to growing boy over the kitchen table. Thus it was that Weldon and Edward learned how to handle, place, and ignite the dynamite with the volatility of the nitroglycerin caps. Accidents, though not common, were a part of this dangerous endeavor. Both boys were adept at setting dynamite charges and their powerful, strong legs were useful for running quickly for cover once the fuse was lit. However it was Weldon who was drawn to create and control the power blasts. He never actually sauntered for cover, but he enjoyed controlling the timing of the event and the timing of his retreat.

Each time a report went off, Bess would go outdoors leaving the confines of the kitchen to verify the safe where-abouts of her men. The little girls were sternly forbidden from going into the fields and Anna specifically was threatened with the switch if she dared disobey.

So it was on an ordinary warm September afternoon that a violent report in the nearby field changed the Bordeau family forever. The men had come upon a boulder the size of a large bull submerged in the field as they finished cutting and clearing the wood from the previous blasting. They attempted to dig and pry out the obstacle to next year's plowing with little success. Weldon lit a few sticks as deeply under the offender as he could get. The huge rumbling report pivoted the rock upward, briefly stirring the sleeping giant. It did no more than yawn before settling down to its sleeping place in the earth.

It was getting close to suppertime. Josh and the boys stood around and kicked the dust with their boots. They talked little; the boys read their father's thoughts by observing where he looked, the frown lines between his brows, and the shift in his posture when he had come to a decision. Nearby, at the edge of the garden, Anna wondered why nothing was happening. She was sitting on the ground in a nest of her creation, a nest of torn grasses, brown-eyed susans, stolen soft brown corn silks, and dried clover. It was placed at the edge of the cornfield and it was easy for Anna to trespass into the forbidden territory a few inches, or a few feet, without calling Ma's attention to herself. "Why weren't Pa, Wellie, and Eddie back?" she wondered to herself. She knew ma would have supper soon and she thought they should be coming back from the field. It had been a half an hour since the last loud bang. She ventured a few more feet into the corn row, looking backward toward the porch where her mother would appear. If her mother caught her venturing toward the men, there would be a whipping and no dessert tonight. Anna squatted in the shade of the towering corn. Surely no one would notice her trespass. She looked down the row of the cornfield. She couldn't quite see to the other side no matter how hard she tried. She looked back toward the porch and with no mama in sight Anna scrambled along the long row.

Pa and the boys built a small mound of dirt over the two sticks of dynamite. They had argued in the heat of the sun about whether to use one or two sticks. Pa had relented though he was tired of wasting good money on blasts that did not get rid of the boulders. He had wanted the boys to dig down about eight feet and using the horses and pry bars they would bury the offending giant forever. Weldon, seeing an entire day's work of digging in the hot end of summer sun, argued for one more attempt at dislodging the boulder. So with the mudcap in place and the fuse ready, Pa and Eddie made their way back towards the cornfield. When they were standing clear, Pa gave the okay to light the fuse. Weldon lit the fuse at the very moment that Ma rang the dinnerbell. When Anna saw her Pa and brothers and heard the dinnerbell, she somehow forgot that she should never leave the yard. Picking herself up she sprinted off toward the direction of the men even as Weldon picked up speed with his long legs making his way farther from the boulder and farther from Anna. Pa and Eddie stood gazing at the boulder as Weldon loped to meet them. As the dynamite ignited, out of the corner of his eye Pa saw the small chubby speck joyfully running toward them and within range of the dangerous fallout from the blast. As he screamed, pointing toward Anna, Weldon stopped in his tracks and reversed his run to save his little sister from the falling rubble. He never made it in time. An errant piece hit Anna as she ran. Weldon threw himself over her in a futile attempt. As the tears spilled from his eyes he could only voice Anna's question from earlier in the spring. "Why?"

The pain of a family that loses a child is not a story that wants telling. The Weldon who sucked the rag of diluted whiskey water at the birth of his brother, the Weldon who fished the streams for trout and taunted his brother to join him for a swim in the pool, the Weldon who made the final plunge into the earth that brought the water, the Weldon who lit the fuse that broke the boulder that killed his little sister; that Weldon left the fold of the family and married a forbidden woman, a beautiful woman of the Bad River tribe of the Ojibwe nation. Josh disowned him for marrying an Indian and in his grief forbade the family to speak his name. Edward grew silent with thoughts of his brother. Little Ella was prone to solitary play with her mother's rosary. In this year following the death of Anna and loss of a son, Bess conceived, and then gave joyless birth to a son named John.

In the year that followed, Edward finished high school and Ella went to school without saying much at all to her teachers. She had no friends. When Edward had the opportunity to learn a trade in the city, his father did not object. Farming had become drudgery. He and Bess grew apart even as they were forced by the birth of John to continue to work together. John was a demanding child, never getting enough attention from anyone in the family.

A VISIT TO SOUTH ST. PAUL 2187

Matt was having trouble putting all the pieces of the puzzle together, the puzzle of his parent's silence concerning family history, the Indian doll his father had owned, the lock of hair, his own discomfort with the statue in the Flambeau Village square. From Callie he had learned parts of the story of the original Bordeau family. How was he, in the 22nd century, connected to them--men from over two hundred years ago, and the woman who lived a hundred years ago on Amy's land?

Matt and Amy went to sleep, on their own sides of the bed; Amy worried about Matt. He was extremely quiet after learning about the death of Anna and about Weldon leaving the family. She went to sleep thinking about Bess, a woman who lost two children. Callie told them very little of John, the last child to be born. What was his life like? Amy's dreams were filled with images of grief and of babies she could not save: bloody babes, with no water to drink or food to eat.

"Amy, I'm going for a run. If you don't mind, I need to go alone." Matt said after a quiet breakfast on the bench under the oak tree.

Amy tried to mask her feelings. "Of course not. I'll do some reading for school while you are gone."

Matt nodded without looking at Amy. He went back to the abode and changed into running clothes. He filled a bottle with water from the well, downed it and filled another to take along on his run.

Amy watched him pace himself as he ran down the driveway. A lump was forming in her throat. She wandered back to the kitchen, cleaned up the dishes and went to the study to work. She found it difficult to concentrate on her readings and she hoped Matt would be back to normal after his run. To feel as if she were accomplishing something, she began to clean vegetables and cook some rice for lunch.

An hour after he left, Amy heard the door open. Matt enter the lav. As she peeled carrots she felt her eyes swim. She shook her head and clamped her jaws firmly together thinking to herself, "Amy Anderson, you are a fool. You have no idea what is going through Matt's mind. You have only known him for five days. He has a right to be alone. He has a right to pack up and leave." The pep talk had the desired effect. She was feeling more in control of herself.

Matt finished his shower. He was now thinking with a clearer mind and in his mind a plan was forming. He stepped out of the lav and into the study. He scanned through each pile from the time capsule on the long table. The last item from the time capsule was a gold ring, thin and worn. It was sealed in a plastic bag along with a tag that labeled this ring as Grandma Bess's wedding band. He finalized the plan in his mind, a plan that included Amy. He knew he wanted a break, wanted to go back to St. Paul, not to get away from this place but rather to try to gain access to a machine which would give him the information, whatever it was, that resided on the memory card. Matt stood momentarily in the doorway of the kitchen watching Amy as she worked. His heart was full as he watched her. She was part of his life now, the reason he could now learn the secrets of his family's past. She was also more important than the past; a life with Amy was his future.

Matt's presence in the doorway was known to Amy; she had been listening for his exit from the lav. She had heard him picking up and putting down the items from the time capsule. She was in control of her feelings at the moment and she knew she couldn't let go of this control, couldn't turn to Matt as she heard him leave the study. The hair on the back of her neck prickled and her breathing became shallow as she sensed Matt moving toward her. Then she felt his arms encircling her and his warm breath in her hair.

"I don't know what I will learn from here on," he said, resting his cheek on the top of her head, "but I know that it doesn't matter to me as much as you do. I love you, Amy Anderson, and I am hoping that you might feel the same about me, regardless of my history, the time capsule, and the information it contains."

Amy and Matt ate lunch and talked as lovers talk in the shade of the old oak by the well. Matt told Amy that he wanted her to accompany him to St. Paul to meet Jim Krantz and to see if he could help them locate the ancient computer equipment. The plan was conceived and the pair prepared for the trip to South St. Paul. They tidied up the abode, pumped precious water from the well to fill a number of bottles for the trip, and took off late in the afternoon in Amy's run-about.

*****

Run-abouts and the Rapid Transport System were the dominant modes of transportation for people like Matt and Amy in the late twenty-second century. Run-abouts served the purpose of quick easy transportation for errands within a 50-mile radius. They were a variant of the 21st century hovercrafts.

The Rapid Transport System, known as the Rapid T was a gridwork for high speed, light rail trains. There were Passenger EMU (Electric Multiple Unit) coaches for walk-on traffic and platform EMUs for run-abouts. The scheduling program for the grid automatically accommodated daily changes in traffic (walk-ons versus drive-ons). They ran every 5-8 minutes in cities and every 15-30 minutes in rural areas. The coaches slowed only briefly at stations, people stepped aboard from one moving platform to another until they stepped into the coach.

The EMU platform cars were marvels of efficiency. They ran at the same speed whether at stations or on long stretches of rail which accounted for their efficiency. Run-abouts drove on a parallel boarding rails, increasing in speed prior to being magnetically drawn onto the platform car. They were held in place automatically until the destination was reached. The detachment of the run-about was governed electronically and there was never any opportunity for operator error.

People without access to run-abouts used Mass Transports in small towns and cities for errands requiring transportation or they resorted to ancient bicycles. A few Segways from the beginning of the 21st century were still being used by lower class people who could afford them, however the batteries for these were never improved and thus did not allow any real distance. The Mass Transports were lumbering slow beasts compared to the quick and light hovering run-abouts. The Governors of the Earth proclaimed that by the early 23rd century there would be a run-about for every living citizen of the earth. Nothing was said about the number of citizens who would die of 'natural' causes before that time.

*****

The sun was low in the sky when the run-about stopped at Matt's building. It was Amy's turn to be silent and Matt's turn to wonder about her thoughts. Amy looked upon the rows of neatly manicured buildings, each building like the next. Within the buildings there were little student pods, one of these belonging to Matt. Few people were about, no animals or insects. The only plants she had seen were in a well-manicured and arranged greenspace. How could one live, really sustain life, in an artificial environment such as this?

Matt and Amy unloaded the run-about, the bulk of what they

carted inside were Amy's heavy bags containing the bottles of well water. "You're not saying much." Matt said. Amy could only shrug her shoulders. She was extremely uncomfortable in this environment. Without Matt, she would never have come to such a place.

The building's computer system immediately recognized Matt from his embedded chip. Amy needed to sign in as his guest using the fingerprint reader. The door opened to Matt's abode. It was as tidy as Matt; Amy's presence seemed to bring disarray into the environment. That evening they stayed indoors; there was nothing to draw them outside. Futile attempts were made to search the web for files containing information about Weldon and John. It was as if they never existed.

Matt slept a dreamless sleep. He blocked his thoughts and unanswered questions. Amy slept very little. She stood by a small bathroom window most of the night that had no view but brought in light. She was troubled by not being home and as she analyzed her mood, she realized she was fearful of using up the bottled water before their mission in the city was accomplished. She wrestled with the problem of conserving the water they brought. Every single potable liquid in Matt's refrigerator consisted of a concentrate reconstituted with water that she was afraid of. Amy's mind wandered to a memory of a story she had read years ago. It was the story of a life raft adrift in the ocean. Aboard the raft were five strangers, one of them a nurse. When they ran out of food and water, the nurse devised a bottle and tubing which she used to give each person a daily enema. The colon absorbed the water for the body and by this method of hydration everyone lived a month at sea before being rescued. Amy shuddered. She lay down next to Matt and in the hour before dawn she floated alone on a raft upon the ocean.

The next day Matt and Amy took the 400 Rapid T to South Saint Paul. They brought some of Matt's clothing and food purchased with passcards at the World Food Market Division, the same WFMD Matt had visited when he first tried to buy lettuce. They hoped they had chosen things they could barter with, not for food, but for some ancient equipment to read the contents of the memory card. They also brought some real food to share with Jim Kranz and Rita.

Jim Kranz, the self-proclaimed mushroom man, did not see them coming. It was Rita who noticed them first. She had a change of heart regarding Matt when he had given her the shirt for her son. Smiling, she waved them over.

She looked warmly at Amy, "Did you like the flowers?"

Amy blushed for the first time. What else might Matt have said to these people about her relationship with Matt? Impulsively she replied, "They were very beautiful. They were perfect."

Rita filled in some information about Jim's failing health. She told them that today was an especially bad day for Jim. His vision had been failing and he hadn't eaten well lately. Rita had taken to bringing little things to Jim to encourage his appetite. "I'm sure seeing you both will have a good effect upon Jim."

"We've brought some great food to share with you both. Amy can really cook!" Matt said proudly. Amy poked Matt and rolled her eyes.

"I'm sure she can." Rita said, smiling, "It is an important craft that has all but disappeared from this earth."

"I cook," Amy responded, "but not gourmet. Can you join us at Jim's stand for lunch? It is good food, not great, but at least nourishing."

Rita remembered her initial encounter with Matt. These two young people were kind and kindness was in short supply in Rita's life. "Are you sure you want me to join you? I don't have anything to really share."

"Oh yes you do. Bring some flowers!" Matt replied. Rita's eyes gave her away. Amy, noticing the emotion at the surface, stepped forward and gave her a hug.

When they parted Rita blinked back a tear. "How soon should I come over?"

"When you can leave your stand, Rita. We'll talk with Jim a little and set up a place to eat. Just come when you are ready," Matt replied. "And bring the flowers!"

Matt picked up the bag with the water and Amy took the food pack. They walked slowly toward Jim observing him as they walked. His eyes were closed and he sat stiffly in his old lawn chair. They did not speak as they walked and the only sounds were their footsteps breaking the dry, brittle grass. It must have been the sound of their footsteps that prompted Jim to open his eyes.

Initially he looked without realizing who they were. However, when he was able to make out that one set of footsteps belonged to Matt, the light seemed to come into his eyes and he smiled the smile that Matt remembered that first day. The two men clapped each other on the back while Amy watched. She immediately liked Jim and was glad that Matt had stumbled upon him that first day at the market.

Jim's smiling eyes took in the owner of the second set of footsteps and they twinkled with a little fun. "Lettuce for life and flowers for beauty; a girl for the heart and a love for the soul."

Amy smiled knowing that she was the subject of his impromptu poem.

They talked about the market, about how Jim found mushrooms, and about Jim's health and vision problems. Amy set aside the newest basket of mushrooms and spread out the tablecloth she brought for lunch. Matt posed the question of how to view the information on the memory card. He showed Jim the device he and Amy found in the time capsule.

"I know nothing of such matters but an old codger, Wally Walczak, deals in electronic salvage. He lives at the edge of the market in a beat-up camping home. He's collected a few of these trailers through his trading and uses them to store parts to sell for the few people around here who use the old technology." Jim added wistfully, "It's too long for me to walk but I can tell you how to get there."

"We have Amy's run-about at my abode. We could pick it up and then come here to pick you up."

"That's a lot of trouble to go through for just another old codger like me." Jim answered, but inside he was pleased that

Matt wanted to include him in the visit to old Wally. He hadn't seen Wally for a few months and was curious how he was getting on.

"No trouble!" Amy chimed in. "We need your expertise!"

"Yes, I am an expert—an expert in mushrooms alone."

"No," Amy answered. "You are an expert in interpersonal relationships."

Jim couldn't think of a good comeback other than to raise his eyebrows. Rita saved him from having to have the last word by joining the threesome with her vase of flowers and a plate of four cookies. Her eyes showed her uncertainty, "I baked these and brought a few for a little dessert after we eat, but we don't have to have them."

"Oh wonderful! I didn't bring any dessert!" Amy assured Rita.

Matt added, "I haven't had real cookies since my mom died."

Rita basked in the warmth of their acceptance of her. The four sat around Jim's table, slowly eating and talking, savoring the flavors of the nourishing foods Amy brought. Amy asked Rita questions about baking and learned a few pointers for her venture into baking bread. Rita promised to share a small amount of starter to raise the bread and told her who to see to trade for enough flour to bake a few loaves of bread. They ended the meal with the four cookies Rita had brought. They were crisp with small bits of dark chocolate. Everyone declared them to be the best dessert they had ever eaten.

When they finished, it was decided that Matt would go back for the run-about and Amy would stay at the market getting a few more baking recipes from Rita. Amy wanted also to wander around the market to see what else people did here. She had brought some dehydrated, prepackaged food for bartering in case she had the chance.

"I never had a daughter," Rita said to Amy as they walked back. Amy reached over and stroked Rita's back.

Amy wandered around the market after leaving Rita. She located the flour vendor and decided to wait until hearing from Matt so that she wouldn't have to carry it around. After a while she used the outdoor lav. It was a small cubicle that incinerated wastes. Amy remembered her parents talking about the ancient outdoor lavs. They had only heard of them through their parents, that they were very smelly and unsanitary. These old lavs, outhouses they were called, were one of the things that was banned by the government at the turn of the century.

After using the lav, Amy wandered into a small bookseller tent. Antique, printed books were always fascinating to Amy. Her mother treasured books and Amy kept the few her mother owned in her study. She added books to the collection when she could find ones she liked. Most books were moldy and too fragile to consider purchasing. Amy looked at them without touching. As she walked along, she spied a book of photographs that made her smile. "How appropriate!" she mused. The author/photographer had put together a collection of photos of ancient outhouses. The book was faded and jagged on the edges but Amy could make out the photo on the cover. It was an old upright timber structure with a little pointed roof. The subtext indicated that this one, from the twentieth century, was from northern Wisconsin. Amy couldn't pass this by and the bookseller agreed on trading for two nutritional snack bars.

Amy's passcard indicated a call from Matt. He was almost back so she went to the stand where she bartered again for the flour before returning to Jim's stand.

The two men got in the front of the run-about and Amy sat in the back storage area. Rita and a few others from the market came over to watch. Run-abouts were not common so Jim was looked upon with some envy. Matt drove slowly through the market so that Jim would have a chance to wave to people he knew. Amy leaned in between the men and asked, "Now, aren't you glad you came along?"

Jim answered without taking his eye off the people in the crowd who were watching him. "This is really something. I never thought I'd ever have a chance to ride in one of these!"

Matt smiled to himself. Even if they couldn't locate a memory card reader, this moment was worth the trip.

"Here we are!" Jim exclaimed, "Turn right and you will see a group of camping trailers. That's Wally's place."

Matt stopped the run-about near the largest, silver-domed trailer. Someone was peering out at them. "That would be old Wally," Jim replied when told about the person peering out of the window. Amy stepped out first, coming to Jim's side of the run-about and offering a hand. The threesome walked toward the entrance but before getting there 'Old Wally' came out, his colorful language bombarding Jim and excluding the two young people. After a few moments, Jim broke into Wally's steady stream of talk. "Walter, these here young people are my friends, Amy Anderson and Matt Bordeau. Matt has a little project where you may be able to lend your knowledge."

Now Wally, like most of the people at the market, would not have helped an outsider, but Jim had brought Matt and Amy into the inner circle. Wally did not even consider keeping his distance, he was so pleased to see Jim and to have his own skills and knowledge valued by someone else. He liked the fact that his friend introduced him by his formal name Walter, giving him the opening to extend his own friendship to the two. "Just Wally to my friends," he answered. "Can you come in for some coffee?"

Jim knew the inside of Wally's home trailer and how its unsanitary clutter would affect his two young friends. He quickly took the opening to sidestep the question. "We've just had some with Rita. You remember Rita from the stand next to mine? She's the flower gal."

"Oh, so that's why you haven't been by to visit; Rita is keeping you busy." Wally chuckled, thinking he had figured out Jim's love interest. Jim let it be.

"So, do you think you'd look at what my fine friend has here and see if you have something he can use to read it?"

Matt took the wafer thin memory card out of its plastic holder and handed it to Wally. He turned it over and peered at the logo then looked at the connection. "Can't say I've heard of the name before, but the edge here," and here Wally pointed to the edge with its silver connectors, "is something that I've seen before on the old consoles and old cameras. To find a way to read it, we need to know whether it was used before or after holigraphic technology. "

"Why is that important?" Matt wanted to know.

"Well, computer technology took a big shift with the advent of holigraphy. Before that time the text and visuals showed up on a liquid crystal display. Then, for a very short time the smaller computers used projection technology on a flimsy, foldable panel. The computer software was basically the same for both of these antique technologies. So to find a device to read your memory card, I would have to find a computer from this era of about a 50 or 60 year time span. The projection screen was nicely portable, very expensive, and many people bought into the concept. In the long run, it wasn't very durable. Do you have any idea what year this might have been used?"

"Prior to 2087," answered Matt.

"Well, Wally," Jim raised his eyebrows, "this should be a piece of cake for someone like you. How many systems could there have been before 2087?"

"Glad you asked that!" Wally was enjoying the subtle sparring match that was occurring with Jim. "Holigraphy became available to the wealthy after 2060. It is possible, if the user of Matt's memory card was wealthy, that the programming to read it was holigraphic, though not of the quality Matt now uses. Or it could be that the system used by this person was the previous technology. I hope it's not one of the portable holigraphic machines. They are as rare as the audio wire recorders of the 1930's and I don't have either one of those. Sure wish I could have gotten my hands on one of those first portable holigraphic machines. It was invented by two old geeks--two brothers. You know," Wally mused, "I have a lot in common with those two guys."

Matt sighed. It appeared that Wally only wanted to talk. Matt was about to thank Wally and simply give up but before he could say anything, Jim stepped in. "The question is, do you have something to read it with or not?" Jim took the card out of Wally's hand holding it up briefly before handing it back to Matt.

"Well now, try to be a little patient with the process here. I'm an electronic doc, and it's good to have all the information before making a diagnosis." Wally was a little miffed at Jim's directness. "We'll have to do some trial and error surgery."

"No surgery, we've just come to try this out with you, but if you don't really know anything, that's okay," Jim concluded.

This, of course, put Wally right where Jim wanted him. Wally led the way to another trailer. Inside, the visitors could see piles of electronic equipment in various stages of disrepair. Wally stated, "This is my operating room. I'll see if I have a device worth resurrecting for your memory card." The fact was, Wally knew exactly what Matt had brought him and he knew exactly what would read it. Still, he continued to create an aura of mystery concerning the card.

First he located a large metal box that he called a tower. It took him twenty minutes to attach a series of cables to the machine. He showed Matt where the memory card could be plugged in. Matt felt hopeful as Wally started up the mammoth machine. It took awhile to come to life with clicking and grinding sounds. Finally the large screen came to life with a low resolution graphic and text

"Okay, it's ready. We just insert your little gizmo here." He pointed to an opening on the front of the tower. Matt carefully tried to place the silver edge of the card into the port. It didn't insert automatically and Wally, to show his expertise, took the memory card from Matt, flipped it 180 degrees and deftly put it in. Everyone held their breath, but Wally was particularly nonchalant. Within a moment a message appeared in text on the screen, *PLEASE INSTALL DRIVER*.

Everyone looked to Wally. He shrugged. "Well, that's that." Wally pulled out the card and handed it back to Matt. He went into a detailed explanation of the PC's of this era and how specific drivers ran specific devices. Evidently this machine did not have the correct driver installed.

"So you don't have anything that will work." Jim stated rather

impatiently.

"Now I didn't say that. I told you a good doctor needs a complete diagnosis before recommending treatment and you didn't let me diagnose!" Again, Wally wanted everything he could get from Matt, regardless of his own friendship with Jim. He rummaged in another room of the trailer and came out with a bulky turquoise blue and silver machine, hinged at one side. He opened it, plugged it into the wall outlet and this smaller dinosaur sprang to life. "Now this here one has all the drivers installed, it is a self-contained computer from the beginning of the twenty-first century. See this logo? This means it's an Apple computer, a brand that vied for the computer market by being simpler to use. It uses the liquid crystal display, a heavy old clunker in the pre-holigraphic era. Maybe it will read your card."

In truth, Wally knew the Apple would read the memory card. Jim glanced at him out of the corner of his eye and understood everything. However, it was impossible to hide the complete fascination the old computer wizard held for Matt and Amy. Wally smiled inwardly. He knew he had them. Jim sighed in resignation.

Inside the memory card was the sum total of all the information Callie had collected. There were scans of family photos, maps, an aerial photograph of the homestead, documents, and scans of letters by people in Callie's grandparents' generation, maybe even earlier. Matt was willing to do anything to have the ancient computer.

Wally invited them in for coffee. Jim shrugged. His interest in the project was waning and he was getting tired. Amy offered to take him home while Wally and Matt shut down the computer and made their way back to the home trailer.

When Amy returned, Matt was looking pale. Amy attributed this to the information on the memory card or to what Wally wanted in return for the Apple or to the strong smell of coffee in the trailer. She was not prepared for what she heard next.

Wally began. "I've given your friend some information and he asked that we wait until you returned. He thinks it may be important to you."

"Basically, I plan to give Matt the apple out of friendship but with a caveat. Some time in the future, I will be useful to you both again, but I will need something in return. Access: access to Matt's console and through his security clearance, access to the world server. That is all I need, I can go from there. I can reprogram your own chips for you and believe me, someday you will need me to do it."

Amy looked to Matt for more of an explanation, but he was silent, sadly looking at Wally. Amy thought to herself that they should just leave, try another avenue for reading the memory card. She was about to say that when Matt put his hand over hers and then looked to Wally to continue.

"I am not what I once was many years ago. I have been waiting for an opportunity like this to occur for almost thirty years. Thirty years of plotting and stewing here with these relics of technology." Wally gestured, encompassing his collections of trailers and computers. "I really began to believe that I had come to a dead end, literally, I would die in this hole; the ultimate victory for our fuckin' Governors of the Earth."

Wally stood up, retrieving three coffee mugs. He turned off the heating element and poured for everyone without asking if they'd want some. He brought out a bottle of liquor, pouring a generous amount into the coffee—again without asking whether the two young people wanted any. "Sugar?' he finally asked. Both Amy and Matt shook their heads. Wally poured a generous amount of the white granular stuff into his mug while his company watched. When he turned his back toward them, Amy gave Matt a look that said, "What are we doing here?" Matt could only give her a small smile in return.

Wally sat down, looking into his cup. "I was a lot like the both of you, thirty years ago. I worked for the World Security System in R&D." He glanced up at Amy, "Research and Development." Wally took a swallow of the black stuff before going on. " I had been there about five years, developing that chip you have embedded in your hand." Amy felt in her left hand between her thumb and forefinger for the little pea size nodule that she often felt for when she was deep in thought. She had never paid much attention to it. It had always been there. The only time she really thought about it was when she was accepted into graduate school and had to go into the regional World Security office to have the chip reprogrammed. She knew at that point that the reprogramming of the chip meant she had a different status and could access resources she could not access before. But even this procedure was rather commonplace. She had been reprogrammed before, just in a different office.

"Yup, that's it, you've both got them and so do I. The only difference is in the programming. I was the one who developed the technology for this damn thing and I am the one who has suffered the consequence of my past accomplishments." He looked up, studying Amy, "At least until now."

This time Amy couldn't meet his gaze and lowered her head to take a sip. The taste shocked her but she didn't say anything. In fact she took another sip. His coffee, like his story, was shocking at first but as she thought about it, his story sounded plausible, sinister, and as evil as her theory about the water. Amy leaned back in the chair, looking at Wally and sipping her coffee. "Go on," she said.

"Well, I met a young woman, a doctor. We fell in love and as I'm sure you both do, we talked about everything, including my work." Amy startled at the parallel she felt he was drawing between himself and Matt, but she tried not to show it. "Sara questioned the outcome of my research. She felt the outcome was sinister and would lead to absolute control of the populace by the world governors. We began to argue about it, about the ethics of it. I was stubborn and wouldn't see it her way. She had lofty values and morals and decided she couldn't compromise her position. It became so bad that we couldn't enjoy each other's company any longer. We'd look at each other and start to argue. One day she just walked out of my life. That was that, she just walked out." Wally sighed.

"So, continuing the path I was on, I became even more sure

of my work and its usefulness to the world's societies. I could envision medical uses; I could envision the elimination of crime and fraud; I could envision efficiency of world travel. I think I must have worked night and day. I didn't want to think about Sara. I didn't want to dream, but when I did sleep, I slept in fear—a fear that she had been right. This fear grew and grew in me so much that I became a hacker, a sneaky monkey hacking into my own work. I looked like I was all gung-ho Governor's control chip by day; and by night I was slowly working on and storing away a parallel set of files, files to allow someone else or some other group to reprogram the embedded chips. I was extremely careful about the storage of my data. Even now, as we speak, no one knows on what server or servers the data is stored or in what cryptic encoding they reside. You are almost the only people that now know of its existence. I basically finished work on both endeavors at the same time."

"The chips were first tested on us at the lab. A beta version was embedded and programmed to give the access, which before had been given using the old passcards and voice recognition. The testing went on for about a year. After FDA approval, the chips were manufactured and embedded in at the birth of each new citizen of the earth. No programming was done at birth, but when the child went to school, the family's financial and social standing was analyzed and the child was programmed accordingly for school. That would be about the time each of you were born and each of you received your chip."

"More?" Wally had stood up to get more coffee. He held the pot and he asked this time. Matt and Amy declined and Wally drained the pot, thick and black into his own mug. "I don't sleep much, never did," He chuckled and added, "wonder why."

"My project, which spanned about seven or eight years in total, was now finished. I was awarded the Nobel Prize for distinguished service at a gathering of the Governors and I was fed a meal of such sumptuousness that I can still remember it today." Wally closed his eyes and smiled with memories of his day of honor. "The Great Hall of the Governors was in a small town in Switzerland. I was flown in on a private hovercraft. There were about a hundred and fifty of these extremely wealthy people. Their clothes were of a fabric I had never laid eyes on. The colors were as beautiful as the colors of all the tropical fish in the ocean. The hall was in many levels. Each had a single support, seeming to float in the larger enclosed space. And that space was of the clearest glass. The view of the snowy mountains and valleys was completely unobstructed by support beams. Sitting at the table of honor in the middle of this extremely beautiful space, I felt I had arrived and I felt ashamed of my lack of trust for these beautiful people. After dinner, there were a few speeches honoring my work and I bowed my head to receive my Medal of Honor. I remember thinking that the two geek brothers would have been proud of me."

"When I arrived home I received the full, unexpected compensation for all of my work for developing the mechanism that allowed the Governors of the Earth to control social justice: I was reprogrammed with no access."

Amy took a quick breath, finally understanding the entire story and its implications if they could believe Wally. She wondered if Jim knew any of this.

Wally shrugged, "Well, many good things did happen as I originally envisioned. There is no crime and in some ways we have a utopian world society. However, our utopia has a sinister side and I am living proof of this. I am locked into a socio-economic status over which I have no control. The Governors of the Earth have control over who is a professor, who is a doctor, and who is an engineer. If they don't like you, they simply reprogram you to reduce your access and status -- to shut you up."

"I understand this. The mighty and powerful are afraid of what I know and what I might do to sabotage their perfect society. So I have been effectively silenced. And now I am fearful that as time goes on, my creation and vision will extend to population control if some other near-sighted geek is stupid enough to create the demonic software needed. And who knows, someone may already have created it. I am even becoming fearful for my life. I'm just glad that I was wise enough at the end of my work for the

Governors to install an encrypted subroutine allowing me to be the chip system manager while remaining cloaked. But to change anything I need access, access to the central system."

Amy's half cup of coffee was cold and Matt hadn't touched his. It sat on the table where Wally had put it down. Everyone was quiet for a time before Wally spoke, "I now fear that they may want to eliminate me because they fear the very thing I am about to ask you to consider---to give me access through your security code. I'm fearful for my life and my goal is to undo this ticking time bomb. I want you to promise me that when the time is right you will come back and allow me access. I give you this laptop in friendship."

Matt stared at the floor and then looked at Amy. Everything she had told him about her fears of the water appeared to corroborate Wally's fears. However, this was too great a leap in his belief system. Matt was silent.

Amy looked at Wally and spoke, "I agree that there is a movement toward population control. I'm not so sure it could ever come directly from this chip."

Wally shrugged, "I don't know why I thought you'd believe me. Maybe because you came with Jim and he has been the only other person I have trusted with some of my thoughts."

"I didn't say I didn't believe you," Amy countered. "It is just that what I know of the biology of the human being suggests that a death sequence could not be triggered by an electrical impulse from a chip."

"I hope not." Wally sighed, "What I do know about death that relates to the chip is that the chip gets its electrical energy from the nervous system in the body. When a body dies, the chip dies. When that happens, the data on the dead person is automatically deleted from the active file. Only basic data is kept on the deceased and it is rarely accessed. One bit of programming that I didn't tell you, is that besides reprogramming your chip, I can set your chip to mimic what would really happen to your chip when you die. Essentially I can delete you from the active file kept by the World Security System. I have the ability to do this if you no longer want to be controlled by the WSS. You would continue to live but under the radar. But you'd give up a lot...and I did not create the software to reverse this, at least not yet. You'd give up a lot also if you wanted to be reprogrammed to a lower status. But by programming your chip to a lower status, we could upgrade at a later time if you felt it was safe."

Matt finally found something to say. "Wally, I just don't know. As Amy has learned, I'm the kind of guy who needs some time to process new information and I am completely overwhelmed at the moment by everything you've said and the implications not only for you, but for us."

"Yes, I understand. But don't wait too long, I'm not going to get any younger." Wally stood up and dumped out Amy's half cup and the grounds in his cup. But he set Matt's cup aside. "I'm sure you can imagine the risks you would be taking if you chose to help me. I also think you are smart enough to imagine the threat to the people of the world if you don't."

Matt and Amy stood up and walked to the door. It was very, very late. They would not be able to go back to Flambeau tonight. Matt extended his hand to Wally.

"Enjoy the laptop." Wally said without smiling.

"I appreciate your generosity and I hope we can find the right way of repaying you in the future." Matt answered.

"Bye Wally," said Amy softening the leave taking. "We will think over what you have said."

As Amy and Matt boarded the run-about and started to leave, Wally called out. "Wait!" He ran back into the trailer and when he returned he placed a small, dirty, golden box in Amy's hand. "When you get home, take a look at this."

"We'll see you again, Wally." Amy called back as she put the box into a pocket and Matt gave a small wave.

That night Matt and Amy opened the small golden box. Inside was a heavy gold medal attached to a woven ribbon of gold. The medal was inscribed with the words '2140, Walter H. Walczak, Distinguished Service, Governors of the Earth'. The back was simply inscribed, 'Nobel Prize for Social Justice'. They talked long into the night about what Wally had said and about Wally's strange behavior in giving the box to Amy. Matt found reasons to disbelieve Wally's statements. However, Amy felt a kinship with someone who was truly concerned with the power and intent of the Governors. Both wondered what Jim would have said, but it would be months before they would find out. For now they had to be content with learning more about Matt's ancestry from reading the words of the woman they knew as Callie.

My grandmother, Elly, was a great storyteller and I always enjoyed hearing her stories, the stories of her childhood. When I was a little girl, I would help her with gardening, picking beans or strawberries and while we would be working she would tell me about what it was like when she was little. When she talked it sounded like she was living the experience of the past. I would see her smile at me but she seemed very far away.

She told me a lot about her father, Edward, but I could tell there were many things that she did not tell me. She would say he was serious and strict but not tell me more. I remember asking her if he ever spanked her. She only laughed and shook her head.

Elly met my grandfather, Joseph while still in college. They bought the homestead next to the farm where Elly grew up after they were married and her grandmother, Bess died. They didn't move to the farm until after my father, James, was born. He was born a few months after a nuclear disaster called Three Mile Island. Joseph had been a nuclear engineer. Elly told me the accident caused him to reconsider his chosen field. I remember him as being very outspoken and distrustful of the government. Maybe Grandpa Joe's distrust all started with the Three Mile Island accident.

My Uncle Robert was three years younger than James. He was born in Flambeau. He met Leanne in Arizona during college. They married and had a daughter, Tiarra, and a son, Tyler. As a family they spent very little time in Wisconsin until after their daughter married. She and her husband, Jonathan, had three little girls in close succession. When the war broke out, Tiarra's husband was called into duty as an army doctor for the National Guard. Tiarra and her parents all moved in with Elly at Flambeau for a few years. Jonathan was killed as he returned to his base after a week-end with his family in Flambeau. After the bombing and her husband's death, Tiarra, her parents, and children moved back to Arizona.

James married my mother in 2003. They were both quite old when I was born and I was their only child. As they both worked in the city in very demanding professions, they sent me on the plane to the farm in the summer to be with my grandmother. I loved Flambeau and the country life. Later, when my marriage failed, I moved to Flambeau to live with and care for my grandmother. Sammy was only four and Marta was just a few months old at the time of our move. Sammy grew up in Flambeau and went to college back east, living with his father. Marta was never healthy and she died at age thirty-three.

Eileen L. Ziesler

FLAMBEAU 1962

The ditch was not full of water but full of ice. There was ice with a space between the top ice and the bottom ice, no soft mud, just cold ice and snow and dried weed grasses woven into the frozen space. Elly broke through the top ice with each step. She dropped down to her knees and peered into the space. It was full of ice crystals -- eerie, beautiful and white. Steam came out of her mouth as she yelled to her friend, "I found a cave! There's a cave here! It goes and goes forever—come here!"

Elly and the neighbor girl, dressed in old snow pants and boots, followed the ditch in the back forty of Elly's dad's farm, often breaking through the top ice. They found wonderful hollow places where they hypothesized ice caves of fairies and elves. They found fuzzy tops of dried cattails and the remnants of green swamp grass trapped in frozen water. On that day in mid-January, the cold, dry jet stream out of Canada gave way to a warm, moist flow from the south. The children played with the steam of their warm breath. They stayed outdoors for hours that afternoon and as the gray, heavy sky darkened it began to snow. Large conglomerate snowflakes, heavy and wet, fell and the girls laughed and lifted their faces to the sky catching the globules of snow, almost drinking the snow melt. They were thirsty, wet, happy and tired. They lay back on the snow covered ground, their wet snow pants and boots shedding the snow and their hats and mittens gathering it. "ELLY! CHERYL! Time for supper!" The call came from the distant farmhouse. The girls rolled over in the snow and stood up. Dutifully, they followed the ditch backwards, not taking time to search for fairies and elves, their stomachs beginning to growl.

Almost thirty years ago other people had taken the same path back to the farmhouse for supper. These were not playful, young girls, but impoverished men--hungry men with families and mouths at home to feed. They were not out on the farmland to play but to work, to work digging a drainage ditch through the farms in the middle of January in 1937. It was the great depression and the men were part of the federal program, the Civilian Conservation Corps, created by Franklin Delano Roosevelt's New Deal. The CCC was designed to help the unemployed and to improve the land devastated by the clear-cutting of Wisconsin's virgin forest and the massive brush fires and soil erosion that followed. In addition it was charged with aiding rural farms by increasing tillable acreage and production with wet land drainage projects and river flood control. On this farm, they dug with picks and shovels in the hard frozen earth; their job was to clear and deepen a seasonal run-off stream.

The work they did then gave Elly's farm additional acreage for growing crops and grazing cattle. Their work prevented erosion caused by the spring melt. The project was a miniature version of the Florida Everglades swamp drainage project. At the time it seemed that only good came of the CCC projects, but the reality was that it changed the wetlands and the natural creek beds forever. The cold natural creeks had held trout in the early 1920's when Ed, Elly's dad, was a boy.

Back at the farmhouse the girls shed their outer clothes and boots. Little feet and hands were red with the damp cold of hours of play in the snow outdoors. They hungrily devoured the tomato soup and grilled cheese sandwiches Elly's mom had made. The telephone rang and Ed spoke with Cheryl's mom. As the girls became aware of the pending separation and end of their wonderful day they put up a protest, pleading voices in the background, "Can Cheryl sleep over? PLEASE???" Ed pretended Cheryl's mom was saying no but then he looked at Mary and winked. In a flash, Elly caught the wink and began to cheer. It was thus arranged and there was an extension to the idyllic day of fairies and elves.

After evening chores and supper, Mary made popcorn for Ed and the two little girls. Mary and Ed watched the children play, delighting in their only child. She was the light of their life. Mary miscarried in the first pregnancy. It would have been a boy. It was years before she gave birth to Elly, their only child. Ed grieved the loss of this son and placed the blame on dirty city air and bad water, pulled from Lake Michigan and treated for drinking. He had planned to name this son after the brother he had lost. He vowed he and Mary would never drink the Chicago tap water again. Each weekend they traveled to an artesian well north of Chicago to fill jugs with spring water, which he deemed safe.

After four years of drinking spring water Mary gave birth to a healthy little girl. For two years, life was simple but their finances were going nowhere and Ed was unhappy with city life. He was a farm boy, a man's man, a hunter. He had gone to the city to leave the sorrow of Anna's death and Weldon's banishment and also to make some money during the depression, living in a rooming house with other men. It was not a good life. However, he learned a trade that let him use his talents, strength, and his mechanical ability to figure things out. Now he had more important things on his mind, namely a better, healthier life for his family. When he had the opportunity to buy his grandparent's farm, adjacent to the farm where he grew up, he and Mary made the big move for a better life. For Edward, moving back to the farm washed away the pain buried in him the day he left. For Mary, it was a commitment to raising a child in a healthy environment where her child would have safe drinking water and fresh, clean air.

But was this a better life? The life they had led in Chicago included running water, a nearby laundromat, neighborhood grocery store, and a Montgomery Wards only a few blocks away. Mary often bundled baby Elly into the buggy--large, gleaming chrome and shiny black. She sauntered up and down the streets greeting neighbors, showing off her baby. She could be out for a few hours in the morning or afternoon and come home with nothing in her shopping bag but a small bottle of baby oil.

This 'better life' was way different. However, as her little girl grew, color in her cheeks and strong, sturdy muscles, Mary believed they had made the right move.

It was a happy life as lives go but one where heavy, hard, and dirty farm work left Ed and Mary drained at the end of the day. They rose from their bed at 5:00 AM and after that wonderful morning coffee and a bite of bread or cake they went out to the barn. Mary did the milking and cleaning of the equipment. Ed fed the cattle, cleaned the barn, and transported the cans of milk into a large cement tank into which the cold well water was pumped with an electric pump. The cold water in the tank chilled the cans quickly and kept the milk cold for the large milk truck, another improvement from Edward's childhood. In the middle of the day Mary baked and cooked. She visited Edward's parents, Bess and Josh, who lived on the farm next door when she needed a reprieve from work. What became of the shopping and the long, lazy afternoons with the buggy? Mary gave the buggy to her brother's family still in Chicago. Shopping was done only on the fifth and the twentieth of each month when the milk check needed to be picked up in town. On those days Elly, Mary, and Bess bundled into Grandpa Josh's car and had an entire afternoon to shop. Josh drove the women folk into town. He enjoyed the afternoon in the local tavern with other retired farmers. Edward never went on these excursions.

Grandma Bess, Mary, and Elly would start with the bank to cash the meager milk checks, depositing a small amount into savings. Then they would walk down the street to the dime store. Elly's mom might pick out a box of Kleenex, a bottle of hand lotion, and some aspirin. Elly and Grandma Bess usually delighted in choosing some penny candy. Bess's eyes twinkled as she gave Elly a few pennies to make the big purchase.

On they would go to the clothing store that carried fabric. Grandma Bess held up cottons against Elly and declared their worthiness to be made into blouses or skirts for the little girl. Elly wandered the aisles looking at the displays of threads and ribbons. The colors fascinated her, especially the thread. A spool of blue could be found in almost any variation from green-blue to purple-blue, the shades of color from almost white to the deepest navy, easily confused for black. Mary moved between the racks of factory made dresses. There was no money to splurge on these. In this place of factory made clothing she daydreamed and recalled her life in Chicago, dancing in a beautiful dress with white gloves as a young woman in the ballrooms of the city to the music of the big bands. Mary thought about her life now--the clothes she wore as a farm wife, her hands, never covered with dressy gloves and chapped from the continuous use of hot disinfecting water and cold air. There was no reason to buy a new dress because there was nowhere to wear it.

Mary checked her watch. Her watch was an engagement gift from Edward. He gave her the watch on the floor of the Aragon Ballroom the evening he proposed. It was real gold with tiny rubies. It had cost a lot. Mary made her way back to her daughter and mother-in-law to let them know the time. They still needed an hour to buy groceries before the stores would close and they needed to get home in time to start the milking. The cows and their needs organized the farmers' day; milkings were at 6:00 AM and 6:00 PM. Everything else had to fit into that schedule; vacations were non-existent. Bess purchased a yard and a half of blue fabric to sew something for Elly. Elly picked out the matching thread.

When the groceries were paid for and packed, it was Elly's responsibility to run across the street to the tavern where her grandfather played pool and drank beer. Elly's craving for independence and responsibility was tempered with her extreme dislike of this task. The tavern was dark and smoky. It smelled of barn, beer, cigar breath, and spittoons. Elly always tried to hold her breath the whole time she was inside. Elly found her grandpa, "Grandpa, Mom and Grandma are done. It's time to go." She didn't wait for him to come but ran outside and gulped fresh air. She knew her grandpa would come even though he would have loved to stay and extend his day with the other old men. He was a farmer and the needs of the cattle came first. They bundled back into the car with their groceries, leaving town and returning to the work of the farm.

Edward tried hard to modernize the farm to make things easier on Mary even though modernizing the house would not come until years into the future. He had put in an electric pump to pump water in the barn for the cattle. All one had to do was plug in the cord and water would fill the large cow tank in the summer. Elly loved to watch the cows submerge their noses and then blow out the water as they drank. It was her responsibility to see that the cows had their fresh water in the tank each day.

One summer afternoon when Elly plugged in the cord to pump the water, she heard an unusual sound coming from the hay barn. She left her station at the pump just for a moment to see what the noise could be. She climbed the rough cedar rails to the top of the hayloft. The scent of sweet clover, and dried timothy filled her nostrils and the buzzing sounds from bees and flies were the only sounds she now heard. Elly stood very still. The sunlight, showing through the cracks in the old barn boards and illuminating specks of dust drifting downward, disturbed by Elly's movement in the hayloft. There it was again! --a tiny high pitched mew. Elly dared not breathe as she waited to hear it again and guage the direction from which it came. Once again she heard it, a little mewing, from the section of the hayloft over the cows' stanchions. Elly made her way as quietly as she could in the direction of the sound. She knew that sound. It was the tiny mewing of newborn kittens. Instinctively, the kittens stopped mewing as Elly closed in and she had to stop and wait for them to forget the trespassing presence. She waited patiently, knowing that they would call again for their mother cat to come and feed them.

Elly loved kittens. Raising kittens, dressing them in doll clothes, taking them for buggy rides, making bright color toys on string for them to chase, this was the way she spent her summers. But first she had to tame them with patience and bits of chicken or cheese that she hid in her pocket as she ate lunch. Tame them by climbing up to the forbidden heights in the barn of sweet smelling clover. The earlier she found the kittens, the easier they were to tame.

Out of the corner of her eye she saw the mother cat--- an old, cagey calico with a crook in her tail where a cow once stepped. It was the cruelty of farm life that one took for granted along with the pastoral scene and impression of peace. Kittens lost parts of their tails, toes, or feet in the barn with the cows, so eager were they to receive the warm milk the cows provided. If they were lucky enough to live to adulthood they learned to avoid being crushed as they lay with the cows, absorbing heat in the cold winter. They had to become clever like this old cat, knowledgeable in the ways and movement of the lumbering cows. Most cats in barns led brief lives.

The old calico had never been impressed with Elly; the child was young when the calico was a kitten. It had not taken to doll buggy rides and dress up clothes. The calico growled.

"Here, kitty, kitty, kitty." coaxed Elly. The calico held her ground. The crook in her tail twitched. Elly tried again, "Here, kitty, kitty, kitty." Elly felt in her pockets for any tempting morsels. Finding none, she took a few cautious steps toward the mother cat. That was close enough for the old calico. She jumped down from the loft and fled.

Elly changed her tactics, "Ma-rare, ma-rare, ma-rare." It was her best imitation of a mother cat calling her babies. It had never worked in previous years but the practice in those years paid off.

"Mew, mew, mew," the babies clamored, fooled by Elly's voice.

"There you are!" she answered as she located the mother cat's nest in the space between hastily tossed bales of hay. There were four babies, with their eyes not yet open. Still they hissed at Elly, knowing that she was not their mother. It appeared quite a vicious defense for the defenseless kittens. Another hour went by as Elly picked up each kitten, studied it and named it. By and by the mother cat crept back, driven by instinctual need to feed and protect her babies. Elly stepped backward ten feet and sat on a bale. The wind blew softly through the openings and Elly yawned. The mother cat came cautiously to her brood and curled up with them, glaring at Elly as if daring her to come closer. Elly smiled, knowing the babies needed feeding. She began to feel hungry herself and somewhere in the back of her mind there was a feeling, a feeling of something forgotten. Elly tried to focus on that thought and closed her eyes to help herself think.

"ELLY!" She jolted awake and all at once remembered that thing she had forgotten. It was the pump for watering the cows! "ELLY!" Her father's voice came crashing toward her. She knew in an instant from the tone of his voice that she had done a very bad thing. She slipped down the shaft and out of the barn to face her father. He had already pulled the plug on the pump. Beyond him stood the cows and an overflowing cow tank, mud all around mixed with the soupy manure.

"Sorry, daddy," she said softly. She knew the value of water and the fear her father had of losing the well. She had grown up hearing the stories from Grandma Bess.

"Don't you ever, ever leave the pump again! If you have to leave, you pull the plug first. Do you understand?" Her father's face was red as he tried to control his anger towards his crying child. He turned away from her and headed to the barn door to let the cattle in. Elly's mother came from the house in her barn clothes. She wasn't smiling.

"Mom, I didn't mean to. I heard kittens," Elly sobbed.

"Your father is very angry. You know how he worries about the water when we are having a drought." Her mother did not stop to comfort Elly, but passed her going straight to the barn.

Elly ran to the house and flung herself on her bed, crying until she fell asleep.

Out in the barn, Mary gingerly asked, "Is it okay?" Edward ignored her question for the first twenty minutes. When he finished cleaning the barn and feeding the cattle, he had calmed down enough to speak.

"Just don't use any more water for the next few days than you absolutely have to, do you hear?" Mary heard and thought unhappily that a bath would be out of the question until the water scare had blown over.

Edward kept to himself that evening. Elly stayed in her room, trying to lose herself in a book about horses. Mary went out to hoe in the garden and sighed when she saw that the tomato plants were so brown. She was too tired to attempt to carry water from the river.

Edward felt a growing fear; a fear of the cost of having a new well drilled. Each hour the fear became stronger and he retreated from conversations with his wife, his child, and his parents next door. Edward's face was a dark mask of fear, frightening and silencing Elly. She visited the kittens but made no attempt to tame them.

It was at supper, three days after Elly's mistake, that fear attempted to take over the Bordeau family but was eventually beaten down by Edward. Elly was not eating her supper and had told her mom that she was done. Her father, noticing her for the first time in days growled, "Eat it!" Elly was silenced and with her eyes cast downward willed herself to lift a small forkful of food to her mouth. She chewed slowly and a lump formed in her throat. The lump in her throat grew bigger and bigger. Tears began to drip onto her plate and she gagged. Mary did not say a word but looked pleadingly to Edward. He was now fully aware of what he had caused and in a flash he understood that this child that he loved should not have to suffer because he was afraid of something that may not even exist. He said quietly, "It's okay Elly, you can leave the table." Elly did not wait for a second invitation but bolted out the door, spitting the food out before another gagging reflex took over. Mary stood up and turned to the sink to hide her own tears of relief. Edward pushed away from the table and strode out the door to the little building housing the well and the pump. He shut off the electricity and dismantled the pump from the casing. After an hour and a half he came back to the house for a reel of fish line and a sinker and a flashlight. It was dark when he reassembled the well but the darkness of fear had left him. There was twelve feet of water in the casing of the well.

Edward took the truck over to his parents. Bess made some coffee and set out the coffeecake she had baked the day before, instinctively knowing what her son needed. Father and son talked for an hour about the cows, the price of milk, and the heifer that wouldn't breed. Edward stood up to leave. "Well, there's twelve feet of water in my well." Josh nodded as he puffed on his pipe. "Tomorrow when you go into town, I'm coming with. I think Elly would like an ice cream at the drug store." Josh nodded again.

"We'd all like some ice cream," Bess added.

More than twenty years later, Elly still vividly remembered that terrible sinking feeling from her father's silent anger and her mother's fear, all because she forgot the water that was running into the cow tank. She had learned as a child that water was precious and this she would never, never forget.

NORTHERN ILLINOIS 1975

Elly met Joseph Hanover in the early seventies. He had just landed a job as an engineer for the nuclear power plant in northern Illinois. They married while she was still in college. When Grandma Bess died, they bought the old homestead from her grandfather, just to keep it in the family.

Joseph was originally satisfied with his career and the opportunities for advancement. Elly and Joseph began to talk of buying a home near Joseph's work and having a family. During her first pregnancy they spent the weekends cruising the northwest suburbs looking for that special place to settle down. Two months before the baby was due they found that little starter home. It seemed perfect.

They made the offer on Tuesday, May 10, 1975. The next day was the 3-mile island disaster, a disaster caused by a faulty gage and human error. To avoid a catastrophic explosion from the built up steam in the reactor containment vessel, radioactive steam was released into the atmosphere. Prevailing winds carried the steam cloud for miles over populated areas. There wasn't as much of a reaction from the local population as there was panic from the political fallout it caused.

The result of the political fallout was the death of the plans for building additional nuclear power plants. Older plants were phased out; security, redundancy, and human error management shook up plant operators. The end result was a 30-year hiatus on the nuclear power industry, all because of a faulty control sensor and the wrong assumption made by the plant engineers at 3-mile island.

James was born two months after the 3-mile island accident that changed the way Joseph would forever view nuclear power. Six months later Elly graduated from college and they moved to northern Wisconsin, back to the family farm they had purchased only a few years ago--back to the land that was once a town named Flambeau, on the banks of the Chippewa and Flambeau Rivers, and away from the threat of pollution. Elly and Joseph used the old well that her father and Weldon helped to dig. The well was tested and the water was found to be pure and as cold as ice. But it was a shallow well and needed to be protected from possible contamination. When Joseph was out of work, he and his father-in-law Edward spent time building a small stone hut by hand from the rocks Edward had collected from the farm fields as a boy. When the hut was finished, a small door provided access to the pump.

About twenty miles away, upstream of the river near their farm, a serious threat to Elly's pure water was brewing. A mining company was obtaining a permit for an open pit copper mine. Protesters came from all over to either help the locals protect their land or to stir up trouble--depending upon whether you felt the mine was a curse or a blessing. Progress was not halted, but stricter mining laws were put into effect and although the permit was granted to mine the ore, no smelting of the copper was ever allowed in Wisconsin. As part of the new mining laws, wells of various depths were drilled and would be monitored for the leeching of the heavy metals into the ground water for forty years.

CLAM LAKE 1989

On Mother's Day, 1989, the Hanover family was relaxing after lunch in a small cafe in Clam Lake, Wisconsin, before driving home to Flambeau. Joseph and the younger boy, Robert, were making plans for deer hunting in the fall. The warm rays of sun from the window had the effect of rousing a few flies that awoke for a brief moment, buzzing on the dirty window pane. James had made a game of impaling the dizzy flies on the end of a straw.

Elly raised her eyebrows at James but remained quiet. It had been satisfying weekend, the four of them working to fill potholes in the cabin road on Saturday. They slept overnight in hard bunks, keeping an uneasy truce with the cabin mice and resident bats in the dark with no light but the embers from the wood stove. Elly didn't want to break that feeling of rewarding work with her sons and husband by disciplining James for his disgusting behavior with the flies.

Intuition, or 14 years of life around his mother, caused James to be aware of his mother's feelings concerning the accumulating pile of flies. Her lack of response amused him. He was unable to control the left corner of his mouth from curling into a half smile. It was a dead give away that let his mother know that he knows that she is watching. She tries but cannot prevent herself from enjoying this silent, playful sparring with her son. Though neither she nor James make a sound, Robert becomes aware of their silent communication. He takes in the graveyard of flies, his brother's teasing grin and his mother's look. He exhales a comment intending disgust from his nose. Joe rambles on for a moment before realizing no one is paying attention. "Okay, if that's all we're gonna do here-just kill time, let's get the hell out before the flies get mad." His wife and sons break their silence and laugh. He feigns naiveté, "WHAT?"

They pile into the car and drive down County Road GG. From the back seat one hears yawning and belching, which either could be attributed to the big breakfast or the social ineptitude of teenage boys. Suddenly Joe turns off the main drag onto a dusty side road. "Dad! Where you going?" The boys are disgruntled at not being consulted with the change of plans. "Well, no one's sayin' nuthin' so I'll just have to decide these things for myself." More disgruntled nose noise comes from the back seat. This time it's Joe's turn to control his grin.

The dry road is dusty because it has been very recently driven on. Not just by a few, but by many, many vehicles. Joe slows the car, as it becomes apparent that there are about a quarter mile of parked vehicles on the side of the road. The boys and Elly are now wide-awake. Elly thinks this is so like Joe. He has a plan and will not divulge it. Ahead they see people gathering in the middle of the road carrying protest signs. A twinge of uneasiness sets itself into the pit of Elly's stomach. Joe knows he has the full attention of his family and he himself feels the unease of the situation. His curiosity cannot be reined in, and he drives slowly forward, one passable lane of traffic between two rows of closely parked cars. "I don't know about this Joe. We shouldn't be here. What's going on?"

"Oh MOM!" comes the chorus from the back seat. Like small roosters, their hackles are up. They want to know more and they want to be in the thick of it. No more bantering with mom, they are solidly behind their dad now. Uneasy but curious, Elly peers out while slumping down in her seat. Someone in authority stops the car. Joe rolls down the window. "If you've come to protest, you'll need to back up and park down there a ways," he states. Joe starts to ask a question but the man has turned away and Elly's fingers have dug into Joe's thigh. Joe makes a huffing noise, puts the car into reverse and slowly backs up the way he drove in. Their car comes to the end of the row of cars and he backs into the parking spot. Before the engine is off, the boys spring out. "WAIT! Wait for your dad!" And to Joe she says, "I don't like this. I don't think we should be here. I want to stay in the car."

"Nonsense," Joe replies as he reaches for a jacket. He pushes the lock on the door. "Then stay here." Elly is out of the car before the boys and their father get two car lengths ahead.

Elly trots up to her family. James gives her an amused knowing look before turning to peer ahead. Some protesters are retreating, thermos and dusty backpacks in one arm, dog-eared signs in the other. They are talking together, hardly noticing Elly and her family. As they approach, Elly sees a somewhat familiar face, a woman with long graying hair. The woman looks straight at Elly, perhaps remembering her also. She was one who was involved in the copper mine protest in the early 80's. Elly makes one more attempt, trying to whisper into Joe's ear, "This is dangerous. We shouldn't be here." Joe gives her 'That Look' and Elly resigns herself to saving the boys first before she saves Joe from whatever trouble they were getting themselves into.

A quarter mile ahead they see what they must have come to see. They hear songs from the war era sung in earnest by long haired fifty-year-old professors from the college in Ashland. They see a man and a woman each with a large spindle full of string. It looks like they are weaving their string across the road. On the ground Elly sees piles of cut string pushed aside and trampled on. On the other side of the weavers' work she sees two men dressed in some sort of military uniform. They seem to have guns. Elly's voice is hushed. "They have guns," she says.

Joe's stride slows. Robert and James instinctively slow with him and the rooster look fades. They stand with him. Robert stands a few inches behind and James a few inches forward. Elly stands very close to Joe. They look on for a few minutes and relax a little. The weavers continue their work. It is the work of two spiders, threading through the already strung threads with new threads. Two dozen or so men and women sing, joke with each other, and hold signs that say, "no more cold war." From behind the gate the sound of a truck or van is heard and dust clouds the view beyond the string barrier. The singers move slightly to the side, the weavers finish one last pass in silence. A few men behind the guards step forward and cut the strings with shears. Elly looks on, no longer fearful, but dumbfounded at the scene. It was a van, a larger one. It came to a stop just behind the string gate. As the last threads fall to the ground, the van crosses slowly over. The protesters, the weavers, the singers and Elly's family move silently to the sides of the road, watching as the van crosses. Once out of range of the crowd, the driver guns the engine and leaves in a cloud of dust. People cough, sneeze, and blow their noses as the dust settles. One weaver ties the end of his string to the post and the other weaver yawns and stretches. "I'll take it for a while." The woman with long gray hair steps forward from behind Elly. Elly watches, fascinated by the scene. "Well, now we've seen it all," says Joe, a little too loud for Elly's comfort.

What Elly and her family have seen is a demonstration by Nukewatch and others against the antenna system built by the Navy called 'Project Elf'. It was a long wave communication system to signal the United States nuclear ballistic missile submarines as a last resort in the event of a communication blackout.

The family turns and walks back to the car without talking. Elly feels the eyes of the crowd on her back. She feels safe, but uncomfortable. She imagines that it was she who stepped forward saying, "I'll take it for a while." She imagines the unspoken gratitude of the tired weaver and the welcoming smile of the woman with the long hair. They reach the car, still not speaking. Joe turns the key, turns the car around, and the boys explode with questions and observations breaking into Elly's reverie.

FLAMBEAU 1997

Elly alternately stands by the window and then sits with Joe on the sofa. She is agitated, agitated by waiting, waiting and anticipating the return of James from college. Although the boys are grown and moving on with their life, she thinks about them every day. Not really worrying, just thinking and wondering what life is like for them. Wondering if they have girlfriends they are not telling her about. Wondering if either is in love.

"He'll be here when he gets here." Joe dismisses Elly's agitation, responding automatically to her body language. There is little he doesn't know about her after twenty-nine years of marriage.

"Right." Elly does not want to get into a discussion or sparring contest with Joe at the moment. Her psyche is concentrating on James. As foolish as it seems, she has always known his arrival moments before it occurs, not through sounds of cars or a call from his cell phone. She simply knows and accepts this phenomenon. Elly stands very still, her heart starts to race. Her hearing is tuned to what she knows is next, the crunching of tires upon the gravel driveway.

Elly is outdoors in a flash. James smiles to himself as he sees his mother's face. She looks as she always looks when she first sees him, a change coming over her face. But James is not thinking about his mother, he is thinking about the face of that girl from Massachusetts. He's only staying for a day, his mind and heart are elsewhere.

During that one day with her son home, Elly tries but is unable to obtain any real information about what is going on in his life. However, she knows something is happening. She feels it. As Joseph questions James about graduate school and work after school, Elly watches. She has never worried about his success in his education or career. She is concerned with his happiness in life. Just as many years ago with the flies in Clam Lake, James knows what his mother is thinking. He is amused by her concern but it is too early to say anything just yet about the love in his life.

The next morning Elly prepares a care package of food and snacks for the trip. As always, she feels sad that he is leaving even as she is happy for his success. James senses her feelings and his resolve to not confide is weakening. To distract his mother and himself from the unspoken questions, he begins to argue about the care package she is sending along. "Mom, how can you buy this crap when you have the best drinking water right here." James pulls the 12 pack of bottled water out of the cooler she bought for him.

"It's just easier for the trip," Elly answers, while trying to put it back in the cooler.

"NO."

Elly sighs, "What do you intend to drink?"

But James has closed the small cooler with the strudel and fruit. He returns with three well-worn acrylic water bottles that he begins to rinse out.

"We could have put them through the dishwasher to sanitize them. You don't want to get sick."

"They'll be okay." To lessen his mother's angst he fills the tea kettle half full with water and dumps out his bottles. "I'll rinse them with boiling water." As they wait for the water to boil, he tries to explain more. "Have you read about the city of Green Bay denying the permit for a foreign company to bottle water from the aquifer? All over the country, the bottling companies are stealing the water from the people, people like yourself, and selling it back to them in these jazzed up bottles like you bought. A gallon of it costs more than a gallon of gas."

His mother counters, "Don't you remember your grandpa telling about the Chicago water. He drove miles just to fill jugs from an artesian well rather than turn the tap on."

"Well Chicago water back then was different. Now these companies turn the tap on and fill these plastic bottles with whatever tap water comes out and sell it along with the hype. People are so gullible. People buy it because the label says 'spring-fed' or some such garbage."

Joe jumps in the conversation, siding with James. The tea kettle whistles and Elly takes it off the stove, rinsing the waiting bottles with the boiling water. She is acutely aware that James has in effect sidestepped any discussion of girls. After rinsing the bottles she lets the tap run until the water is icy cold. She fills the bottles and Joe gives the covers an extra twist. It has always been this way. Joe and Elly mechanically working on a task to prepare a son for leaving, not speaking about the emotion they both feel.

"Bye." James gives his mom a hug and she kisses him back. He and his father shake hands and then slap each other on the back. James climbs in, starts the car, and rolls the window down.

In sudden inspiration, Elly grabs the edge of the window, putting her face down and into the car, "So when are you bringing her to meet us?" James laughs and waves. He keeps chuckling to himself all the way down the driveway, knowing his mother knows and wondering how it is possible. Once out of sight of his parents, he uses both hands for a moment to loosen the cap on the bottle before taking a drink of the water, the precious water, the water he has always taken for granted.

FLAMBEAU 2187

The old I-Mac from Wally was slow to boot, but Matt was not impatient. The computer was like Wally, Jim, and Rita. It was from another generation. Running the photo program, Matt viewed the photos in the wedding and funeral folders. Callie's handwritten notes from the time capsule lay on the table next to the computer. When Amy arrived he was still studying the last photo of Weldon, the one with Callie on his lap.

My father James, and his brother Robert were married just a year apart. I imagine Elly and Joseph were thrilled about their sons' marriages though I am sure they were sad that the boys would continue to live so far away from Flambeau. Edward and Mary were still alive at the time and can be seen greeting guests in the photos of both weddings. In some of the photos there is a man seated in a wheelchair. He has steely gray hair and is very thin. He looks much older than Edward but it is Edward's brother, Weldon, who is only a little more than a year older.

Edward died before Weldon even though in the wedding photographs he looks very healthy. He had a stroke. Elly told me that the doctors tried to bring him out of it, but the stroke was from a bleed, not a clot. In those days, there was no treatment for a stroke that came from a bleed in the brain. Elly and her mother, Mary, made the difficult decision to let him go—no intravenous fluids or nourishment. Elly told me this story many times. It must have been a very difficult time for her and her mother.

Weldon is pictured in one photograph from Edward's funeral. He is holding a newborn infant in his lap, with Elly and Cathy on either side. I am the baby in the photo. Cathy is my mother and James, Elly's oldest son is my father. This is the last photograph taken of Weldon. Elly had no additional information about what became of him until much, much later.

ARIZONA 2047

On a warm winter day in Arizona Robert Hanover sat with his cup of coffee in the Oasis Café reading the newspaper and pondering the question of housing his daughter's family. The newspaper headlines proclaim skirmishes in states north of Arizona around the various construction sites of the aqueduct. The Great Lakes Militia won a significant battle, taking over a large pumping station near the Wisconsin-Illinois border. Their engineers and sharpshooters behind the militia lines were creating havoc with the water supply to the southern states by having completely disabled the large pumping station where the aqueduct met the Mississippi River. Robert thoroughly reads the article, learning that the militants are moving under cover to the next pumping station down the line in Iowa. It was getting personal. Jonathan, Robert's son-in-law, was being pressed into service by the National Guard to patch up the wounded hurt by the militia. Tiarra would be bringing the girls to live with Robert and Leanne.

Robert sighed, folded his paper and got up to pay the bill. Leanne would be expecting him home for lunch but he was not eager to be home. They would be arguing over their own personal issues concerning how to house Tiarra and the three girls in their tiny condominium. Robert sighed again. His bill was 12.50 with tax just for a cup of coffee-no refills. The complimentary glass of water with an order had been deleted from restaurant service for over 15 years. The price of a cup of coffee was up again-almost too much to even consider for someone on a fixed income. Of course he could have ordered Purefz coffee at 8.50 a cup with one refill. This was advertised as being every bit as good as the coffee made with real water, but he couldn't go there quite yet. He wasn't used to this newfangled water concept. It almost made him shudder to think that water was being produced as a bi-product of a nuclear reaction and the average human being couldn't even tell the difference. Right now the drinks produced using Purefz had to be labeled as such and the cost was about 2/3 the cost of real water products yet he was sure it cost more than that to produce. Robert wondered how long this price subsidy would last. How long would it be before people would be tricked into forgetting the water was not real water. Then the cost would go up he figured.

As angry as he was about the cost of water, he found it easier to think about these and other current events than the pending discussion with Leanne concerning their daughter and grandchildren. It wasn't that he didn't want them underfoot. It was more that the undercurrent of Jonathan's service to his country challenged his belief of what was happening in the US over the water war. He hadn't thought of it as a war until he read online an editorial in the Wisconsin State Journal. Printed alongside the editorial was a cartoon. The cartoon showed a child-like President Garr, looking victorious, shooting water balloons from a cannon at the Iraqis. The people being shot looked surprisingly unharmed, dancing in bathing suits with brown faces turned upward to the falling water. The caption said, "We win."

Robert grew up in Wisconsin, attending the UW in Madison, WI in the late 1990's. It seemed such a long time ago. At that time, it was predicted in the Wisconsin State Journal that there would soon be a war about oil. In the early turn of the century, following the bombing of the twin towers in New York, there really was a war about oil, hidden in the rhetoric of a war on terror. He went with a group of friends to Washington, DC on a lark really, to protest the war in Iraq. He carried a sign that said, NO BUSHIT, NO WAR. He had a great time with his friends, laughing and snapping pictures of the other protest signs. He had a great time until he and his friends lost track of each other and Robert ended up alone on the White House lawn. The organizers of the march had placed white crosses to simulate a cemetery with rows and rows of white crosses. When he came upon the simulated cemetery, his trip was no longer a lark and his experience no longer funny. He was holding back tears and his throat and head hurt with the effort. He wandered the lawn and the one-day cemetery unsure of whether he would connect with his friends before boarding the bus to go home. Now when he recalled that moment he felt it was a premonition of the 10,000 dead US soldiers from the war in Iraq. Following the war, a memorial was built in tribute to the seven men from Robert's community who had died in Iraq. Among those honored was one of his childhood friends. It was one of the friends that he had lost in Washington DC that day of the peace march long ago. Now he was lost forever, but memorialized on some piece of granite in a small community park.

It was estimated that 100,000 protesters marched in Washington that day and it was only a blip on the radar screen of the mainstream media.

These wars, as bad as they were, were localized; they were being fought by individual nations to gain and control the diminishing natural energy resource, namely oil. So what if 3000 were killed on 9/11 in New York, or 50,000 soldiers in Korea, or a million in Darfur. This new war, a Water War, was worldwide. People were fighting skirmishes on all fronts. There would be no winners in this war, only a slow creeping death blanketing the continents as insufficient food could be produced for the populations of the world. Robert was almost to his little modular home, his own little oasis in the heart of the vast Arizona desert, in a vast expanse of row upon row of identical tiny pods with all the modern technology one needed in January, 2047. It was home.

With a heavy heart, Robert stood before the door of his little home and looked at the iris detection sensor. An uncomfortably human voice said, "Hello Robert Hanover." He could hear himself being announced inside before the door unlocked and opened. His wife Leanne was busy at the computer console. "Hi Hon," she said, her greeting covering the tension between them. "Hey yourself," he replied as he placed a deliberate kiss on the top of her head. He knew this woman so well. He met her after graduate school. They married within a year and moved to her home state of Arizona. They had one daughter, Tiarra, and a son, Tyler. They traveled over the years with the children back to Wisconsin at regular intervals to visit Grandma Elly and Grandpa Joe. They always went in the summer, avoiding the searing heat of the Arizona sun for a few weeks. Tiarra and Tyler relished these trips to the northwoods of Wisconsin and the freedom to roam the 160-acre farm where Robert, Robert's mother, and even his grandfather had grown up. Leanne was never at home there. She preferred the Arizona desert to the woodlands, rivers, and farms of northern Wisconsin. She was always happiest when it was time to go home.

Now they must consider how to manage the space constraints in the tiny pod. And Robert must consider how to handle his opinions concerning this war when his daughter's southern-born husband, Jonathan, was around. Most importantly, he did not want to add more pain to Tiarra's life by arguing with Jonathan. However, it would be hard not to verbalize his opinions. He had learned from his father, Joseph, to think critically and hold his own in a discussion. In this case, his son-in-law seemed to feel it was a personal affront. Jonathan had his own opinions about the equal disbursement of scarce resources, namely water. He actually believed that the south was entitled to share in the Great Lakes watershed.

The Federal legislation that allowed vast quantities of water from the Great Lakes to be diverted by the southwest coalition of Arizona, Texas, New Mexico, Colorado, Utah, Nevada, and California was ultimately the piece of legislation that brought another civil war to the tottering government of the United States of America. Of course, it wasn't called a war in the media outlets Robert had access to. No longer united, legislators from each of the coalitions fought among themselves in the Congress and eventually authorized the National Guard to bring down the militant groups.

The fighting was carefully labeled as localized skirmishes, which they were. Localized skirmishes occurred on every continent: in Africa; in the former rain forests of South America; in the vastly depleted mountain streams of the Northern Hemisphere. Many of these areas were once thought to be able to provide an infinite amount of water to the valleys of Europe and northern Asia. When seen from a world perspective, these were no isolated outbreaks between a relatively few angry men. These were the battles on the ground of a worldwide water war. Not many civilians in any country knew and understood the scope of the fighting. But Robert knew.

He knew because he had always followed and analyzed world news. Before the death of his father, the two of them would discuss the news and world policy. No one, Robert now knew, had the depth of knowledge Joseph had, and the foresight regarding the future world concerns and events like his father.

Joseph had been predicting a water war before Robert had any interest in world events. When in the 1980's a Great Lakes Consortium was first established, Joseph read the newspapers with great interest. Here was the beginning of divergent groups banding together to protect what they considered a regional resource. The Great Lakes Consortium members included the Native American tribal groups from Canada, Wisconsin, Michigan, and Minnesota--along with the governments of the Canadian provinces of Ontario & Quebec, and the eight United States bordering the Great Lakes. The individual entities had their own specific needs and priorities, but they eventually signed a pact in the first decade of the 21st century to agree that they would vote as one voice when faced with significant changes to the great watershed. They agreed to ban, with limited exceptions, new and increased water diversions from the Great Lakes water basin unless approved by all signers.

The concept of forming coalitions to facilitate the management of regional resources was not isolated in the Midwestern and southwestern states. In the 1930's the southeastern states of Tennessee, Kentucky, Alabama, Mississippi, Louisiana, and Georgia implemented many joint ventures, harnessing the power of water for the purpose of generating electric power and controlling the annual flooding. Rivers such as the Ohio, Cumberland, and Tennessee were dammed and locks and canals were built to tie together these rivers for the purpose of facilitating the movement of goods with barge traffic.

With the development of highways the trucking industry took over much of the freight movement in the country. The vast canal systems of the 1930's were now not needed for transportation of goods, but this old infrastructure lent itself with only minor adjustments to its new purpose of moving water to where it was needed. The people of these southeastern states were lucky, lucky at least for the time being, to not have their young men thrust into a civil war with young men of angry neighboring states over the lack of water.

The people in the southwest coalition were not so lucky. It was here that the lack of water was felt the greatest and with density of population in these states the situation was dire. They were hurting for water. This crisis developed over a period of about 25 years but the precursor to the crisis began to build a hundred years ago. Back then, in the early 1930's, the Hoover Dam was built to provide power for the growing population. It created a huge reservoir called Lake Mead that stored the water allowing it to be metered out through the year. This was necessary because the Colorado River and its tributaries were replenished only from the snowmelt in the spring. The Glen Canyon Dam, a decade-long project beginning in 1956, was added to provide additional water storage and electric power. The lake it created was named for Major John Wesley Powell, a civil-war veteran and explorer. Other minor dams were added to control flooding, provide electric power generation, and give the government the ability to provide water to the seven western states. However, in the beginning of the 21st century, less and less water flowed down the Colorado River due to lack of snow pack in the winter from global warming and the increase in housing development requiring additional water. The headlines from an associated press story read, "NOT ENOUGH TO DRINK: Dwindling freshwater supplies project a coming global crisis, and governments are pinning plans on conservation and technology."

"I've been on the webcam with Tiarra, Jonathan, and the little girls." Leanne always approached difficult topics from the back door.

Continuing to skirt the meaning behind the webcam discussion Robert asked, "How are my little sweeties?" He always wanted to know how they were doing. There was comfort in knowing that in the midst of the angst the adults were feeling that the little girls were happy and healthy.

Leanne smiled, remembering her recent call. "Oh, they are so cute! So funny!" Maria, Angelia, and Jen were the three darlings of the family. The amusing thing was that Maria, the oldest, ruled over the two younger ones usually in conflict with Angelia, who was anything but an angel. Dear little Jen simply kept up with them both as well as she could. She was just beginning to talk and her mission in life was to get between her two sisters, adding her baby comments to their arguments. "Jen was siding with both her sisters at the same time. I couldn't understand a word she was saying, but she said everything with great authority. Maria and Angelia stopped their fighting to gang up on her. It was so funny, I could hardly concentrate on my conversation with Tiarra and Jonathan."

Here it was, the lead in to the argument Robert was sure would follow. He tried to keep his voice nonchalant. "So what did you talk about?" Robert said this out of habit. He knew Leanne would tell him whether or not he asked this question.

"Well, as bad as it will be, Jonathan and Tiarra believe having all of us stay with Grandma Elly in Wisconsin will be better than trying to fit everyone in here." Leanne turned in her chair towards Robert and indicated the small living room with a sweep of her hand. Tiarra wants us to go with her and the children to lessen the stress on Elly having three little ones underfoot.

Robert's heart did a little leap. This was a completely unexpected and pleasant turn of events. He had avoided offering this suggestion as long as he could. He had planned to argue his point with Leanne today. Now it was a moot point; Tiarra and maybe even Jonathan had rescued him.

"Tiarra has called your mother and it is all arranged. Although it may be more difficult for Jon to arrange to travel to see us, going north instead of south, his trip will only take a few hours rather than twenty four hours of driving back to Arizona." Leanne sighed deeply. "You and I could make occasional visits back here," Leanne added, "to check on things as long as Elly isn't overwhelmed with the children."

Robert glanced at Leanne. This was really hard on her. She would have loved to have the children to herself. Now she would be sharing them with his mother, Grandma Elly. Even at the age of 90, she was never overwhelmed with children. She exuded a magnetic presence with them. Then there was the winter in Wisconsin. Leanne hated the cold. "How do you feel about this?"

Robert asked.

Leanne gave him a look and swiveled her chair back to the computer screen. Robert came over and stroked her arms. Leanne sighed again. She felt guilty about her feelings concerning Elly. "You've always done what is best for the children," Robert said comforting. He stood behind her chair with his hands on her shoulders. Leanne crossed her arms, her hands reaching for Robert's hands. They silently stood together, with each other's hearts in their separate thoughts.

My grandfather, Joseph, was the one who instilled in me a major distrust of the government. He read everything he could get his hands on concerning current events. He tried for hours on end to find alternate news feeds on the computer. He was highly critical of politicians, and believed they made decisions that were only in their own best interest. I'm sure he had conversations with his sons over this. Robert, not my father, seemed to have inherited his father's passion for current events.

Grandpa Joe was also extremely distrustful of chemical additives to foods. He took no pills nor would he allow his wife to buy processed foods. I remember eating out with my grandparents during one extended visit to Wisconsin. I was about twelve years old. He forbade me to order orange soda because of the artificial flavor and color and made a scene about it with the waitress. I was so mad and embarrassed that I refused to talk to him the next day.

I never forgot that experience and I never really enjoyed orange soda after that. But I did learn to cook real food from scratch when I visited the farm and helped my grandmother *in the kitchen. I learned to love the taste of these foods and although I couldn't find enough time to devote to cooking while in college, I tried my best to eat healthy foods while I was pregnant with Sam and with Marta.*

QUAD CITIES 2047

Jonathan's regiment in the Arizona National Guard was stationed outside of the quad cities. The states of Arizona, New Mexico, California, Utah, Wyoming, Nevada, and Colorado had banded together to fight off the militia of the Great Lakes Consortium. The consortium held that the battle in congress to allow the pumping of water out of the Great Lakes basin to the southwestern states had been won illegally.

The President and the Republican controlled congress of 2025 had enacted into law the National Conservation and Distribution of Water Resources Act. This eminent domain legislation expanded the ability of regional utilities to divert water from natural rivers and lakes for the greater public good. Key to passing this legislation was the language in the legislation concerning protection of low lying communities such as New Orleans. New Orleans and other, similarly situated communities suffered the now routine breaching of levies from the ever raising of the levels of the oceans. The first phase consisted of diverting the Mississippi to provide water for Arkansas, Texas, and Oklahoma. Although a few people complained, these diversion canals from the Mississippi to its border states proved successful. It relieved the flooding pressure on New Orleans and provided drought relief for Texas. Texas, at this time was the state most critically affected by lack of water for agriculture.

These Federal emergency rulings in 2025, which allowed for the diversion of the Mississippi, created problems for the consortium. Now the underground aquifers feeding Lake Superior and Lake Michigan were being depleted at an ever-increasing rate. The dropping of these levels affected the other three Great Lakes. Activists in Wisconsin, Illinois, Michigan, Indiana, and

Ohio worked to inform the public and held demonstrations at the pumping stations. When they went beyond peaceful demonstrations, and began to use sharpshooters to take out electrical transformers at the pumping stations, they were referred to as the Militia.

Initially the Great Lakes Consortium had nothing to do with the Militia. The men of the Militia were self-appointed, grassroots activists, self-proclaimed protectors of the water very much like the demonstrators of the later twentieth and early twenty-first century against Project Elf, the Flambeau Mine, and the 250-mile, 350,000-volt electric transmission line from Manitoba through Minnesota and into Wisconsin. Many were older Americans from Nukewatch, GreenPeace, S.O.U.L. (Save Our Unique Lands), and the Sierra Club. These old timers of civil resistance between 1980 and 2000 reminisced about the victory they won in 1996 when the two men who effectively crippled the Elf project by cutting a few poles, won a jury acquittal on state sabotage charges. This was nothing when compared to the highly organized Militia. Three men blew up the first pumping station, destroying the buildings and killing the maintenance staff, electrical engineers, and civilians who were luckless enough to be near the pumping station that night. The three men were sacrificed to the water gods: death by lethal injection. The Great Lakes Consortium denied any connection to the bombing.

In the next twenty years, more canals and pumping stations were added under the emergency rulings to provide water to the southwest. The demonstrations were never peaceful, but made world news as men from the Militia sacrificed themselves for the cause. As the pumping of water out of Lake Superior and Lake Michigan into the grid work of canals and locks leading to the Colorado River system became imminent, the Great Lakes Consortium undertook the huge step in organizing and financing various factions of the militia, effectively inaugurating a new civil war. The United States executive branch downplayed this activity, suggesting that it was all a big bluff.

Eileen L. Ziesler

FLAMBEAU 2187

Matt and Amy sat together on the outcropping of rock at the top of Flambeau Mountain. It had become a favorite place in the warm weather to hike and indulge in a picnic lunch when they needed to be away from their studies and reflect upon the past generations. It was here that they came to try to make sense of Callie's notes and photo captions and when they couldn't make any headway, they had other things to consume the time they had away from their studies.

"We'd better get back if we want to hear the information from the main capsule." Amy said after some pleasant moments in Matt's arms "We should be there before 7:00."

"Do you really think we have anything to add?"

Amy had also been wondering the same thing. It was wonderful to spend the time on themselves and difficult to motivate to do something else. "We could at least provide some factual information the council might want."

"Hmmm. I could do with less facts, and more..." A long and deep kiss finished his sentence.

But in the end they did leave their idyllic site to sit through a rather uninformative hour in the community room. Most of the presentation detailed the names of the past city council members and mayors. Matt and Amy learned about the rebuilding of many of the businesses in the county seat, Ladysmith, following the tornado in 2002 and the hardships of the drought upon Rusk County. They found out that the ancestors of Amy's water deliveryman, Ned, had also purchased an individual time capsule, but that Ned and his parents had declined the opportunity to claim it. Ned's family time capsule became public at this meeting. Ned and his parents sat in the back row. When Amy smiled at Ned, he averted his eyes and didn't acknowledge her presence.

The community time capsule presentation gave special honors to the three young men of Flambeau who had joined the civil war against the southwestern coalition. These young warriors of the Great Lakes Coalition all died one day in 2048, almost like suicide bombers of the Iraq War, by blowing up a bridge over the Mississippi River. The bridge was key to the building of the first pumping stations. These pumping stations were to be built to bring water to the dry Colorado River basin. Innocent travelers on the bridge lost their lives, many burned in the blast and were never identified.

At one point in the program, the person giving the presentation gave some interesting insights from the time capsule into the general health of the community. A serious cancer, pancreatic cancer, was found to occur in a very high frequency in the county. As Matt and Amy listened to the chronology of other events taking place in the community, it became clear—at least to them—that the increased cancer rate occurred ten to fifteen years after the completion of the first installation of Purefz water tanks or about 20 years after the Water War had ended. Yet the Purefz tanks and the free water along with the technology of carbon scrubbing was uniformly thought to be the much-needed solution to global warming.

JONATHAN 2049

Jonathan straightened up, rotating his neck from side to side and around. His shoulders hurt. His back hurt. He was more tired and depressed than he had ever been in his life. He looked down the long row of beds in the temporary tent hospital. There was nothing more he could do tonight. The night nurses and orderlies would page him if there were a crisis they could not handle. Jonathan walked back to the mess tent and sat alone with the food he dished up for himself from the refrigerator. No one was on duty to serve him. It was a little after midnight and for now, all was quiet.

Quiet. Quiet meant his mind could think about his family. His darling, Tiarra, and the three little girls, Maria, Angelia, and Jen had been living now for over two years with Tiarra's parents and grandmother on her grandmother's farm in northern Wisconsin. Jen was now three and a half. She had spent her toddler years without him. He had visited whenever he could but that was nothing, nothing at all. Jonathan chewed his food mechanically. It was cold and tasteless. His heart ached with a longing for his family. He tried to picture them asleep in their warm beds at Grandma Elly's. They would be piled sideways on a mattress on the floor upstairs. Tiarra would be sleeping on a cot next to them. She refused to be alone in the bedroom down the hall when he was not there. She kept that room ready for them, should he come unannounced. His in-laws would be sleeping in Elly's bedroom and Elly would be in the living room on another sofa.

Jonathan honored his mother-in-law and father-in-law as the parents of his dear wife, but he and his father-in-law had far too many differences to allow them to be close friends. Leanne, his mother-in-law was from the south as he was. They seemed to have more in common, but by an unspoken mutual agreement they only spoke of the children and left many other things unsaid.

Jonathan's thoughts went back to his little daughters. Maria would be in kindergarten, soon to 'graduate' into first grade. He had missed every kindergarten program because of this war. Angelia would be in preschool, half days. He had wanted to visit them both at school during his last furlough, but Tiarra was concerned that his uniform would stir up angry feelings among the school staff that would somehow find their way to the children. He agreed and stayed on the farm with Elly and Jen while Tiarra went to pick up the girls from school.

It had been lonely for Tiarra, giving up her friends and cousins in Arizona. She and her mother, Leanne, had disagreements about the little things. Living in such close quarters in Grandma Elly's house day and night had put a strain on their relationship. Leanne regularly drove back to Arizona with Robert. She tried to talk Tiarra into coming with her as the girls got older, leaving Robert and his mother to care for the two girls in school while she and Tiarra would take little Jen who was not in school. Tiarra adamantly refused to have any separation from the girls and she refused to travel to the south. Tiarra was becoming accustomed to the brutal northern climate. She saw her children growing strong with the big open spaces and outdoor projects that Elly contrived.

Tiarra could relate to her grandmother. Elly's belief in the value of the land and the water was something Tiarra had never experienced with her friends and family in the south and it was somehow both romantic and reassuring. From Elly, Tiarra learned to prepare simple meals using the foods they grew and harvested on the land. The work was hard, but it was a joy to see the children learning about real food. Grandma Elly never once outwardly questioned Jonathan's beliefs, Leanne's longings, or the war as Robert did. She went about her life as older people do, taking pleasure in the simple joy of watching her great-grandchildren play, never pushing her own beliefs on Leanne or Jonathan.

Only once did Tiarra overhear Elly praying, if that's what it was. Elly was leaning on the large oak next to the pump house, her head resting on the rough bark and she was caressing the bark the way a lover caresses the beloved. She spoke to the tree. "You and I, we are the elders, and we must be quiet to allow the young people their time. We both value the same things: fresh air, warm gentle winds, and cold pure water. Let us pray that our children grow to value these things also." With that Elly patted the bark and turned toward the garden. Tiarra never forgot that moment.

Jonathan was startled out of sleep by the sounds of sirens. He had been sleeping three or four hours, dreaming pleasant dreams of his family. He was well aware that he needed at least another three hours to function well in his twelve-hour day at the hospital. Jonathan pulled on a pair of clean white cotton pants and a faded tee shirt. Tiarra had helped the girls make handprints all over this shirt in many colors. He wore the same uniform every day as he went to work in the hospital, plain cotton pants and a bleached out tee shirt decorated by his girls. He had a collection of almost two dozen tee shirts, decorated with fabric paint by his little girls. Each tee shirt had come with a letter that described the antics that went on as the shirt was being created and a picture of the process. Sometimes reading the letter made him laugh. He kept the letters even after the tee shirts slowly wore out. When he couldn't sleep he would read through the stack of letters and cry.

His 'uniform' gave him a connection to his patients, men his age and younger who were missing their sweethearts and their children. They would have a far-away look in their eyes as they looked at the shirts. Jonathan knew seeing the shirts was helpful to these men, but he never shared more, never shared the letters and pictures that arrived almost monthly with the tee-shirt package. He never shared the information that his wife and children lived with her grandmother in the north, in the home of the very militia they were fighting. He kept this information from everyone. Only the man who sorted the mail knew anything at all about Jonathan's connection to the north by the postmark on the big envelope, and thankfully kept his thoughts to himself.

Once in the hospital, Jonathan shook off the chill of the early morning and stamped his shoes to remove the snow. He grabbed a banana and a hot, sweet coffee loaded with cream. This might be the only thing he would eat for the first few hours today. When the sirens blew, it meant injury and death. Jonathan would try to prevent the latter.

Today the orderlies had a man of about thirty-five on the surgery table. His body was bloody and convulsing in pain. Jonathan barked out orders for pain medication after looking him over and feeling for telltale signs of internal bleeding. The orderlies would prepare the man for surgery. It appeared he had shrapnel embedded in his flesh and two broken arms. He was a tall, dark-haired man, dressed in the uniform of the militia. Jonathan didn't give it a second thought; he was simply one of the wounded who needed care.

When Jonathan returned, the man's body was quiet and his eyes were open. He looked directly at Jonathan with no emotion. Jonathan spoke.

"I'm Doctor Campbell. I will be operating on you shortly to remove the shrapnel and to set the bones in both of your arms. Other than that, you have no life-threatening injuries. Do you have any questions before we start the IV?"

"If you can work with a spinal, I would prefer that."

Jonathan looked up quickly into the man's face. He realized he hadn't even checked the patient's name, so intent was he on getting the job done. Jonathan looked at the anesthesiologist and nodded. It would take the team fifteen minutes to make the procedural shift. Jonathan pulled a stool over to the man's bedside.

"It will take a few minutes to make the changes. Do you mind if I sit here with you?" Jonathan expected the man to close his eyes to the pain he must still feel. This would give him more time to carefully review the chart and at least be able to address him by his name.

"That would be fine. By the way, my name is Michael Bordeau." He smiled knowingly at Jonathan.

Amused by this accurate assessment of the situation, Jonathan smiled back, the first genuinely felt smile he had in a long time. "May I ask what brings you here?" he asked, surprised at his own spontaneity.

"Well," Michael looked away for a moment, "I guess the same thing that brought you here."

Jonathan shook his head and looked down at the charts given to him by the orderlies. All around the two men, there was the constant stream of hospital activity. He and Michael Bordeau seemed to be separated from it by a protective bubble. It was a strange feeling being so comfortable in the presence of the enemy, this Michael Bordeau. The name was familiar. Had he heard that name before? "Is Bordeau French?"

"I suppose it is." The pain must have overcome Michael as he closed his eyes and did not offer any more conversation. The surgery lasted over two hours. Jonathan checked his patient's face often for signs of increased pain or anxiety. Michael's dark eyes watched him work but there was no fear in them, just simple quiet observation. While his assistants went for supplies or cleansed areas of blood, Jonathan himself took the cooling sponge from the nurse and wiped Michael's forehead, pushing the straight black hair away from his eyes. He wondered at his own behavior. War and the caring for injured bodies had numbed his emotions. This unusual man awakened Jonathan's feelings for his fellow man.

"I'd like you to sleep now," Dr. Campbell said to his patient after the nurses transferred Michael Bordeau to a regular hospital bed. "Do you want anything to help you sleep?"

"No thanks, but I'm really thirsty."

"I think you could have small sips of water. Don't overdo it. You don't want to be throwing up." Jonathan was surprised at how easy it was to communicate honestly with Michael and to leave the rules to Michael's discretion.

That evening, Jonathan finished in the hospital earlier than other nights. He was tired but had a feeling of satisfaction. Before he left he stopped at Michael's bedside. His patient was asleep and he stood looking upon him for a long time.

He left Michael's bed in time to be served a hot supper with the other hospital workers and doctors. His team sat with him and they all made small talk of calls from home and rumors of the end to the fighting. The anesthesiologist shifted the conversation to the man they patched up from the other side.

"This guy we worked on certainly didn't trust us. He wouldn't have the general, just a local. It was eerie how he watched ol' doc set the bones and dig out the shrapnel. I would have died before going through what he went through on the table this morning."

Jonathan nodded but he didn't agree with his colleague's assessment on the trust issue.

"I don't know," a young nurse offered. "I think some people

are fearful of going under and not ever coming back. I don't think it was an issue of trust. He seemed very brave to me. He looked to be Native American, don't you think, Dr. Campbell?"

Jonathan smiled, glad for her faith in another human being. "Well his name, Bordeau, is French." He hoped that would end the conversation.

"Hmmm, maybe he's French Canadian. If he was from Quebec, he could be."

Jonathan nodded and then asked if anyone wanted dessert.

"You serving? The Doctor Omnipotent?" teased the anesthesiologist. "We saw you wiping the guy's brow. Are you going soft on us?"

"Dessert or no? Make up your mind or the next time we are together I'll operate on you sans general, sans local."

"I'm shaking in my booties—dessert please."

Serving the dessert had the desired effect. His colleagues forgot about Michael Bordeau.

Jonathan didn't forget. In fact, after his supper, when he was alone in his tent he reached for his cell and called Tiarra. His father-in-law answered.

"Great to hear your voice, Jonathan! I picked up because Tiarra left the phone here while she went to get Jen and the others ready for bed. I'll call her for you."

"Just a minute. I have a question for you before you put Tiarra on."

Robert was surprised at this. He and Jonathan rarely had questions for each other.

"Shoot." he said without thinking. Once out of his mouth he couldn't take it back. It was the wrong thing to say with the war going on.

Jonathan seemed not to notice or at least he was not irritated by faux pax. "Does the name 'Michael Bordeau' mean anything to you?"

"Well, not specifically Michael Bordeau. Elly's maiden name was Bordeau; her father was Edward Bordeau. Her father's oldest brother was Weldon Bordeau, Elly's estranged uncle who was reunited with Elly's father when my brother was married. Luke Bordeau was Elly's youngest uncle, but I never met him. I don't think he had kids. Weldon Bordeau came to my wedding and then to Elly's father's funeral. I believe he had children but I never met them. His story was one of those skeletons in the closet. If the family talked about why he left for so many years and why he returned, I never heard. And I would guess the Bordeau name is a fairly common last name. Why do you ask?"

"Today we had a casualty come in, from the militia. We've taken care of them before, you know, but this guy was different. I was making small talk with him. I asked him how he had gotten himself in this mess and he answered, 'same way as you'. It was an unusual and rather calculated response. We were waiting for a change in the kind of anesthetic that was to be administered. We had to wait because he chose a local instead of a general and he was well aware that the surgery would be no walk in the park. I had to pull shrapnel and set two broken arms. It was a two-hour ordeal. He was not afraid, but watched me throughout most of the proceedings."

Jonathan continued, "He gave me a funny feeling. Not a bad feeling, more of a feeling that we knew each other —which of course is completely impossible."

"Tiarra's not done yet but Elly is looking this way, maybe she knows something else. I'll put her on." With that, Robert handed the phone to his mother.

"Hi Jonathan, how are you holding up?"

"I'm holding up fine here. What about yourself? Are you ready to send those little troublemakers back to Arizona?" Jonathan was very fond of his wife's grandmother and happy to make small talk with her.

"Oh, heavens no. I love them too much. I might even try to sneak them away from Arizona when this terrible war is over."

"How about if we sneak you away from that farm of yours and plant you in Arizona?"

"Now Jon, you know how much trouble I'd stir up for you there and there isn't enough water in Arizona to transplant me.

The whole war would start again." They both laughed, and both knew it was true. "Tell me," Elly changed the subject, "why are you interested in Weldon Bordeau?"

Jon repeated much of the story he told Robert.

"What did he look like, Jon, this Michael Bordeau?"

"He was darker skinned than Tiarra and with straight, shiny black hair. He had high cheekbones and one of the nurses thought he looked Native American.

Elly was quiet on her end of the line.

"Elly?"

"I'm here Jon. I was thinking that the only thing I remember about Weldon Bordeau is that he had no daughters. When his wife died—she was full-blooded Ojibwe Indian—he stayed with each of the sons and their wives. He was not very happy as I remember but I know my father was grateful that he came to my sons' weddings. He also came to my father's funeral. I didn't talk to him very much other than to ask how he was. He did tell me that he had three sons and a grandson and that his wife had died. After the funeral I lost track of him.

The weeks following Michael Bordeau's capture by the Guard were fascinating days for Jonathan. He spent all his free time with Mike.

"Dr. Campbell,"

"Mike, I've told you before, please call me Jon. None of my friends address me as doctor and if we are going to attempt this crazy rendezvous we'd better at least be on first name basis."

"It's hard to get away from the formality drilled in by one's upbringing."

"Your father was strict about those things? How was he addressed by his patients and friends?" Jonathan and Michael had discussed Michael's family heritage and potential ancestral link to Elly, Robert, and Tiarra. It was because of this, Jonathan was planning to bring Mike to Elly's home to see if any additional connections could be established when Elly and Michael had a chance to meet and talk face to face.

"His closest friends called him 'Doc' or if it wasn't a close friend, but rather a long time patient, it was 'Doctor Bill'. I hardly heard his first name except when my mother was angry with him. Then it was 'WILLIAM', with all capital letters! My mother ruled the roost with all of us: my sisters, our dad, and me."

Jonathan's belief in rights of the southern states to the water of the Great Lakes basin had been shaken considerably since he befriended Michael Bordeau. Things that he may have heard from his father-in-law, but blew off, he now debated openly with Michael. Michael's arguments for protecting the Great Lakes water basin were beginning to make sense to Jonathan.

Michael was healing fast and would be sent to a POW camp in another week. Jonathan planned to drive him to Elly's on Sunday. He asked for a 24-hour emergency family leave. He and Michael would leave after midnight rounds. He would have his signature on the discharge papers for Michael and that would probably provide some confusion to the staff. Their tent hospital had zero security clearance and the alcoholic sergeant was not known for following the rules or being concerned with mistakes. Maybe he would also not be concerned with a temporarily misplaced patient.

"Why would you take such a risk?" Michael demanded to know. He also genuinely liked Jonathan and knew that if this didn't work, it could mean a court martial for his friend.

"I guess family is more important to me than this damned war. I may have been on the wrong side of the fence with my wife's father and this could be a way to say that I truly care and want to make amends. You are taking a risk also you know."

"I am happy to make an attempt to get out of the POW camp. If I fail, I'm no worse off than I am today. If I succeed, I go home to my wife and kids. I have connections in the city, a place to stay until she can get to me. My old friends will feed me and give me a bed."

So it was about ten minutes after midnight on a warm spring evening that Jonathan quietly stripped the hospital bed and helped Michael Bordeau into civilian clothes. They got into Jonathan's jeep and drove north. It was so simple.

It was a joyous reunion for Tiarra, the little girls, and Jonathan. Tiarra couldn't stop smiling as she and Elly prepared a meal for the two soldiers. After supper, when the children were asleep, Jonathan and Tiarra cuddled together listening to Michael and Elly exchange memories and find places where knowledge of family intersected. They talked long into the night and would have talked longer if Jonathan had not put a stop to it on behalf of his patient.

The next day, after breakfast, Elly and Michael Bordeau walked the plot of land upon which their ancestors had walked. They talked about the well that Elly's father and Michael's great grandfather dug by hand, the well that Elly still used today and they talked about the war that was being waged for access to water. Michael told Elly about his two little boys, one who was a little older than Tiarra's oldest child.

They sat together on the bench in the shade of a young oak tree and shared what each knew about the death of Anna. Elly knew the story by heart. Her father had told it to her many, many times. Edward always told it with great emotion, a tear forming in his eye. This from a man that never cried.

"I am so grateful to you, Elly, and to Jonathan for bringing me here." Michael said, knowing that even if he could return some day with his children, Elly would no longer be alive. "I told Jonathan that it was a great risk to his career. It still is a great risk," he concluded sadly.

"It was a joy to meet you, Michael. My father would be so pleased if he were alive. Weldon's disappearance from the family created a hole in his heart."

Tiarra was holding Jonathan tightly as Michael said his good-byes to the little girls and to Elly. She could not hold back the tears as they drove away. "Be careful my love." she whispered as the jeep pulled out of the driveway. Three hours later both men were dead, killed by the blast of a bomb, placed by the Militia under the bridge of the Mississippi River. The bomb took out a major pumping station and killed almost fifty people. Tiarra did not learn of Jonathan's death until her father returned to Arizona a week later. He brought the newspaper clipping that spoke of the bombing and the loss of a southern coalition doctor. A formal condolence letter from the army arrived a few weeks later. Intelligence was never able to trace Jonathan's trip to Wisconsin that put him on the bridge at the moment the bomb was detonated. Of Michael, and his death, no one ever heard.

I left Jordan and the lifestyle of the east coast just after the government began to provide free water. PureF2 water put an end to the civil war. There is a series of pictures that were taken at about that time: Elly, my Uncle Robert, Aunt Leanne, cousin Tiarra, and her three little girls. There are a few pictures that also include Tiarra's husband before he was killed and one picture of Elly with Michael Bordeau. What I have learned from Elly is that Jonathan and Michael met by chance when Jonathan served as the army doctor in the Quad Cities. He evidently patched up this soldier from the Militia who happened to be distantly related to us.

When I asked Elly about this particular picture, she told me the story about her Uncle Weldon marrying a beautiful Native American woman and his father, Josh Bordeau, disowning him because of it. No one heard of Weldon until my father and uncle were married and Weldon attended the weddings.

I missed the meeting between my grandmother and Weldon's great grandson by only a few months. While the war was coming to an end in the Midwest, I was in the last stages of my pregnancy on the East Coast. I was very nervous about this birth and Jordan and I did not agree on many things at this time. It was a sad and stressful time in my life. My parents had died soon after my marriage and I felt I had nowhere to turn with my two young children. So after the birth of Marta I turned back to my childhood memories and Elly.

There were more changes in the world than just the provision of free water at this time. One of the changes was in the postal system. Because we were no longer dependent upon mailing hard copies of written material, the postal system was abandoned. This almost led to another war except that the transition to electronic mail had been developing for over fifty years. The postal system was a dinosaur that finally became extinct. When I returned to Flambeau, the rusty old mailbox that had received communications between family members for almost one hundred and fifty years was barely standing. I believe the last mail delivery occurred three weeks after Robert's family returned to Arizona.

A NEW WELL 2049

Elly's heart ached for her grieving granddaughter and for the loss of a father to the three little girls. As her own grandmother before her, Elly summoned the courage and strength to provide the stability, the food, and the child care necessary as Tiarra, Leanne, and Robert prepared to return to Arizona. It was determined that Tiarra and Robert would go first, put both homes on the market and search for a home they could afford which would meet all their needs. Leanne would have to stay for the week alone with Elly and the children. She did not want to do this, but could see it was the only sensible short-term solution. Her feelings for Elly had not changed over the eighteen months they had lived under the same roof. The girls sought Elly for any little thing they wanted to share and Leanne had felt the pain of not being needed. Now, things would change though even Leanne would never have wanted the change to come about from this horrible catastrophe in their lives.

This finally changed for the better in the week the two women were alone and allowed Leanne to feel sadness for losing Elly when she took her leave. It happened in the way all healing happens. Elly hid her own pain during the day when the children were about, but in the night when she could not sleep, she stood at the kitchen window, looking out past the oak tree, the bench, and the well. She saw in her memory her own father in different stages of his life. She saw him through the stories she was told: of his youth, of his digging of her well, his marriage to Mary, his role as her parent, his caring for Bess and Josh in their later years, and finally of his last words to her before he died. She saw Leanne's plight and Robert's dilemma. She grieved for Tiarra.

On this one night Leanne could not sleep either. She tiptoed to the kitchen to get a glass of water where she saw Elly standing and weeping at the window. Her former feelings towards Elly were swept away as she took the old woman in her arms to comfort her. Leanne was finally needed. That night she became the rock her family would always depend upon. Kindness and love that had always resided in her heart now came into full bloom.

When Robert and Tiarra returned, they felt something had happened for the better though neither would ever really understand the difference in the two women. Robert worried for his mother, thinking she would have trouble when they left. He tried, unsuccessfully, to have her move along with them. Now he had to put his energies into making sure the heat would be reliable and the water pump would not freeze in the below zero weather of a Wisconsin January.

The children appeared to fare the best. They had become accustomed to Jonathan's absence and seemed to adjust to the changes that would be forthcoming at the end of the school term. Of course, no one would ever know what they would be feeling and thinking about when they grew into the age of self-awareness. They knew their father had died. They were just too young to understand. They were excited to take their first trip south when school was out with their Grandma Leanne and their mother. They didn't have the awareness that they might never see their great-grandmother again.

As they say, 'when it rains, it pours'. In a complete reversal of the old saying, the summer following Jonathan's death heralded severe drought conditions in Wisconsin. To add to Elly's concern about the well water being enough for her family, the Holcombe dam was scheduled for a draw down in late August in order for the electric company to repair the turbines. Homeowners along the man-made lake were fearful for the loss of their wells and rightly so. Most homes had been built in the second half of the twentieth century, which meant the wells had been drilled after the water levels of the riverbed, rose to make the lake. The electric company that was responsible for the draw down offered a monetary compensation for people to help pay for the drilling of new wells in the event their wells went dry. Elly's well was created long before the building of the dam. She need not have been afraid of loosing the well. The ancient rock formations and sand veins would have provided plenty of water. But, as it was, she determined to have a new well drilled.

Robert oversaw the drilling of that new well. The well was created by pounding rather than drilling, forcing a point deep into the earth. Each time the machine lifted its arm high over head and then forced downward, the point was driven in six to eight inches. When the point sank down two to three feet at a time, Robert had the well driller stop. He had heard too many stories of how well drillers went past the sand vein either because they did not watch the pounding process closely enough or because they were paid by the foot. The well driller tried to argue with Robert. Better water would be deeper he said, but Robert held out and requested the water be pumped at that point to determine the quality and the flow rate. It was as good as was needed.

Elly chose not to cap the old well, but to purchase a new, state of the art hand pump and replace the existing water pump that had been installed at the time when the farm became electrified. A lovely little stone building was built to house the hand pump.

Robert shook his head. It all seemed like foolishness to put money into this. He felt the stone building was simply a home for all of his mother's memories. Water from the new well, a seventy-two foot deep well with a submersible pump, provided the same flow of water and quality of water as the old well. Robert smiled and shook his head. He may never understand his mother, but he loved her just the same.

With the well project completed and the outdoor heavy work accomplished, Robert was the last person to bid farewell to Elly. "Come and visit us, Mom," he asked, knowing what her answer would be.

"You know I'm not going to set foot on a plane again in my lifetime."

"Well, you don't need to fly. I'll drive you to Arizona to visit."

"There's no good water in Arizona and I need to take care of things here."

And so it went, on and on, until Robert hugged her. "Bye, mom. Thank-you for being here for all of us."

Elly smiled at her son; she would cry later. "Did you get enough water bottles filled for your trip?"

"Yes. Love you. Thanks again." Robert drove down the driveway, and turned at the old crooked mailbox. He looked at the mailbox through blurred vision. He should have fixed it before he left he thought. The steel pipes holding it up were looking as though they would rust through. Robert sighed and drove on, unconsciously unscrewing the lid of a water bottle and taking a drink even before he was thirsty.

PUREFZ 2049

Soon after the horrible bomb attack that took the lives of Jonathan, Michael, and many, many citizens, the United States government, with the powerful water corporation conglomerate, ended the war by federalizing all ground and surface water and guaranteeing water for personal consumption. The only water allotted for human consumption was Purefz and tanks were installed at no cost to landowners who previously depended upon water from their own wells. The ground and surface water was only to be used for agricultural purposes.

This plan had been quietly in the makings for 20-25 years. Purefz water had been on the market for at least that long, sold as a less expensive alternative to regular bottled water. In those fifteen years, it had lost its stigma as a bi-product of nuclear reactions. It became cheaper to produce and there was an over-abundance of the stuff. It could not be used for some applications. Indeed Purefz water had undergone extensive testing with the hopes that it could be used for agricultural purposes. This was not the case; healthy plant growth could not be sustained with Purefz water. Plants did grow, but the plant metabolism was speeded up and this produced plants with less vitality. Seeds from these plants had a greater percentage of sterility. Seed crops such as corn, soybeans, rice, and wheat gave a diminished return per acre. Vegetable crops matured too quickly with a reduced size and could not be stored. Leafy vegetables and fruits were the most affected being essentially unpalatable.

However, the effects of Purefz water on rats, extensively tested, produced less obvious problems in the one generation of testing. Over multiple generations there were some difficulties because, as with the plant testing, testing on mammals resulted in an increased metabolism. This metabolism change resulted in decreased vitality, shortened life span, increased sterility, and susceptibility to disease. Testing on the human population had begun quietly by offering the much less expensive Purefz water in soft drinks, coffee, and the omnipresent bottled water.

People were now willing to make the change to Purefz and the added perk during the change was that the government guaranteed the water at no cost! States would be targeted based upon current need. The population of the southern coalition states would be the first to have the water holding tanks installed and water delivered. Highly populated areas would be targeted, and the rural areas would be phased in as time went on. As each rural customer was outfitted with a new Purefz tank, the old well, by federal statute would not only be capped, but the pipes and pumps pulled. It was said these fittings would be recycled for additional tanks and pumping equipment. The plan was perfect.

In other parts of the world this plan was already in place. Purefz was trucked in to desert regions of the earth and people were joyful for the water. With global warming abating and adequate water at hand, a spirit of peace slowly spread across the earth. Little did the citizens know the price they really were paying for these gifts.

COMING HOME 2050

Callie stood at the local transport station with little Sam holding onto her leg. In her arms, half hidden with her blouse, little Marta nursed and then slept. A wave of fear swept over her as the guards passed by and she reached to stroke Sam's blond head. Did she do this to comfort him or was this in preparation to grab onto him should danger threaten? A guard, a boy really, glanced her way and in his eyes Callie thought she saw the same fear. She tried a smile and he lowered his eyes. These were the guards left behind after the Governors of the Earth took control, abruptly ending the worldwide Water War. They had no apparent reason for guarding anything. The war was over. The fear was still present. There was a real reason for the fear but not many knew what it was.

Sam looked up at her, "I'm hungry mommy." "Soon, Sweetie. We just need to walk a little farther." When the guards were out of sight, Callie crossed the tracks with her young children. They skirted the main road and found a wooded and brushy patch of land near the tracks. She spread her jacket upon the ground and released her heavy backpack. Sammy dove into a pocket of the pack, pulling out a granola bar. His little teeth could not tear the wrapper. "Do it mommy!" he demanded and a moment later with a mouth of granola, "I'm thirsty." Callie lowered herself and Marta to the ground and smiled. She put her finger to her lips to signal Sammy to be quiet and pulled out a water bottle. In the shadows of these trees she felt rather than saw other moving shapes and sensed fear.

She also felt intense anticipation. If she were a girl again, she would have run until her lungs burst. It was less than two miles from here, but Sammy was tired and she couldn't carry the baby, Sammy, and the pack. Sammy lay back and contently munched on his granola bar. "Bite mommy?" he offered. Callie signed thank you and pretended to take a huge bite. She was hungry for more than food and thirsty for more than the bottle of warm Purefz in her pack. Rest a bit and then try to make for home she decided. The summer night was warm and the ground was very dry. They could sleep on the ground farther along if needed but she was keen on getting away from here and even more anxious to get home. Little Marta whimpered. Callie unwrapped her baby and looked down at her. Marta was not well. Fear overcame Callie again. Not fear of the guards or what she would find when they arrived at home, but instead a mother's fear of danger that cannot be seen and will not be gone in the light of the morning. Sammy snored quietly, crumbs of granola and drool in the corner of his sweet mouth. With Sammy asleep, Callie allowed the tears to fall and to feel not only the fear but also the intense loneliness of missing Jordan. He wouldn't come with her, indeed he was angry that she would leave the comfort of their modern home. "What do you think you will find?" he demanded, "A old or dead woman and a dried up well?" He had turned his back towards her and would not accompany her to the air tram.

Jordan was everything modern: the Insta-Food, the new mail, and the modular apartment. He loved it all and was eager to grasp the usefulness and simplicity. "Don't be so old fashioned," he told her. "Look, all you do is pick the meal you want to eat, place it on your plate and put the plate into the Food Preparation Device. It is perfectly safe, the FDA has tested it and you read the results yourself. You'll love it! By the time you pour your Purefz, it's ready to eat! I really think we should invest in this. The money we will save on using Purefz instead of the old stuff will more than pay for this in three or four years. Callie feigned support of these ideas. They started to use Purefz to save money. Five months later she miscarried. When she became pregnant again, she used money to buy real water and tried to drink only this when Jordan wasn't home. She gave Sam the real water also.

One day Jordan found out what she had been spending money on. He was furious with her and was not convinced of the danger that she believed was inherent in the new water. Marta was born a little premature. She was tiny and Callie thought of her as frail next to the stocky little Sam. Callie had a gnawing fear of this new water and what she believed to be the serious health effects on her children. Jordan wouldn't give in.

And then the dog died. Musty had been around before Sam was born. For about a year now, Jordan had been feeding him the IF dog ration along with Purefz. Callie could tell that Musty didn't like the IF. Callie told Jordan that the IF or the Purefz must have killed Mutsy. Jordan wouldn't listen and wouldn't talk about it. He put in a voice order for a one-year's supply of IF for human consumption on the spot. It was the last straw; Callie had to leave.

Her whole being ached to see Grandma Elly and the farm. She was thirsty for water from the old well. Her belief in the danger of IF and Purefz and her fear for her children's health was more compelling than her love for Jordan. While Sam slept on, Callie dozed and dreamed that Jordan was holding her. She felt safe and warm. In her dream he was talking, telling her something, something very important, but she didn't understand his words. Abruptly, a loud voice called out in the dark and jolted Callie awake. She turned on her phone and checked the time, surprised to see she had slept 3 hours. There were five messages from Jordan. Sadly she turned the phone off. Sammy moaned and Marta yawned. "Sammy, we're going to take a little walk under this beautiful moon" she whispered when he opened his eyes.

Sammy was surprisingly cooperative with this suggestion. He asked about finding a toilet and was awed and intrigued by her suggestion that there were no toilets here but that he could just pee next to a bush. Toilets and everything to do with them were currently one of his greatest interests. Marta's diaper was changed. Sam took the task of burying the packet very seriously. He found a stick and scraped the dry earth. When he wasn't successful in creating a deep hole, he proudly piled twigs and grass on top.

Finished with their preparations, they left the little woods and came to the road. To her relief, Callie found the roadway deserted and without road lights. She paused for a moment and took a deep breath. This was the road, wasn't it? She had not been back for over 25 years. Sam chattered on about the moon and sang a little rhyme he had been taught. Callie looked back--no one, no transports were in sight. She sang with Sammy and immediately felt better, happy, and more hopeful that she had been in months.

The night journey took them almost two hours. Sam did not tire or complain until they were only one quarter mile from the old homestead. He had nibbled along the way on dried fruits and had some more Purefz, the only liquid drink left in the pack. Callie was very thirsty, her milk wouldn't flow for Marta. She took a sip of Purefz, rinsed her dry mouth and spit it out. The light was showing faintly in the east. Soon she would drink. Soon she would be home.

The mailbox she remembered was hanging askew from the heavy pipes that supported it for so many years. Callie turned with Sammy and slowly made her way to the house. Sammy was openly crying now and little songs no longer amused him. Callie coaxed and prodded. Marta started to scream. They made it to the door. What would she find? She tried to put the fear away someplace deep inside. Her hand reached for the doorknob but before she touched it, the door opened. The old woman and the tired, fearful young mother took in each other's eyes. "Oh, my sweet Callie!" Her grandmother was here and she was home.

THE REMAINS 2187

Amy and Matt walked from the bench under the oak to the end of the driveway. They had been talking about where the mailbox had been when Elly was living. Trees and grass and brush with their tangle of roots had encroached upon the road squeezing it to the narrowest possible width necessary for the water transport to make its way through. The town's government spent little on maintaining these secondary roads and trails. Run-abouts did not need anything more than a six-foot wide trail and the water transports could make it through almost anything. Plowing of the snow on the roadbeds in the winter in northern climates was a water reclamation, a snow melt process made possible by the abundance of electricity. Utilities were either underground or over the airwaves. Maintenance for the underground electricity was unnecessary with the new technology.

Matt stepped off the driveway into the tall grass and brush. He kicked about for a while and then went to the other side of the driveway and did the same.

"The pipes are probably buried under years of debris. If we had a magnet or something like a heavy metal rod or shovel, we could probably locate them."

Amy sprinted back to her abode and returned with a heavy iron bar.

"Where did you ever find this?" Matt queried as he took the heavy bar from her.

"There were so many things that I saw a potential use for when my mother and I cleaned up the property prior to installing the new pod on the foundation and building the addition. I stored what I could and set aside things like tools and shovels and this bar. I tried to cover them with a heavy plastic to protect them. It didn't work too well, but here you are with the perfect tool for sleuthing out a lost mailbox." Amy finished with a flourish.

Matt was now lifting and dropping the heavy bar into the soft ground. He could hear and feel when the bar hit a rock underground. He moved along poking into the ground every foot or so in a westerly direction. After about the tenth easy plunge into the earth, the bar hit solid metal. Matt continued to poke about, the bar stopping hard against metal about half of the time. Amy went back for a shovel, handing it to Matt and taking back the heavy bar. Matt dug and pried until the sweat glistened on his neck.

"Voila!" he shouted, climbing up out of the brush and waving a length of rusty pipe over his head. "The great archaeologist unearths the ancient ruins." He was sweaty and dirty, his skin covered with dried weed seeds, and he was grinning from ear to ear.

Amy laughed at him. "You look like a back to nature man!"

Matt growled in fun, "I am a big black bear, coming out of the woods to eat Little Red Riding Hood." He bounded out of the depression next to the driveway, dropping his prize and the shovel as he grabbed Amy, pretending to be a bear.

Amy screamed and giggled. She had almost forgotten how this whole thing started, with the social, emotional need for friendship, love, and bonding that was not part of her academic world. It felt good, felt great, to be in love. Only for a moment did she feel a pang of guilt over the losses of the former inhabitants of her land.

ON THE BANKS OF THE FLAMBEAU RIVER 2056

Sammy grew tall and strong in this life on the banks of the Flambeau River. Under the watchful eyes of his mother he learned to swim and fish and canoe. With his close friend and next door neighbor, Tubby Nader, he climbed the hills of the old Flambeau Mountain and made forts and dens among the ancient rocks and fallen trees. They played out ancient stories of the Ojibwe Indians canoeing the Flambeau and Chippewa and used old canoes from the Nader resort. When they were old enough they were allowed to paddle the canoes for real between the two homes. They attended a community school a few days in the week. Callie, Tubby's mom, and other mothers taught in the school, housed in the old church near the bridge. It was more of a home schooling system with parents coming together to give each other support and respite. Each parent took responsibility for different areas of the curriculum. There were only 12 students.

Little Marta would make thirteen. She grew but continued to be a weaker child. Her enjoyment for the most part was hanging out with her Grandma Elly in the kitchen, drawing lovely little pictures with her crayons and watercolors. She was loved and protected by all and on the days she was strong enough to go to school, her mother took her on the back of her bicycle. Sammy ignored the pull of roughhousing with Tubby and the other children at recess time to stay by his sister's side and push her gently on the empty swing. He was the strong, important eight-year-old brother and protector of little Marta.

On those days when Marta went to school, Elly made chicken soup with a chicken from the neighbor and with carrots, onions, garlic and parsnip from her own garden. Elly had great faith in the healing power of chicken soup. She made the soup in sort of a reverie, dreaming of the distant past and her own grandmother Bess. When the soup was finished she let the meat cool and carefully de-boned it, dicing the meat into small pieces so that Marta would eat a good quantity. Marta preferred the broth and the noodles so Elly tried to cut the vegetables and meat into tiny pieces.

Callie and Jordan never did resolve their differences concerning Purefz and insta-foods but their relationship was cordial. Jordan visited the children every year at Flambeau, staying at a hotel in the larger town of Ladysmith. Sammy went to visit him in New York at least once in the year. During these visits Callie was fearful for Sammy. She sent along a great deal of food and drinks, trying not to cause Jordan to become angry, but trying to quietly register her concern for his safety. Marta never went on these visits. The stated reason was that she was too young but the real reason was that she was too fragile and this frailty affected all aspects of her social, emotional, and intellectual growth. Jordan accepted the fact that Marta never visited him in New York. Maybe, somewhere deep inside himself where he chose not to go, he knew that the water he insisted they drink before Callie became pregnant had affected little Marta.

Jordan aged greatly in the years since Callie left. His hair was thin and mostly gray. His skin had the pallor of a smoker and hung on his large frame like some old coat that is too big for its owner. Jordan continued to eat and drink insta-food and Purefz exclusively. His belief system did not change. Callie avoided Jordan as much as she could when he visited.

Life in Flambeau moved at a slow pace just as the river flowed slowly past Elly's home. But each spring as the ice broke up at different rates in each of the two rivers, the full power of the water could be seen. So it was with the governing boards of the townships in the state when conflict arose. The rumblings began soon after Callie arrived. Some people were angry at the federalization of the ground water along with the wide-spread use of the free or inexpensive Purefz. These were the same sort of people who years earlier had joined the militia fighting for the Great Lakes Consortium, protested the building of the highline from Canada, and demonstrated at Clam Lake against the underground antennae. Callie initially attended these board meetings concerning the eventual capping of the wells but chose not to become active. She had her own set of problems. She was single-parenting an active eight-year-old, a developmentally challenged five-year-old, and providing support and care for her aging grandmother.

Callie did take action to protect the well when it became clear all county wells would be capped. Her plan, concerning the pump house, stemmed from a discussion a few years back with Elly. Elly had told her how the old farmers often stored rusty old equipment in and around outbuildings that were never used. Callie experienced this first hand when she tore down an old chicken coop. It was full of rusty old parts and held up from the outside by parts of old farm equipment. It had been a terrible job, chopping out the weeds and blackberry bramble that had intertwined itself in the metal framework. This was the last building to go from Elly's parents' farm. Callie was glad when the task was over. The work had been awful. She collected all the remaining tools and scrap iron, draping the pump house with an old car door and propped the other scrap iron and broken fence posts around the outside of the beautiful little pump house Elly had built only a few years before. Then she transplanted the blackberry bushes around the pump house and farther out, a variety of trees and bushes. Only the oak tree was left slightly separate from the chaos she created.

Elly looked on with sadness from her bed. She was not strong enough to help her granddaughter with this year's outdoor work. Callie tried to time her planting when it was likely that Elly would be asleep.

"Why, why?" Elly thrashed and screamed in the middle of the night waking Callie with a start. She came to her grandmother's bed, soothing her with quiet words and wiping her forehead with a wet cloth. Callie was sure the end was near and as she sat, ministering to her grandmother she began to talk, not the typical talk one says to a dying person about everything being all right, but talk about the future.

"Grandma, I want to thank you for all you have done to protect this land and our water." Elly's movements became less frantic as Callie spoke and her breathing, the rattling sounds from her chest, remained even and slow. "I've been working on the pump house, to hide it from the people who will come one day to fill and cap our well. I've hidden the pump with some old metal and I've placed junk around the building. Then I planted blackberries all around." Elly was breathing comfortably and it was cool in the room. Callie, not wanting to leave, but feeling cold and sleepy, crawled into bed with her grandmother. Her grandmother's body was very warm and for a moment Callie wished she could give her a drink of cool water. She knew she could not, as Elly could no longer swallow. "I've planted birch, maple, pine and spruce transplants next to the blackberries. I hope that the blackberry brambles will cover the little stone pump house within a year or two and then the trees will begin to grow and eventually shade the blackberries. I think this will prevent the feds from finding our precious well though they will of course find the one you drilled just before I came here with the children. The townspeople say they will be here in five to eight years and then we will not be allowed to pump water. But I will have saved your well for Sammy and Marta." Elly was resting quietly and Callie pulled her grandmother's hand to her cheek. She closed her eyes and squeezed out the tears that would not stop, wiping them on her grandmother's pillow.

*****

"Mom?" Marta called out; and more loudly, "Mom!" Marta could not take her eyes off of Elly. Though it was cool in the room, her great-grandmother's white curls were damp with sweat. Elly's breathing had been shallow for almost a week with long stretches of apnea. A few minutes ago, Marta had been entranced with the plot of one of her favorite stories, one that she had known by heart from childhood, when something made her stop reading and stare at the form on the bed. "MOM!" She called as loudly as she could. The stretch of apnea went on and on. "Mommy," Marta whispered; she could not move, could not reach over to touch Elly's hand, could not stop her great-grandmother from taking her leave.

Marta truly did not understand what was happening to her great-grandmother. Elly had been the center of her life since infancy.

When Callie taught at the school or went to meetings in the town hall Elly became her comfort. Marta was a fragile wisp of a child, innocent and unknowing. Elly let Marta be herself. Callie pushed and prodded Marta to memorize addition facts, practice piano, and explain stories she read. Elly let Marta help with baking and laundry. With Sam and Callie off at school, Marta enjoyed beating her great-grandmother at canasta, choosing flowers for the vase at the table, or stitching clothing for her favorite doll.

In the kitchen, Callie was putting the last touches on their noon lunch. She was listening to the local radio station with great interest. People were calling in with their complaints concerning the number of illnesses and deaths occurring in the community. Everyone had something to say in this town where everyone was related and had a connection to someone who was sick. There would be a town meeting next week. Callie hoped to go. She felt she had an insight into this; however, she was loath to actually tell people why. When a commercial came on, Callie was startled to hear Marta's voice. Marta was distressed and Callie knew in an instant that Marta's distress concerned Elly. She rushed to the bedroom.

Elly was dead. Sensitive little Marta must have known intuitively that Elly was gone, for she was sobbing, sitting in the chair by the window. She hadn't moved since she looked up at Elly. At first Callie felt sorry for herself. She had wanted to be there when Elly passed, to hold her hand, to stroke her forehead, to kiss her cheek. She had even rehearsed the scene in her mind so she wouldn't break down and cry. She wanted Elly to feel safe, leaving her and Sammy and Marta. Indeed it was Elly who had kept them all safe in her little farm home, with the garden and the connection to Elly's friends and neighbors. Elly had been the rock in Callie's life since she left Jordan. Now Elly was gone.

Callie went over to her grandmother and kissed her forehead, "Thank-you, gram. We will be fine. You have made sure of that. Go in peace."

Callie turned to her daughter, the little fragile one who would never be fine, who suffered because of the artificial water her parents drank before she was even conceived—or so Callie believed. Anger welled up in Callie's heart, guilt, blame, and anger. She told herself she would never, never forgive Jordan. Then she sighed and took her daughter in her arms and rocked her until Sammy came home from school.

Tubby's mother, Janet, helped Callie get through the next few hours and days as the body of her grandmother was removed and prepared for cremation. Robert and Tiarra came from Arizona with Maria and Angelia. Little Jen was sick so Leanne stayed back with her. Tyler, Tiarra's younger brother came in from New York. Even Jordan came and spent a lot of time with Marta who could not comprehend the significance of this event but was nonetheless affected by what she felt from the people around her. Sammy stayed to himself and no one could help the eight-year-old. Everyone grieved this loss harder than would be expected, maybe because Jonathan's untimely death was a dagger-like pain driven deeply into the heart and the hole left behind had never filled, but only became larger with this next death.

Callie scattered her grandmother's ashes on the land, in the river, and around the pump house of the old well. In the empty meadow beyond the well she planted a tree. She saved Elly's thin wedding band and encased it in a small acrylic plaque along with the Joseph's wedding band that Elly had saved.

In the second year, following Elly's death, the blackberries bloomed in the spring in tremendous quantity. Callie watered the plants cautiously that summer, still concerned about how much water she could pump from Elly's new well without pumping up sand or damaging the pump. Elly had often told the story of how as a child she forgot about the pump as it filled the tank for the cattle and the emotion behind that story had carried it through two generations after Elly. Now Callie told the story to Sammy and Marta. Marta who loved kittens would listen to the story each time as if it were new. Marta learned to call baby kittens that still roamed feral on their land and Callie wondered how many generations of kittens would have been born since Elly was a little girl.

Callie and Marta picked giant, juicy blackberries around the pump house in late July. Callie juiced and froze much of what they picked, remembering the ways Elly had fixed luscious desserts and jellies for breakfast from the frozen juice. Marta recited words from a preschool book 'one berry two berry, pick me a blue berry' as she helped her mother. Later, as Callie fixed supper, Marta continued reciting from Peter Rabbit, "Flopsy, Mopsy, and Cottontail who were good little bunnies had blackberries and milk for their supper." Callie looked with love and sadness upon Marta. Marta had a memory for rhymes and stories like no other child, but her ability to make friends and learn in school was completely lacking. Sammy was always kind to his sister, but his friendships and interests were far in advance of what Marta would achieve.

Each year the blackberry bramble grew thicker and more intertwined. The thorns on the canes prevented the pickers of the fruits from entering the tangle. The metal that Callie placed years before became part of the framework upon which the berry canes grew. Callie never pruned back the dead canes but let them become additional support for the new vines. The birch, pine, and maple planted a distance from the stone building grew more slowly. They did not shade the blackberries but the blackberries grew outward from the building encroaching upon the trunks of the small trees. Callie smiled and recited with Marta, 'billions of berries in blackberry bramble'.

Thus it was in the year 2061 that a team from the Federal Water Conservation Corporation arrived in Ladysmith, Wisconsin. It took them three months to locate, test, and fill all the wells in Rusk County. Callie's property bordered Chippewa County and was one of the last wells to be filled and capped. The young engineer supervising the project evidently had his fill of the people of Rusk. When Callie offered him and his team some blackberry lemonade and cookies, he was moved by her kindness and sat with her under the oak tree about 20 feet from the ripening blackberries.

"You've been watering these berries, haven't you?" he stated more than asked. He knew a great deal about trees and bushes and their requirements for water. These ripening berries were the size of his thumb and he knew they didn't get that way without adequate amounts of water.

Callie smiled sadly but didn't answer.

"You know, it is against the law to use unauthorized ground water for growing. You will need permits to gain access to the ground water for this purpose. It's a pretty expensive process. Don't try to use the tank water. It isn't formulated for plants."

Callie sighed deeply and looked out towards the stand of young pine trees growing on and around Flambeau Mountain. She didn't answer, and her companion was quiet. He was thinking about how his team was destroying a way of life in this beautiful place. He was not a mean man. He was only doing his job.

Callie was still a little nervous about what was hiding in the pump house covered with brush. Because the well had been dug, it was not registered in any documents but Callie knew that the planes above probably detected the little outbuilding, but it could no longer be seen from the bench by the oak tree.

"Well," the man went on more kindly. "You could keep a few of the berries watered by hauling pails of water from the river when there's no rain. Don't pump with a sump pump; it would take too much water from the flow. If you were caught, it would be a very stiff fine. And please don't tell anyone I told you to do this. Even drawing water a bucket at a time sets you up for legal proceedings."

The tank blazoned with the words 'Purefz for a better environment' was installed close to the house and the pipes connected to Callie's existing pipes. The tank was filled and the pressure system tested for water flow. A meter was installed on the pump but Callie was assured that this was not for billing purposes but rather to monitor the household's water use.

Before the team left, Callie inquired as to the upkeep and how often the water company would be filling the tank. She was given a brochure on the standards and procedures. Callie had one more question.

"We have been used to drinking very cold water and I am

thinking this water is rather tepid from storage in the tank."

"Oh, your refrigerator has the capability of chilling the water. You should draw water from the refrigerator for drinking."

Callie smiled inwardly; she was prepared for this. Her neighbor, an old gentleman just a little younger than Elly, lived a minimalist life style. He had a root cellar and he cooled his milk and eggs with spring water. He was given a water cooler for drinking water. "Well, when I buy a new one, it will be fine, but we've never used the water ice cube maker or water cooler and a few years ago when I tried it, the internal pipes were clogged. I believe my grandmother had shut off the refrigerator for a year when she traveled (this was a deliberate lie). The piping is full of algae."

The technician, eager to move on to supper and a return trip to his family, sighed. "Well in a few cases, we've left water coolers with people. I have one left. It is not recommended that you use it, but it is legal for the time being. I'll leave one with you. It's old technology and the company cannot vouch for its safety, but you could use them on your counter if you prefer cooler water. I guess it would make more sense than keeping a heavy pitcher in the refrigerator." With that, he brought in a beautiful water cooler. Callie thanked him and he was on his way.

The new Purefz tank at Callie's house, the last to be installed in the county, had hardly been there a week when the township met in the evening. Angry men and women stood up and blamed the township officials for the illnesses that had begun to sweep through the community. The township officials blamed the county government. Everyone was fearful of what was happening. One after another families were struck with a cancer: leukemia, pancreatic cancer, colon cancer and other types of cancer that no one had ever heard of. The town hall was packed with people. Everyone had something to say and everyone was impatient waiting his or her turn, everyone except for two unknown visitors sitting near the back at the aisle. The two were the only ones Callie did not recognize from the eight years she had lived at Flambeau. A few older individuals who spoke voiced their belief that the old Flambeau Copper Mine, north of Callie's home had finally leached the heavy metals into the ground water, into the river, and into the wells of the families downstream prior to the Purefz tank installation. They blamed government officials for not being on top of this and they blamed the old timers who had allowed Rio Tinto-Zinc, the parent mining company to enter the community.

Callie wondered if she should speak and add to the fray. Callie believed that the illnesses were connected to the Purefz water that many of the residents had been consuming for almost a decade. The Naders had been one of the first families who had chosen to take the free water over ten years ago when their well did not provide adequate amounts of water. Other families who had opted for Purefz also had family members who had become ill. Should she speak of this?

Undecided, Callie became more than curious about the two unknown visitors in the aisle whispering to each other. Who were they? She wanted to ask Tubby Nader's mom, whom she was sitting next to, but Janet was listening carefully to the speaker. Callie sighed and divided her attention between the two visitors and the current speaker.

The town chairman was speaking and members of the audience were grumbling to each other. Jerry Urmanski, an old timer sitting in the row directly behind the visitors, stood up, swore at the town chair and stomped out of the hall. More disgruntled town of Flambeau residents stood up, booed the speaker and created additional disturbance. The chair, trying to regain control of the crowd, pounded the gavel, and shouted, "I'm calling for a twenty minute recess to this meeting."

More grumbling. A number of people stood up, some probably to leave for good. Others held their seats. Callie stood, and eyeing Jerry's empty chair, walked casually forward. She slipped into his chair unnoticed by the two visitors ahead of her. They were speaking intently to each other, slightly above a whisper, and Callie strained to hear their conversation. She couldn't hear much but guessed the gist of what they were talking about. They were speaking about water and Callie could tell that they were humored by the crowd and the crowd's focus on the old mine. The folder held by the man on the right had no identifying information on the cover. As he spoke, he opened the folder slightly and Callie caught sight of a single sheet of paper. It was something like corporate stationery, and the header was blazoned with a single word that made Callie's blood turn cold---Purefz.

The kind of town meeting that Callie attended was duplicated all over the state. Rice Lake, a nearby community, had the same unknown two visitors with the nondescript folder, whispering to each other as the discussion heated up. In Rice Lake, blame was laid upon a massive garbage dumpsite near Weyerhaeuser. The dumpsite opened in 1980 and served a large geographic area including metro Minneapolis and St. Paul. The locals both hated and were beneficiaries from the money that came into the community via the garbage.

Eileen L. Ziesler

THE CABIN

Callie's life continued as it had been even though Elly was gone. Not a day passed that she didn't think of her. Not a day passed that she thought of the great gifts Elly had given and continued to give in the well, the water, and the restoration of an old hunting cabin that Sammy had grown to love. Before Elly was too frail to travel, the four of them had taken a trip to the federal forestland where the old log cabin stood. It had been Elly's dad's love. He hunted there in a tent on the banks of the Torch River before the cabin was built. Callie's own father and uncle had spent many an overnight there in the winter, skiing or hiking in with snowshoes, on the two mile long road which was never plowed. When Elly had seen in her great-grandson that sense of wonderment in the wild, she arranged for the cabin to be rebuilt, complete with a sandpoint well to provide that precious water. It was of course, an illegal well, but the people of the north were not inclined to bother with permits and such when you greased their palm with cash. The entire operation cost Elly a pretty penny but what would she spend her money on? She had hoped Tiarra's girls would be interested, but they were girly little girls and had no interest in enduring the mosquitoes and flies that plagued hikers in the north.

Sammy loved the new cabin and begged to go up whenever

school was not in session. Tubby had been there but was a little more "ish-ish" about the whole experience. Callie went more in memory of her grandmother and great-grandfather and to please Sammy. They stocked the cabin with a few select dried foods, not the insta-food, but rather the foods Callie grew and dehydrated in Flambeau. There was no running water or electricity that could be counted upon, but there was a composting toilet that worked fairly well and a way of taking a shower with water heated on the wood burning stove. A small solar panel provided the occasional need for electricity and the cold storage under the cabin was reminiscent of the old cellars from Edward's time.

Callie lived in both great joy and great sadness. Joy in Sammy as he grew to manhood, looking so much like the Jordan she once knew and sadness as she watched Marta lose ground in her development. Callie refused to feel sorry for herself. She lived for the happiness of her children. Each year Jordan came to Flambeau, staying for the weekend in a local motel and each year Sammy visited his dad returning with the invitation from Jordan for Callie and Marta to visit also. Callie would smile at Sammy and say, "Sometime, maybe." She never reciprocated on the invitation until a much later event.

While their personal lives continued, other events were taking place on a global scale. A massive conglomerate slowly bought up all water distribution and food distribution in the US and abroad. Eventually, the conglomerate owned all power generators, scrubbers, water & food production, and distribution of goods worldwide. The world population continued to grow without war, high tech medical advances, and adequate food and water. However, hidden from public knowledge, the median life span slowly decreased, fertility rates decreased, and infant mortality increased. This happened around the world to varying degrees and no one, not one radio station, not one television station, nor any Internet news media outlet caught on to the slowly eroding world health status and insidious control of resources.

A GRADUATION PRESENT 2063
Sammy and Tubby were in their final days of schooling at

Flambeau. Tubby would graduate and move on to continue the family business. Sammy would be off to school. He would be living with his father on the east coast in New York, attending college. Sammy had a small inheritance from Elly to use and Jordan would co-sign his loan. Jordan was employed, making nice money. He could have completely paid for Sammy's education but that was not the way he saw it. Jordan wanted Sammy to live with him. When Sammy saw the amount he would save by living with his dad, he readily agreed.

As graduation drew nearer, Callie asked Sammy what he would like for a graduation present. Callie had very little money from part-time teaching and her stipend from her secretarial position in the township but she wanted to give Sammy something important.

Sammy did not take long to answer Callie's question. "I'd like you to invite dad here for graduation."

Although Jordan had visited each year, he always stayed in town and Callie had avoided speaking with him as much as possible for 14 years. She had almost been able to pretend that those first years of being in love never existed. Callie looked upon the face of her child, almost a man, who looked so much like his father. "Of course, Sammy, you can invite him."

"No, mom. I didn't ask you if I could invite him, I asked if you would invite him, invite him to stay here on Grandma Elly's farm during his visit."

Callie couldn't help but smile at the intelligence looking her in the eye. "Of course, Sammy, I will."

Sammy hugged his mom and bounded off to school. Callie sat looking out at the melting snow over her garden and wondered how she would manage this visit. Of course Jordan would come and of course he would accept her invitation to stay in the house with them. He would not miss this.

Callie made that difficult call to Jordan. She felt he was rather quiet on the other end of the line. The last time they had any real conversation was ten years ago at Elly's death.

"Are you sure you want me to stay at your place?" Jordan

finally answered.

"Of course!" Callie feigned cheerfulness and then added, "I would like us to have a better relationship not only for Sammy, but for Marta."

At the other end of the phone, Jordan gave no reply.

"I would like you and I to feel at ease in each other's company, to..." here Callie paused, trying to convey a feeling that she had. Without Sammy, her life would have an emptiness that Marta could not fill. She took a big breath and continued. "to share more time together if ...." Callie trailed off. Why would Jordan want to spend more time with her when she had never been open to this and why would she even suggest it?

"Yes," Jordan answered slowly. "It would be good for us too."

"Thank-you, Jordan." Callie was holding back a flood of emotion. "Call me when you have your flight arranged?"

"Sure thing." Jordan replied.

The month of May went by far too quickly for Callie. She went through the motions of planting her garden and preparing for Sammy's graduation. Besides teaching a couple of hours, Callie went to town meetings, spent time with Marta, cooked, gardened, and pumped water from the well each day. But at night she gave way to the sadness of her loss. Sammy would be moving away and she realized how empty her life would be without him.

FRIENDSHIP 2189

Matt's quest to learn more of his ancestry and his joint quest with Amy to uncover the governmental control of the lives of common people like Jim, Wally, Ned, and Rita came to an abrupt halt with his own pending commencement. He spent most of his waking hours cloistered in Amy's study with his console; the holograms of his many professors were his only companions for hours at a time.

Amy, for her own part, lived in four separate worlds. She lived in Matt's world where she shopped and prepared food and where she shared brief moments of bliss with him when he dared take a respite from his work. She lived in her academic world, working on her degree still two years away. She lived in her garden, having

given up running over the summer months in order to devote time
to a personal goal: learning to grow food. The fourth place Amy
lived was in her imagination: in Elly's world, in Robert's world,
and in Callie's world.

In her imagination, she experienced the joys and sorrows of
these people from the past. These three people and the ones they
loved became Amy's constant companions, imaginary friends
through whom she experienced the emotions of a lifetime. Elly
lived within Amy's mind as Amy petted a stray cat hunting for
mice. Tiarra lived in her heart as she thought about this woman's
lost love and her own great love for Matt. But it was Callie
living within her soul who was her constant companion: Callie,
the woman who came to this place as a young mother seeking
solace and healing from a beloved grandmother and who left this
place as an old woman; Callie, who believed in the health giving
water from the almost magical well; and Callie, whose sleuthing
opened the door to Amy's new quest to uncover the most diabolic
plot by the Governor's of Earth: the manipulation and control of
the lifespan and livelihood of the common people.

Amy sat on a large rock that anchored one corner of her garden.
The scrawny mother cat, a calico, had become unafraid of Amy
and Matt the previous summer. Now Amy petted the warm fur
of the old mother who must have given birth within the week.
Only a few days ago she had walked with a sagging belly and
had lain upon Amy's lap after eating the carnivorous leftovers
of Matt's lunch. Now her mammary glands were hard and her
nipples showed the recent suckling of her young. Amy would
have liked to have seen the birth of these kittens; her chosen field
was obstetrics.

Smiling to herself, she called the way Elly would have called
almost 200 years ago. "Ma-rare, ma-rare, ma-rare." Nothing.
Amy wondered sadly if the kittens would make it. The old cat
did not seem to have the physical resources to sustain and grow
a young family. There was no reason to call the kittens and tame
them and help care for them. It would be better for the old cat
to lose these offspring, to go about her own pleasurable life in

the meadows with the mice and baby birds. Or would it? Should she, Amy, have control over the destiny of these helpless beings in the way that the Governors controlled the helpless beings in their world? Amy stood up and stretched her sore back. She felt hungry, but with an unsettled queasy feeling. Brushing the dirt off her pants, she surveyed the progress she had made. Then she walked to the abode to have a shower, to be cleansed of these thoughts, and to make dinner.

Matt would be taking a break this evening from his studies. They had invited Ned and Ned's girlfriend to dinner. Matt and Amy had befriended Ned one day in the spring by helping him when his water transport became stuck in the soft earth. They found him to be quite a happy guy, more knowledgeable than they would have guessed and much younger than they had guessed. For his part, Ned was fascinated by Matt's knowledge of nuclear and water producing systems. Ned was hoping for a different position and a raise in salary when the Chippewa scrubber became activated. He wanted to make a good impression on the management who would be hiring and Matt was helping him with this. Ned had always been interested in Amy, the newcomer to the community. Maybe he was even a little infatuated with her. Luckily, a young woman entered Ned's life, a social peer to whom he was attracted. The feeling was apparently mutual. The two of them would be guests for dinner and Susan was feeling included by Amy who sought her gardening and sewing expertise.

Because of Ned's connection to Purefz, Amy was afraid of divulging too much information about her well as the friendship between the four young people grew. She referred to the water cooler in the kitchen as an antique found on the property when she purchased it. This seemed a reasonable enough explanation. But now that Amy and Matt knew something about Sammy's friendship with Tubby Nader, they decided to see what Ned knew about the history of the property during the time of his great grandfather.

GRADUATION 2063

On Sammy's high school graduation day, June 9, 2063, Callie

woke with a heavy heart. Jordan was already in the kitchen sitting with Marta. He had been working hard ever since he arrived on Thursday to re-establish a relationship with this child he hardly knew. Now it was Saturday and Marta was at least comfortable in his presence. Callie put on a smile and gave Marta a hug. "Morning, you two early birds."

"Good-morning to you too, sleepy head." Jordan said.

Finding no reply to the same endearment Jordan had used in their romantic years, Callie went about preparing breakfast.

After the graduation ceremony Jordan left and Sammy began to prepare for college. He would be leaving soon, eager to get on with his life. Jordan called every few days and during one of those calls, Callie let down her guard and unhappily shared her sorrow at losing Sammy. Jordan was surprisingly kind, the Jordan she remembered. Beginning with this call, the fourteen years of anger and detachment from each other slowly began to fade.

Callie had never traveled back to the east. Sammy, though wrapped up in his own young life, had moments when he thought deeply about his mother and his father. He knew about the well, the water, and he knew why Callie had left his father when he was four. He also overheard one of the recent telephone conversations between his parents. Although he possibly would have preferred to jump on a plane and start his new life, he asked Callie for one more gift.

"Mom, I would like just the three of us to take a road trip."

"A road trip?"

"Yeah. I mean, you and I and Marta have never really had a trip by car together. We've flown a few places for vacations, and we've gone to the cabin. But I remember some of Grandma Elly's stories about how she and Joseph would take Robert and Grandpa James in a camper all over the states, staying at state parks. I'd really like that, just the three of us. I was thinking we could do that and you could drop me off at Dad's. I mean if it wouldn't be too hard for you to drive back alone with Marta."

Callie smiled sadly, thinking about how quickly time had passed. She found no reason to deny Sammy this experience.

It wasn't that she had any reason to be afraid of the trip back without Sammy's help. It was more that she was face to face with another lost dream from her early years with Jordan, the dream of taking family trips with their small children, introducing them to the beauty and wonder of all the parks she had been to as a child. And of course there was the inevitable meeting with Jordan at his home, the home they had not shared all these years.

So it was arranged. They left on a two-week journey that would take them away from the precious water and the home that Callie loved. Marta would be fine on the trip as long as she had her headphones and a stack of her favorite picture books. Jordan got involved in the planning, renting a small motor home for them. Sammy bought a tent and minimalist camping gear, intending to sleep outdoors when he could. They would arrive in New York State on July 2nd. Jordan would meet them and drive them to his condo. Then a few days after the fireworks on the 4th Callie and Marta would leave, leaving Sammy behind. If Callie was fearful of the drive alone, she never let on.

What can be said about letting go? Sammy's excitement at beginning the next phase of his life was matched by his mother's sadness when she thought of him being gone. Without intending it to happen, Sammy had become the rock in his mother's life. Now it would be gone. When, as a complete family they sat together, watching the fireworks, Callie was grateful for the darkness that hid the tears streaming down her face.

But Jordan observed the reflection of bursting light on Callie's cheeks and knew. His fourteen years of anger and sorrow were washed away. As Jordan watched the fireworks, the spark of an idea kindled and grew.

The next morning Sammy took Marta on a walk in Central Park. Sam was struck with the difference between the two of them and though he could not change the events contributing to Marta's disabilities, he realized that her loss was his loss also. He never had and would never have a sister to challenge him intellectually. Marta would always be little Marta and he, Sammy, would always be the caregiver, the big brother.

Jordan and Callie sat quietly for a while after Sammy and Marta left. Jordan asked if there was anything Callie would like to do or see in New York. When she didn't respond, Jordan suggested a day trip to the United Nations building. Callie looked up at him quizzically.

"Why?"

"Well," Jordan began slowly, not knowing whether he would open all the old wounds of the past, "I've read that they are preparing for a world summit."

Callie did not say anything, waiting for more information.

"You know, all the difficulties with the water, --we've had, you've had--well, the problems are not just here." Jordan trailed off. He began to think this was a bad idea.

"So what is the summit about?" Callie was genuinely curious but it would take some doing to interest her in something beyond her grief surrounding Sammy's move.

Jordan tried to choose his words carefully. "The summit is about outsourcing the production and delivery of water worldwide. I thought you might get some interesting information to take back to your town board." Callie had told Jordan about her involvement in town government. Jordan was thinking that anything that helped Callie focus on something other than Sammy would be a good thing.

Callie, for her part, was only mildly interested, but she saw an opportunity to walk and spend the rest of time that she had with Jordan in a way that didn't conjure up old and painful memories.

Marta held tightly to her mother's hand as the four of them made their way into the subway station. She had never experienced a city with its overwhelming noise and smell. Marta whimpered and Sammy stood beside his sister with his arm around her. The scrawny little fourteen-year-old looked like a child of eight or ten next to her brother. Jordan took in the scene of Callie, Marta, and Sammy clumsily following the stairs and underground passages. When the train came to a halt, and Marta froze, he saw Sammy give her a hug before giving her a push onto the train. Someone else on the train noticed and gave up a seat for Callie and Marta. Marta sat on Callie's lap for the duration while Sammy stood with his father, watching over little Marta.

Once out into the open areas and sidewalks around the United Nations building, Marta recuperated. Her headphones were on and she hummed her little songs. Sammy stayed outside with his sister while giving Callie and Jordan the opportunity to browse the displays inside the building. Callie picked up a few brochures, one describing the summit for the summer of 2065. It would be an event studying the world health issues arising from the water delivery systems. Outsourcing water delivery worldwide was to be one of the topics covered. Callie mused; two years from now, Sammy would be half through with his education. What else would happen in those two years?

"Our township is talking about these same issues." Callie shared some of her thoughts with Jordan.

"Well, why don't you see if you can get involved at the state and national level. You could come back to New York for the summit."

Callie nodded. Jordan not only had aged greatly in the last fourteen years; he had also grown emotionally. He seemed more at peace, less determined to have every last piece of gadgetry that was coming out. She had noticed also that his stock of bottled water was of the very expensive type, advertised as spring water. Whether it was truly natural water, Callie did not know. She realized she could not protect them all forever.

The following day, the four of them toured Sammy's college campus. While they were all together Jordan gently expressed concern for Marta and Callie driving the motor home back alone. With Sammy concurring, he arranged a short leave for himself and an airplane ticket from Wisconsin back to New York. He said that it would give Sammy time to be on his own and make his own space in Jordan's home and that he, Jordan, would feel better if he could see Marta and Callie back safe at Flambeau.

Callie had no energy to dispute the decision. She was barely able to get through the leave taking with Sammy and once they were on their way, she left the passenger seat to sleep. She slept until Jordan stopped the motor home for gas. They ate a lunch and she slept again. Jordan wondered if he would see her at all during the trip. He didn't regret his decision to drive them home; in fact he was glad he had finally made the right decision.

When they stopped again it was very late in the afternoon; Callie did not get up. Jordan paid for the camping permit and coaxed Marta to come with him for a walk. It was still hot outside and they walked down to a sandy beach on the banks of a river. Jordan took off his sandals and encouraged Marta to do the same. They splashed their feet in the cool water. Marta saw a large frog on the edge of the beach and then some minnows in the shallow water. She delighted in standing very still in the water, watching the minnows close to her feet. When they came close, she giggled softly. Jordan sat in the sand watching her simple enjoyment. They stayed at the beach as the sun made its way behind the trees on the other side of the river. Jordan sat dozing while Marta played in the water.

Jordan didn't hear Callie coming up behind him. She stood watching for a long time. She sighed and sat next to him in the sand. Jordan startled and looked over at her, wondering what she was thinking. Callie smiled at Jordan, first a small smile and then a bigger one as she recalled a pleasant memory.

"What?" Jordan queried.

"Morning, sleepy head!" Callie teased. For the first time in fourteen years, they were both overcome with the giggles and Marta came over to join in the fun.

CONNECTIONS 2189

Amy set the small table for the foursome. In the center she placed a large pitcher of water from her well, hoping that she would not need to refill the it with tank water. She was looking forward to this evening, yet her concern for the well continued to be in her thoughts.

The two young couples ate and laughed together. It was a relief for Matt to have an evening with friends and not his constant hologram companions. They finished eating and decided to take a hike up Flambeau Mountain. Ned and Matt took the lead with their wide strides while Susan and Amy talked quietly together. As Amy and Susan reached the top, they noticed the guys deep in serious conversation. Amy had a sudden intuition that the guys have shared something important together and she hoped fervently that Matt has not spoken about the well to Ned.

"Amy!" Matt called out excitedly, "Ned's family owns a cabin that was once in the Bordeau family. I believe it is the cabin that Elly rebuilt for Sammy! You know, the cabin from Edward's generation." It was impossible for Matt to contain his excitement that the Bordeaus and the Naders had a connection that extended to himself and Ned.

"Why do you think this?" Amy questioned Matt sharply; thinking ahead to the time capsule story of the well and worrying that Matt may have shared too much.

"Ned has the abstract. His dad turned the property over to Ned before he died. The first owner of the forty acres was the state of Wisconsin. The second and third owners were Edward Bordeau and then his daughter, Elly. Callie Nelson and Sammy Nelson were the next two owners. Sammy Nelson sold the cabin to Tubby Nader and Tubby was Ned's great grandfather!"

Matt grabbed Ned by the shoulders; "We are practically related!"

The trip down the Flambeau Mountain provided an entirely different experience. Ned and Matt grew closer as they made plans to visit the cabin. Susan tried to engage Amy in conversation, but realized Amy's mind was far away. The girls made their way down in silence.

That night, after Susan and Ned left, Matt and Amy had their first argument. Amy tried to impress upon Matt the danger of sharing too much with this long time resident of Flambeau who worked for Purefz. Matt couldn't agree with Amy on the danger of Ned's knowing too much, feeling her fears were unfounded. He argued that they both needed to learn to trust others in this small, tightly knit community.

The week went by with little change in their respective positions.

Amy was too distracted to engage Susan in any conversation and Susan felt the distance between them. Matt focused on his professors and blocked any thoughts of Amy's dilemma.

Towards the end of the week, Susan confided in Ned.

"Something is wrong. Amy is not herself and I'm afraid it is something we have said."

"I'm sure you are imagining things." was all Ned could say.

MARTA'S INDEPENDENCE

Callie continued her life and routines of her life at Flambeau without Sammy. She found she spoke very little in the day when she was home with Marta. Each night grief would envelop her and then guilt concerning Marta. Slowly as the weeks turned to months, she formed a plan for Marta: a plan that would allow Marta to become semi-independent of her.

Sammy was well into his academic and new social life. He occasionally remembered to call his mother to tell her about college, but not nearly enough to fill the hole that was in her heart. Sammy and his father had dinner together once a week. Jordan, like Callie, would have preferred more time with his son. He thought a lot about Callie these days and called after each evening with Sammy. They talked also about Marta; Jordan concurred with Callie's plan to build a friendship circle for Marta.

In the meantime, a number of citizens of Flambeau had been diagnosed with pancreatic cancer. Tubby's dad, Fred Nader, was one of them. Callie took Marta along with her when she went to Janet's house to help. She helped in whatever way she could, peeling vegetables for a meal, unloading the dishwasher, or just sitting with Janet in the final days of Fred's life. Marta, in her quiet way, became a comfort to Janet and after the funeral was over, Janet encouraged Marta to come more often. Janet confided in Callie that Marta's quiet, unassuming presence helped her feel at peace with all that had happened. Callie always sent along a water bottle for Marta. Marta drank water only from that bottle, although if offered tea or lemonade, she would drink that. Janet grew more and more curious about the water bottle. One day she couldn't contain her curiosity any longer and gently asked Marta about it.

"Marta, why do you bring water with you? Our tank is full of water."

Marta looked around for some support. She had never been left alone to explain the water that she and her family relied upon. "Momma says I have to drink this water," was the best that she could do.

Janet could see that her own interest in the water bottle had made Marta very nervous. Janet and Callie were close friends. Why had Callie not said anything to her about the water?

SHARED SECRETS

The trip to the cabin had to be put off until Matt finished his degree. Then it was put off a little longer because Matt landed a job for GEO, Inc. a global engineering firm whose subsidiary was located in Chippewa Falls. It was the job of his dreams, a design engineer for the next generation of power scrubbers. He learned that past scrubbers provided dangerous levels of nuclear reactive ions in the water, the same Purefz water that Callie had been so skeptical of. Today's water controlled for this. GEO, Inc had the contract for building the new small-scale prototype carbon scrubber and water bottling operation.

At first Amy was not pleased with Matt's new position. She was thrilled that they could continue their life together because of the proximity of Flambeau to Chippewa Falls, but on the other hand she was worried that he would become a convert to the Purefz camp in the same way that Callie's husband, Jordan had. She decided to verbalize her fears, and learned that Matt was intrigued with not only improving the quality of the water, but also in finding out more about Purefz from the inside.

In early September, months after the foursome had learned about the Bordeau family's connection to Ned's cabin, the trip to the cabin became a reality. Both Amy's and Matt's run-abouts would be used. Neither Ned nor Susan were of the social status to be able to own such a technologically advanced vehicle. It would have been fun for Ned to drive; unfortunately, the programming in his chip prevented this.

They packed for an overnight trip, unsure of whether the cabin would be standing when they arrived. Ned took a small hatchet, should he have to clear trees from the path that was once a road. Susan and Amy collaborated on provisions. Amy brought a five-gallon tote full of water from her precious well. Amy, and especially Matt, had never had an experience like this, traveling deep into the Chequemegon National Forest, home to elk, deer, bear, and wolves. Without Ned's confidence (and possibly his hatchet) they would never have gone.

The trip on the side roads from Flambeau to the end of the forest road system two miles from the cabin took an hour with the two run-abouts. Once they turned off the established roadways and trails onto the cabin road, the going became more difficult and the run-abouts did little except provide a means of carting the supplies. Ned and Susan went ahead most of the time; walking and breaking brush on each side of the trail. Occasionally, Ned used his hatchet to break bigger limbs. Matt and Amy drove the run-abouts up to each obstruction, then got off to help remove the debris. In this manner, the trip on the cabin road took another forty-five minutes.

Ned suddenly announced, "We're almost here." He picked up the pace and Susan ran to catch his hand. Matt and Amy smiled at each other from their respective run-abouts. They hung back a bit, letting Ned and Susan have the first glimpse. Ned didn't turn around towards them but bounded up the small hill to the cabin door. It was never locked against human trespass, just tightly secured against the trespass of curious animals.

Ned finished unlatching all the hooks and the heavy door creaked, its hinges slowly recalling movement. He propped the door open and the sunlight from the west threw beams of dusty light on the cool interior. Ned turned around, grinning at his friends; "It's still here!" he happily called out.

Without unloading the run-abouts, Ned's friends made their way into the cabin. Ned opened the door on the other side to let the breeze freshen the musty air. Looking around Amy noticed first the heavy varnished picnic table sitting under a wagon wheel chandelier. There were dark scars in the surface of the wood where hunters had stuck their knives deeply into the grain, knives used both indoors for slicing hard salami and bread and out of doors for gutting a freshly killed deer carcass. Of this, Amy knew little. Instead she rather felt the history of the place than knew it for a fact.

At one end of the L-shaped cabin there were some roughly hewn bunks with thin mattresses. A centrally located potbellied wood stove stood ready to heat the cabin and to keep water hot in an old teakettle. On the backside of the kitchen wall was an indoor composting toilet, a small sink, and a tiled floor with a drain. There was no running water, not that the young people expected any. The cabin layout matched exactly the description Matt and Amy had read in Callie's journal. Amy looked at the expression on Matt's face as he discovered each thing they had read about. Callie had included two pictures, a before remodeling and an after remodeling picture. The old cabin was a log cabin and the logs at the foundation had decayed during Elly's lifetime. The new cabin exterior was of a synthetic material, barely touched by time. However, the work on the inside of the cabin had preserved its rustic nature. The table, the potbellied stove, the kitchen, and the bunks were original. The logs that formed the walls and the roof supports were also originals. Elly had paid dearly to preserve the interior of the cabin in the style of its original construction. It was a preservation of love.

Now the cabin was in Ned's hands. Although his family did not build the cabin, he had his own set of memories from four generations using the cabin. Rarely was Ned ever able to visit the cabin but it was the one thing he valued as an heirloom. He held an irresistibly romantic feeling about the cabin as it was completely inaccessible, landlocked in the midst of a National Forest. Even the roads and trails in the forest were slowly returning to the days before the timber was harvested.

Ned dutifully paid the taxes each year. He probably could have let the forty acres revert to national forest, but about this he was very stubborn. His reasoning was simple: if he paid the taxes, he owned it.

Amy wondered to herself what Ned would tell Matt about the well at the cabin. She knew from the time capsule that Elly had a well driller drive a point in the sandy soil between the Moose River and the building. She would explore this area before she left even without Ned's knowledge or blessing. But she hoped he would talk openly about it with them. Was the well a viable well? If so, it would be, like all private wells, completely illegal. If it had been filled, like most of the private wells, what did Ned know of this story? It was an intriguing puzzle and it somehow put them on equal footing. Maybe a deeper level of trust would develop between the two couples. Maybe the secret of the well would deepen their differences.

"Hey, isn't anyone hungry?" Susan queried. "Some host you are Ned, starving your guests!"

"Well, we'd first better unload our supplies." Susan's teasing did not affect Ned. "You don't want to go out with the bears and wolves in the dark, do you?"

"No, not me," Matt answered. "But you know, Ned, the ladies are not at all afraid to be out in the dark with the ravenous animals." With that he lunged at Amy, who screamed in fake terror.

"Okay, behave yourselves you love birds. Work now, eat later." Ned enjoyed his role as the most knowledgeable and thus leader of the expedition. Matt and Amy went about unloading the gear and supplies while Susan and Ned swept off the dust from the mattresses, the floor, and then wiped off the table. "I'm going to get some water." Ned announced in an offhand way.

Amy perked up her ears upon hearing Ned refer to water. She would have loved to follow Ned, but Matt touched her arm and shook his head, signally her to wait with her questions. "We will be in a much better position in the future if we can have a mutually trusting relationship with Ned," he said to Amy when Susan was out of earshot.

Amy nodded. She had been so careful, so distrustful for such a long time that it was difficult to break the pattern.

With the bedding out and the food stacked on the counters,

Amy and Susan set out to make a meal. They had brought one precooked ready-to-eat meal that had thawed on the trip. Ned came back from his hunt for water. He set a bucket on a bench and without any emotion in his voice stated that they could dip water from here to wash, but that it would be safer to use the water they brought for drinking and cooking. That arrangement was certainly fine by Susan. The pail was a dented old galvanized bucket. Even if the water had been good before it went into the bucket, it was certainly contaminated by being in the bucket. Nevertheless, they used the water to wash a few dishes before using them.

Ned showed Matt how to start a fire in the stove. He then poured some bucket water into an old teakettle to heat up for washing dishes after their meal.

When they finished eating, Matt cheerfully took the lead in cleaning up, admonishing the others to relax. Susan and Amy sat with the rest of their wine, served in big old coffee mugs while Ned sat quietly watching them. They made small talk about the cabin and its beauty. They talked about Susan's family and her work as a nurse. They talked about Amy's pending internship as an obstetrician. "Maybe we will work together some day," Susan smiled. She was comfortable with her position in life as most people were. The programming of the chip had a great deal to do with her acceptance of her class standing.

Ned suddenly stood up and poured the rest of the bucket into a teakettle that he placed on the potbellied stove. He took the bucket and went to the door. Amy asked quickly, "Want some company---to ward off the wolves?"

"No thanks, it's better if someone survives to carry my uneaten bones back to Flambeau."

Susan laughed. Animals didn't at all frighten her. She was the only girl in a family of boys. How she grew up to be so feminine was baffling. When Ned left, she seemed pensive. Amy wondered what she was thinking.

"Amy, Ned is trying to decide whether to share something with you. I hope he will. I have been telling him that you both would be trustworthy." But before she could say more, Ned was back with the water. He looked straight at Susan, as if knowing what she had just shared.

Matt had finished the dishes and sat next to Amy, pulling her close. Ned stood looking out into the dark. The one battery powered electric lamp was moved from the kitchen closer to a place behind the chairs by the potbellied stove. The flickering light partially illuminated the thoughtful faces of the four friends. Ned took in a deep breath and let it out slowly. He walked to the pail and filled his cup with the water he had just carried in. Then he sat down next to Susan. No one spoke as Ned slowly drank the water.

"You know, don't you?" he began, looking at Amy. Susan hooked her arm into Ned's and laid her head upon his arm.

After an uncomfortable silence, Amy spoke. "We read Callie Bordeau Nelson's journal. We read about the cabin and its reconstruction by her grandmother for the grandmother's great grandson, and we read how a sand point was driven into the bank of the hillside between the cabin and the river. We didn't know what had happened since then, whether it had been filled in and capped like other wells in Flambeau. Or," here Amy hesitated, "whether it survived as did one of the wells on the land I own in Flambeau."

There, she had divulged the most important secret she had. Susan and Ned looked up, speechless, at Amy.

"It looks like we both value the forbidden waters." was all Ned could muster.

Amy was drained of emotion. Matt stepped in. "Ned, Callie's journal has given us some amazing information of how she and her ancestors treasured the water in the local wells. Callie's grandmother, the person who paid dearly for rebuilding this cabin also hid and protected her well at Flambeau." Matt stopped talking and hugged Amy, kissing the top of her head. "Amy has been very worried about our friendship with you because of your employer and your possible allegiance to Purefz."

Now it was Ned's turn to confess his fear of exposing the secret of the well. When he finished, Amy stood up and walked over to Ned. Taking both his hands in hers she knelt before him. "Thank you. Thank you very, very much."

A LITTLE WHITE LIE

Callie was puzzled by Janet. Her friend seemed to be creating a distance between them. Janet still encouraged Marta to come and visit often, usually on a weekly basis or more, but she never called Callie just to chat or to come for tea. Callie invited Janet to come to her house, and sometimes Janet came. Sometimes she excused herself, stating she had other things to attend to. When Janet did come, she engaged Marta in conversation most of the time so that any real communication with Callie was extremely limited.

Without Sammy and without Elly, Callie had no confidants. Jordan had been good, surprisingly, wonderfully good, but he was far away. He now knew about the well and was supportive of Callie's use of this water whenever he and Sammy visited. He even pumped the water himself and brought containers to take back as much drinking water as he could the few times that he and Sammy drove. But this was not enough in Callie's life. She had friendships with a few of the teachers and with others in the town of Flambeau, however there was no one who offered the kind of relationship Callie needed most. She had been close to Janet and now did not know why Janet continued to shun her.

As Marta's sixteenth birthday approached, Callie decided to have a sweet sixteen party. She asked Janet if she could bake one of her special cakes, knowing that Janet would not refuse. A number of women and their daughters would be invited. It was to be a ladies' tea in the garden in June. Marta was interested though not exactly excited about the affair. She was slipping, slipping slowly but steadily into a place where she was less and less present. It had come about so slowly that neither her mother nor Janet had really noticed.

The day of the party, the weather was perfect, warm and sunny. Elly's flowerbeds bloomed with splashes of pinks and whites, the many peonies that Elly had loved. It made Callie smile, to see that the flowers were in full bloom for Marta's birthday. "Thank you, Gram," she thought to herself. A few neighbor ladies brought extra tables and chairs. Janet brought a three tiered layer cake, a chocolate cake with pink roses on a butter crème home-made frosting. Callie made cold lemonade with water from the well and hot chamomile tea served with lemon and honey. Marta was enlisted to put the place cards at the tables and add a small bouquet of pastel colored tulips on each of the five small tables. Callie had made small goat cheese and arugula tomato sandwiches early in the day along with fruit salad. Marta helped make a raspberry finger gelatin, cutting out small cookie cutter shapes.

Janet and Callie were almost able to dismiss the distance that had widened between them in their joy at creating a party for Marta.

Everyone arrived on time and Marta seemed to really be enjoying the party though at times Callie believed she saw touches of sadness on the always-pale face of her beautiful but childlike daughter. Marta seemed to take great delight in opening the little gifts of soaps, chocolates, lipstick, and stationery. The party wound down around five in the afternoon and after all the guests had departed, Janet and Callie sat together with one last glass of lemonade while Marta sat with her gifts in the swing.

"Thank you for everything today. Especially thank you for your friendship. I've missed you greatly this past year. It seems as though we've grown apart and I don't know if it is something I've said or done to hurt you." Callie had decided to tackle this problem for better or worse.

Janet studied Callie, unsure of whether to speak of her talks with Marta about the water. Janet had felt Callie wasn't trusting of her. It had hurt her feelings greatly. It just seemed easier to do without the close friendship they once had. And then again, Janet was beginning to emerge from the grief she experienced at Fred's death. Maybe it was time to be honest and try for a fresh start with her old friend. "I guess I should tell you about something that has hurt my feelings. It happened a while back, but the situation continues to emerge each time Marta visits.

And in an instant, Callie knew what it was. The thing she treasured and the thing she kept hidden. The thing only Sammy and Jordan really knew. Callie had kept this secret hidden even from Marta, Marta who took everything at face value and had no questions.

Callie could have told the truth to her friend Janet and that would have bound them even closer together than before. In fact, she almost did; but as she spoke, a piece of the truth convoluted itself almost on its own. Her words flowed not from herself but from that secret place hidden by blackberries and rusty old machinery. The words flowed to protect the well.

The story that flowed so easily from Callie's mouth was a partial truth. She told the story of Marta's frailty at birth and blamed it upon the water, not the water in the Purefz tank, but of an imagined contamination of the bottled Purefz water before Marta was born. Maybe this was not so far from the truth, maybe the Purefz water that Callie drank during pregnancy was infected and that infection weakened the babe who was now the child, Marta, causing her disability and frailty. "So, I continue to fear for Marta's susceptibility to infection and I boil and cool the water we drink."

It seemed plausible and preposterous at the same time, but Janet, was happy enough to trust the story. She had also had concerns about Purefz since Fred died and she now shared those concerns with Callie. Callie and Janet renewed their friendship though it was built (on Callie's side) on a little white lie. Together the two of them wondered about the possibilities of impurities in the Purefz water that might have contributed to Fred's early death.

"You know, Janet, when I went to the summit at the United Nations, I heard a great deal that makes me fearful. The break out session was on the benefits of a single corporate structure running the utilities in each of the union nations. So, in our case, Purefz, may be the single utility that would handle all water production and distribution, carbon scrubbing, electricity production, and waste management. We were told that the benefit to the people would be in keeping the cost of utilities to a minimum. The UN is pushing for this model to be replicated in the other unions around the world."

Janet looked thoughtful. "I can see where keeping the costs down will benefit the people. After all, aren't there something like nine billion people in the world right now? I mean, can we really afford to produce enough food, water, and other necessities of life the way we do right now?"

"Yes, that is what they were getting at. But I was thinking how very controlling this would be if you have one utility that not only handles your drinking water, but also processes wastes. We might be going overboard on this recycling concept. How healthy can that be for us? You know I wouldn't be surprised if they will go ahead and do this consolidation in the other sectors of the economy. You know what I mean?"

"Hmmm, I think you mean that we might have only one conglomerate handling all transportation and one handling all food manufacturing."

"Yes!" Callie became very excited with the sudden insight she and Janet were having into the possible management of the world. "We would have only one giant corporation handling all transportation, from cars to trains to planes! And there would be another giant corporation that would handle all communication."

"You know," Janet said sadly, "we can't do anything about this. It is way beyond us."

"Well, yes and no," Callie said. "We can help ourselves, our families, and our community. And we can keep ourselves informed of the world events. Jordan invited me to come for the next summit. I think I'll take him up on the invitation. It's at least a start. And you and I can focus on the water problem here in Flambeau."

Callie and Janet talked about the artesian springs that were said to be at the surface in many places on Flambeau Mountain. They made a pact to explore portions of the mountain together to see if they could locate an artesian well. They decided they would enlist the help of the old timer Stephan Linski if they couldn't find a spring by themselves. Linski sold eggs from his farm. He was very old, and had lived a self-sustaining lifestyle his entire life. He might just know something in regard to the whereabouts of one of those springs.

One morning, two weeks after Marta's sweet sixteen party, Callie and Janet walked with Marta up one side of Flambeau Mountain. They took a few pieces of cake, some fruit, and a thermos of hot tea. The path up the mountain was overgrown with grasses and fern. Four years of unhindered brush had encroached upon the sides of the trail that had once been a road. The best walking was on a deer trail that followed the old roadbed.

When they reached the top they sat on the logs and ancient rocks, resting and musing about how and where springs would be. They had no real idea of what to look for, but going for this walk together was a start. The spring flowers were long gone and the ferns had unfurled. Flies buzzed about and pestered them when they sat in the sun eating. When they moved to the shade, the mosquitoes took their turn. Still, it was pleasant and even if they found no water, they were enjoying the day.

Marta walked amongst the fern and rocks stopping at each tree. She put her hands on the rough bark and leaned her cheek near her hands. She seemed to be smelling the bark of the tree. After a few moments she would circle the tree and repeat the procedure on the other side.

Janet and Callie watched her. They were both aware of how she seemed to fit into the woods, a wood sprite in communion with the trees. Callie started to notice that Marta seemed to be comparing the smells or textures of the south facing trunks of trees to the north facing side. Standing up she copied her daughter's actions to better understand Marta's experience. The south facing trunks were rough and dry, the north facing trunks had a growth of soft green moss, damp and cool.

"Janet!" she called excitedly after a few moments, "I think Marta has given us a clue. I think we need to locate outcroppings of rocks where we see more of this moss. I think if we locate moss in places that do not necessarily face north, we will find water."

They did not find an artesian spring that day on Flambeau Mountain, but they both felt they would and they both felt the urgency to do so.

Watching her beautiful daughter slipping further back into childhood fueled Callie's urgency. Callie worried that if something should happen to her, Marta, wherever she would be, would be consuming Purefz. In Callie's way of thinking, Marta was the victim and she stood for all the children who were victims of Purefz water. Callie might not be able to save her own daughter, but she would put all her energy into helping save the children of Flambeau and future generations of children of this very special community.

The next time Callie went to the Linski farm to buy eggs, she baked a cake to take to Stephan. If everything went well she would enlist his help in finding a spring.

Old farmer Linski initially balked at any discussion of spring water, but slowly he came around. Perhaps it was the cake; perhaps it was the realization of the closeness of the end of his life. Perhaps it was his curiosity. There were stories in his oral history, passed down from one generation to the next of the original Ojibwe, Linski's ancestors living on the banks of the 'Flaming River'. It was said that when they left this land, they buried some of their sacred artifacts near a spring in the side of the Flambeau Mountain to be ready for them. As a child, Stephen hiked the woods of the Flambeau Mountain.

He agreed to come with Callie. They would drive his four wheeler around Flambeau Mountain and he would try his best to witch the water for her. The two women did not want to risk Linski having a change of heart so Callie took Marta to Janet's home before picking up the old farmer. Callie's vehicle would pull Linski's four wheeler to the base of Flambeau mountain. Stephan Linski was far too old to walk the distance, but he reveled in the thrill of adventure. After unloading the four wheeler from the trailer, he climbed slowly on and beckoned Callie to sit behind him.

Callie could have walked faster than they drove. However it was pleasant to sit astride the ATV behind the old man in his red plaid flannel shirt. Her intuition about rock outcroppings and moss had been correct. Farmer Linski stopped whenever he observed this type of outcropping. With a heavy pick and shovel, they checked out the soil below the outcropping. Linski would pick up a handful of the dirt Callie dug up and would squeeze it with his large muscular hand. He passed the soil on to Callie to feel and then he pronounced judgment on the place that they explored. "Nah, this soil is too dry. See? You can't get any wetness to come out. We are looking for soil near the surface that will ooze some water when we squeeze it. If we find that kind of soil, sure as shootin' there will be a spring not far above."

They had been out over two hours and Callie was considering how tired Stephan might be. She was about to call it quits for the day when Stephan beckoned to her. He had been walking around with a forked willow branch and had evidently felt something in the movement of the branch. "Now here! Get a handful of this soil and squeeze it." Linski had not waited for her, but had dropped the willow and was clawing away the moss to get a handful of soil. "See how your hand is wet with the mud. It's different than the other times. Right?"

It was different. Stephan sat on a nearby rock while Callie went for the crow bar and shovel to try to unearth more of the surface rock and surrounding mud. She was unable to get any further than sixteen or eighteen inches down, but her efforts allowed a muddy ooze to quickly fill the small hole. Stephan came over to inspect.

"Well, you did it. You've allowed the water to come up to the surface. Now put some of that moss into the hole to line it. Ya gotta keep from churning up the mud next time you dip your hands in for water. If you leave it alone for a day, you should have some clear water in that hole. If you go deeper, and create a small spillway, the water will always flow. You could drive a point into the ground and attach a horizontal pipe at the surface, extending a few feet. If you did that, you'd keep the water flowing and pure."

Callie wiped her muddy hands on the grass near by. "Thank you so much, Mr. Linski! I can't believe we found this. I'm so grateful!" She stepped toward him, giving him a hug."

Old farmer Linski looked bashfully away for a moment. Then he became serious. "Now Callie, you mustn't tell anyone about this. If you either decide to enlarge the hole or have a point driven to let the water flow, you must be very careful. The damn government will bulldoze the whole thing in if they find it."

"I understand what you are telling me and I will be extremely careful."

Nothing else was left to do so the odd pair collected the crowbar and the shovel. They boarded the four wheeler and made their way slowly down the mountain.

After Callie and Janet found the spring and drove in a shallow sand point, they pondered the problem of whether to enlarge the circle of beneficiaries of this forbidden water. Obtaining water from the spring was not a simple process. One had to have a few clean, empty jugs, and drive as close as possible to the hidden spring, walking the last 500 feet. This would not be a bad walk, but how much water can one really cart away in this manner? And what about creating a well-trodden path for no apparent reason. Would the path be seen from above by airplanes or satellites? These were the questions they pondered without a solution for the next four years.

The solution finally came to them when one of Fred Nader's old business partners tried to change Janet's mind concerning the buy out of the restaurant portion of the Nader resort. Janet had initially resisted but had found it increasingly hard to manage her share of the enterprise with Fred gone. But now, with the sale of the business, Janet was able to purchase a few acres of Flambeau Mountain that encompassed the spring in addition to gifting monies to her children. She and Callie decided on building a small wayside chapel close to the well. The trodden path could now be explained away by the construction and subsequent visits to the small stone chapel. The little chapel, complete with a Madonna, was built by Tubby and the landscaping around the chapel provided cover for the little spring. Callie and Janet put the finishing touches on the landscaping. Elly, an atheist, would have been amused.

The development of the spring and chapel should have signaled a better time for Callie and Janet had it not been for Marta. Marta, now twenty-two, was having seizures more often. The seizures were worse and no medications diminished their intensity. Marta needed bed rest a day or two after a seizure. Callie could no longer leave Marta unattended during the day and at night Callie's sleep was interrupted by fear.

LIFE 2191

Amy's two years of internship and then residency in obstetrics passed uneventfully. In fact, the big event in those two years was a small, unassuming wedding, to which a handful of Flambeau residents were invited. Amy's father and his wife came, looking very much out of place. There were also three other strangers, not from Flambeau, at the wedding--a woman who brought flowers for the bride and two older men. Ned and Susan married within the same year. Susan went quietly about her work as a nurse, saying little about the nagging fear deep inside. She was worried she would be unable to conceive. This troubled her greatly, but she kept her fears to herself.

Matt, working for GEO, stumbled upon documents that indicated that the old generation scrubbers did not adequately remove nuclear reactive ions in the water that was distributed to the public for general consumption. This piece of information corroborated Callie's fears. He was also very relieved to learn that in the past fifty years the newer units effectively removed all reactive ions. At least this was what he read this in the reports from the EPA

Matt and Amy were able to commute together with one run-about to Chippewa Falls about half of the time. Some days the hours she put in made that impossible. After the residency she took a position as a medical researcher and part time doctor at the World Health Organization, Chippewa Center. Matt and Amy could see that living in the small Flambeau abode, with a round trip drive of an hour and a half, was just too demanding. They opted to invest their new wealth in a spacious double pod on the banks of the Chippewa River, just west of the city.

Life in the double pod had its advantages. It was within walking distance to everything if they chose to walk. It was clean to the point of sterility. Food was delivered in rationed portions for them to easily prepare as Matt had once done when he lived on his own. This method of modern food preparation was discouraging for both of them. They tried to use real produce to augment their meals, purchasing real food in Flambeau and carting jerry cans of their precious water from the well for the week.

Matt and Amy drove to Flambeau almost every weekend to take care of the little abode and spend time with their friends. Though they talked about visiting Wally and Jim, they never found the time. They talked also about the spring they found with Ned and Susan on the Flambeau mountain three years ago, but again, they never found the time to go back and do anything with it to help others in Flambeau. However, Ned and Susan quietly collected the spring water for their own consumption. Amy found it sad to think that the city of Chippewa Falls originally grew and prospered because of the pure spring water that the residents in the twenty-second century were not allowed to drink.

One Friday afternoon as they performed the now familiar rituals of preparing for the drive to Flambeau, Amy shared with Matt some of the research she had been doing, the most recent numbers from the population studies. "Look Matt, just since we've married, the birth rate has dropped, owing to decreased fertility, choice not to have children, and premature births. The rate of births for women just in Wisconsin is about one woman in two thousand women of childbearing age, and Wisconsin has a higher birth rate than most of the states, only Alaska and Vermont have a higher rate, but not by much. I am positive there is a connection to the Purefz water."

As he finished packing the run-about with the groceries and their clothes, Matt said very little in response to Amy's findings. He had also quietly been doing some research after he stumbled upon GEO's documents. The original Purefz water bottled and sold as a by-product of the carbon scrubbing had many reactive properties. Today's Purefz water truly was at least more pure than a hundred years ago, though not perfect. To make matters worse, he found he did not have the access level needed to obtain all the documents. They were classified. He had also been thinking that he and Amy should start thinking seriously about having a child in the next few years if they were going to. He was almost thirty. He wondered sadly if they would ever be able to have a child.

Matt and Amy arrived at their Flambeau abode as the sun was setting. They stepped out of the run-about and stretched. As was their custom, they held each other close for a few moments breathing in the fresh, cool air before getting to work. Amy secretly wished she could be a young child again and run down to the river to check on it. She took in another deep breath and sighed in resignation. She was not the little girl who could run around carefree while her mother took care of the details.

Matt smiled and put Amy at arms length so he could look at her. He could almost read her mind by now; they had shared so much in the past three years. "Why don't you have a look about while I start unpacking. We have about twenty minutes before we have to leave for Ned and Susan's abode."

Amy's eyes twinkled. "You know me too well!" She stood up on her tiptoes to kiss Matt on the lips before she trotted off to the river. "I'll just run down to the river to take a peek. Then I'll help."

Matt turned toward the run-about and began carting in the groceries and the bag of clothes for the weekend. He'd leave all but one of the jerry cans for fresh water in the run-about. They'd fill them just before they would leave Sunday evening. He took one out and placed it on the bench under the oak tree. It was another ritual that they had maintained after he moved in with Amy. In keeping the ritual alive, she was always the one who pumped the water.

Amy trotted up the hill and sat on the bench next to Matt. "Want to do it?"

"The question is, do you really want me to do it?"

That comment got him another kiss as she dropped down off the edge of the bench with the jerry can in tow. They had stopped the Purefz water delivery transport a few months ago so the collection of jerry cans would not seem odd if authorities caught them with cans of water. And now Ned knew of the well and carefully guarded their secret.

After filling the ancient water cooler on the counter in the kitchen, Amy and Matt took off for Ned's place with the salad Amy always brought for supper. A Friday night supper with the young Nader couple was another ritual they looked forward to each week. On Saturday, Amy and Matt cooked and Susan brought a dessert. In this way the friendship they had grew stronger and stronger. After their greetings, Susan and Amy went in to set the table, put the finishing touches on supper, and dress the salad. Matt and Ned took the run-about to Flambeau Mountain to the hidden spring where they drew fresh water. They had to be very cautious and rather than using a large jerry can, they used liter-sized water bottles that were carried in and out of the woods in backpacks.

Ned and Susan had their own daily ritual for obtaining spring water. On workdays, Ned completed the task while driving the Purefz water transport home at the end of his deliveries. On week ends and holidays, they found time to hike together always varying the times of their hike, the color clothing they wore, and taking slightly different routes to and from the spring. Amy had cautioned them about the satellite vigilance of their activities.

Amy, Matt, and Ned were engrossed in discussions about another trip to the cabin. They were planning to do a big spring cleaning, to throw away old and stale food, to bring back bedding to be cleaned, and to cut weeds and small trees threatening to encroach upon the cabin and the roadbed to the cabin. They even planned to brave the mosquitoes and horse flies of the summer so excited were they about preparing the cabin for fall and winter activities.

"You doing okay?" Amy had noticed that Susan had been unusually quiet.

Susan's eyes gave her away. They held a great sadness that threatened to break through in tears. She couldn't speak.

Amy called out to Ned and Matt, still planning the cabin renewal, "Hey guys, would you please handle cleanup? We are going for a short walk while the moon is out."

Matt looked at Ned and Ned shrugged. This was highly unusual for Amy. She loved completing the small rituals in Susan's big old kitchen and had never asked this favor before. "Sure thing." Ned called back as he pushed his chair away from the table and stood up. Matt could sense that something was wrong and he felt uneasy as he began collecting the dishes.

Ned silently began to store the leftovers as Matt made the trips back and forth. When they were married, Susan and Ned had bought his parents abode, a comfortable old house. It needed a great deal of updating in Susan's opinion. However, it was pleasant though definitely stuck in the end of the twenty-first century.

Matt finished the task of clearing the table. He stood in the kitchen with his friend. "What's up?" There was no point in pretending this was an ordinary Friday evening.

Ned kept his attention on loading the dirty dishes. "Susan." He stopped with a plate in his hand and looked at Matt, unwilling to put words to the emotions he was feeling. "Susan is beginning to fear that we will never have a child."

The unwanted thoughts Matt had earlier in the day about whether he and Amy could have children came back suddenly and took away any logical thinking he might have had to help Ned.

Ned didn't seem to notice. "We've been trying. Actually we didn't ever take any precautions. We both knew we wanted a family. Now, two years later, Susan is getting discouraged, depressed. I don't know what else. She keeps going to work; we keep a semblance of normalcy in our personal lives." Ned trailed off.

Matt sat on the stool at the counter where Ned stood, still holding the same plate. "I've been wondering the same thing about us." Ned looked up at his friend momentarily and automatically resumed his task.

"But Amy is not crying her eyes out every night, right?"

"Well, we haven't gotten that far in our discussions about having a family. Amy's research is important to her right now. It's actually about birth rates in different parts of the world."

"Would she have any hopeful information for us?" Ned didn't really want to hear the answer to the question he had blurted out.

"Not that I know of. Sorry." Matt responded as well as he could to Ned's question but his mind was racing. He had a sudden gut feeling about the embedded chip. It was time to visit Wally again.

MARTA

Jordan came as quickly as he could when Callie called, taking a red-eye flight and arriving mid-morning. Sammy and his wife arrived the next day. Fragile little Marta was barely aware of what was happening to her and her mother refused to leave her side, concerned that Marta would awake with no one there to comfort her.

Marta's seizures had been going on for years. Sometimes she would experience a few in a day and then go weeks, even months, with no episodes. Then, without warning she would fall to the ground, unconscious and twitching. For the past three days these seizures had gained in ferociousness, giving Marta little time to take a few swallows of water. She was in the intensive care unit at St. Joseph's in Chippewa Falls, hooked up to intravenous fluids, and seizure medications. The medications did not control what was happening in her brain.

Callie knew this was to be the end but she wouldn't let herself grieve, not yet. There would be time enough later. When Jordan arrived, and she told him what to do, what to expect, she lay down upon the bed next to Marta and immediately fell asleep. She awoke in an hour to Marta's whimpering knowing she and Jordan were powerless to help. Jordan put his arm around her and she let herself be held.

Marta was quiet when Sammy and his wife arrived; her breathing was shallow and with great pauses as her brain worked to keep her body alive. She never regained consciousness, taking one last deep breath before leaving the world forever. The three held Callie who dropped to the floor, finally giving in to her grief, leaning on the cold white sheets of the hospital bed.

Sammy and his wife left for their jobs in Oregon a day after Marta's memorial service. They encouraged Callie to visit them. "Someday, maybe." she answered softly. Jordan stayed on with Callie. He was loath to return to the city. The friends he had were all sick or dying and it was depressing to go out for coffee without his old buddies. All they talked about were the ones who were gone. Callie did not argue with or even wonder about Jordan hanging around with her at Flambeau. They slept in separate rooms. He got up before her, made coffee or tea and read the news reports. He waited patiently each morning for her to wake up. They made breakfast together and for the most part sat silently, speaking very little. Callie usually went out to the garden; Jordan watched her for a while through the window. Then he shaved, dressed, and went into town to be around other people with whom he could have some small conversation. After buying a few grocery items or other things, he came back. Callie would be reading or in the kitchen. She tried to make some small talk, such as asking whom he saw, or the price of electricity. Jordan was grateful for the effort, knowing the pain she was in.

He never asked if he could stay. After three months he told her he needed to close up the apartment in New York and asked if she would like to come.

"No, no. I need to stay here." was all she could say.

So Jordan took a week to go back to New York. He toyed with the thought of calling Callie to say he had decided to stay in New York, but he didn't. Instead, he shipped anything he thought was worthwhile to keep from his years without her. There was very little. He signed the contract with the realtor and moved to Flambeau with Callie.

The week that Jordan was gone was the loneliest week in Callie's life. She slept very little and ate very little. She used the week not to continue grieving, but to think about the future and what she wanted to do with her life. Two days before Jordan arrived back she called Janet, asking for her help. The two women cleared out the old furniture in Elly's room where Jordan had been sleeping. They repainted and created a study with the computer and a modern desk. In the study Callie hung pictures she had stored for over thirty years. Pictures of her childhood, her grandmother, her father and mother, her wedding. Callie stood looking at herself and Jordan in the picture, young and fresh and modern. She turned toward the window. It was night and she looked at her own reflection in the glass. She was aging but as she squinted at herself, she felt some new desires, long hidden. Callie slept a deep, refreshing sleep alone in her bed. It would be the last night alone for many years to come.

THE VISIT

On the way home, after that weekend, Matt and Amy had a good deal to discuss. They projected reasons for different birth rates for different social groups. Their focus was on Susan. Amy continued to believe in the evils of Purefz even as Matt steered the conversation to another evil.

"I just can't buy it," Amy argued with Matt. Her opinion concerning the potentially tainted water was so strong that she could not see another possibility.

"I am just saying this," Matt pursued his line of argument, "that we should take a trip to visit Wally---and Jim for that matter. I'd like to see what they have to say about this. It's the least we can do. We haven't seen the old guys since we were married. For all we know, they could be dead."

Amy's eyes flashed up at Matt. He had finally hit a chord that resonated in her being. But she was torn with the problem of getting water from her well for them for the week.

"Tell you what," Matt said. "Why don't you go to Flambeau as usual and I will take the transport to St. Paul? I'll let you know what's up when I get there."

Amy was still not convinced even though the plan did accomplish both things. Why was she so stubborn about this?

"Listen, we'll only be away from each other for one day, maybe two."

There he went again, reading her mind. This was the stumbling block she had. "You're right. Let's do it."

That week the administrator of the engineering department for GEO became the father to a new healthy boy.

SOUTH ST. PAUL 2191

Matt did not know what to expect when he arrived at the Exchange. He wondered whether Jim, Wally, or even Rita would be there. He walked slowly into the open market area and his eyes sought out the mushroom stand. When he did not see it, he grieved. Jim had been the first one to befriend Matt. He looked for Rita and her flowers. She was not there either. He swallowed hard as he made his way to the edge of the market in search of Wally. If Wally was also gone, he and Amy would never learn what the Governors had in mind for the world.

Matt walked through the Exchange, uncertain of whether he would find Wally. Suddenly, there it was, the conglomeration of old trailers that marked Wally's territory. They looked somehow different, maybe a little more presentable? There were more trailers it seemed and the grass around the trailers was not as untidy as he remembered and as he approached he actually saw clusters of coneflowers and yellow yarrow growing raucously in the sun. A stone path led him to the central area connecting the cluster of trailers. Then he saw them, Rita, old Jim, and Wally, their backs to him, sitting looking out into the small wooded wasteland that bordered the exchange on that side.

The rest of the day was devoted to hearing their story. After they had all returned from Matt and Amy's wedding, Wally invited Jim to set up shop with him. Rita joined them, last year. The two still sold flowers and mushrooms, but in a single stand just a ways from the trailers. Rita's son came with Rita to lend a hand at the heavy work of creating a more pleasant outdoor space. The three now lived here year round. "Well, my boy, you and your pretty little bride helped us come to this. We get along well and we need each other." Jim Razor sat smiling with a bowl in his lap. He was cleaning the beans Rita would be cooking for their supper. The three looked healthier and happier than when he first met them.

They were older, but that didn't seem to matter.

That night, when Rita and Jim retired to their respective trailers Matt had time alone with Wally. In a round-about way the story was told of Amy's research, Matt's work, Susan's depression, Ned's cabin, Ned's employer, the forbidden wells, and the spring on the Flambeau Mountain. "So, Amy and I are wondering first about Susan. I guess I am also wondering about our fate. Will we be denied children because, as Amy believes, the water we have been drinking is tainted? What do you think?"

"Can you discover anything in the history of the carbon scrubbers at work with your level of access?" Wally was quickly putting two and two together. His own personal ambitions were stirred, even at his age. After all these years, he still seethed with anger over his life's work being used against him.

"I will continue to try, but it will be slow."

"Well if you let me reprogram your chip, you'd learn what you want to learn almost immediately." Wally looked at his feet. He wondered how quickly Matt would ask about the risks. He didn't have to wait long.

"That seems pretty dangerous. Someone from World Security Systems is sure to be watching those files pretty closely."

"True." Wally pursued, "But if I gave you only a slightly upgraded access, it may go unnoticed."

"I can't decide that alone. I'll need to talk this over with Amy.

"It could be that there will be very little risk involved." Wally was beginning to get excited about the possibilities if he could only convince Matt to give him access. "Remember my telling you about how I embedded an encrypted subroutine which would allow me to access the system configuration as program administrator?"

"Not really. What do you mean?"

Jim sighed. There was so much Matt didn't know and for that matter there was so much that may have been altered in the programming since his original work. But he could hope, hope that the embedded subroutine he added would still work. "I created a cloaking mechanism whereby my access would not be detected by others having administrative rights, until of course it would be too late." Wally smiled to himself. It felt good to recall how crafty he had been. "The way I did this was to bypass World Security's central chip reading processor and to give myself access to the subroutine with an old fashioned DOS password!" Wally began to laugh hysterically. "Can you believe it? A password of all things!"

Matt was skeptical. "But passwords can be easily broken."

"Of course they can!" But first you have to know that you are looking for a hack. And then you have to make the leap to thinking it is an old-fashioned DOS algorithm, something from about 1970 and not an access code." In the back of Wally's mind there was a small nagging doubt. After thirty years, someone could have stumbled upon his subroutine and deleted it. Or worse, found it, broken the password, and hacked into the system for their own gain.

"Wouldn't it be possible to simply change your access level?"

Wally looked at Matt. "Do you recall how many years ago I created that program. I really don't know what has gone on since then. If I have access and take, say even a week to figure out what the Governors are up to, I will be noticed. However, in your case, I could upgrade your access for a short time and then reinstate your current access when you are done. That is much less risky."

Matt shook his head sadly, "I guess the real question is whether all of us want to take these risks or whether we want to hold onto our lives as they are, running the maze with our little joys and little sorrows under the Governors' watchful and controlling eyes."

"You got it, boy. I'm going to bed. You can bunk in there." Wally motioned to the trailer where they once had sat looking at the apple laptop. "Sleep well, my friend."

Matt didn't sleep well. He struggled with questions of morality, ethics, and how he was choosing to live his life. So much had happened since he first met that girl with the brown ponytail. He fell asleep before dawn and dreamed a dream of holding the hand of a small child. It was a little girl and she was pulling away from him. They were in a hayloft and hidden somewhere in the hay they could hear the mewing of newborn kittens. The brown haired child pulled her hand out of his to get to the kittens. He tried to grab her but she was falling, falling down the hay chute and then it wasn't a chute at all, but a stone lined well and she fell into the icy water. Matt woke drenched in sweat.

FLAMBEAU 2084

In one sustained movement Callie moved the covers aside, sliding her legs out of bed and sitting up. She sat on the edge of the bed and listened for Jordan's easy snoring. She assessed the stiffness and little pains in her back and feet and hands. Slowly she wiggled her toes and then made circles with her feet and then with her neck and head. As she yawned the muscles in her back and neck tightened. Cold air under her pajama top reminded her that it was winter and she really didn't need to get up because her garden too was sleeping, blanketed in white. She had almost convinced herself to crawl back into the warmth when Jordan's easy breathing ceased and he mumbled, "Morning?"

"Uh-huh," she mumbled back as she slid her feet into the slippers on her side of the bed.

She padded into the kitchen and, as was her routine, poured two glasses and one mug of water and then she poured the last of yesterday's well water into a teakettle for later. There would be enough for coffee for each of them. After they were dressed Jordan would go out with her to help her carry two fresh gallons back to the house. This would last until the next day. She heated her mug of water and steeped a bag of chamomile. Then she sat down to read the news summaries of the day.

Callie and Jordan had grown old together. The passionate love they once had before Callie left with little Sammy and Marta was replaced with a deep, respectful love. They enjoyed each other's company, shared each other's sorrows, and depended upon each other for the things they each could bring. What Callie brought to the relationship could not be measured in money. She provided good food, a loving relationship, and of course, her precious water. Jordan brought love, stability, and his retirement money.

Elly had used up her money on rebuilding the cabin for Sammy and updating the house and the well. Callie was used to living off of her own employment as a teacher and clerk for the town. Jordan's retirement gave them something more: the flexibility to travel as often as they liked to see Sammy's family. In the years when they had more energy, they traveled also to interesting places in the world, with Callie always curious about how people around the world got their water.

It was harder and harder to stir up the passion she once had in uncovering the covert operations of Purefz. It was enough to keep pumping the well water and cooking meals. In the summer, gardening was added to the tasks Jordan and Callie undertook each day, though on a much-reduced scale.

Callie tried to focus on world events in the news. The countries within their respective continents united as continental unions, just as when the countries in Europe united as the European Union. Callie's interest in these unions arose from her concern for the welfare of the little people, the ones who starved when there was no food and perished from disease when the water was contaminated.

Only recently had a pandemic arisen that essentially deleted the poorest of the poor in each of the unions. It began soon after Callie and Jordan returned from one of their visits to New York.

Callie and Jordan visited New York almost yearly after Jordan came to Wisconsin. At first Jordan asked Callie to return so that he could reconnect with his east coast friends. He had hoped that he could interest her in something from his former life. When he realized she had little interest in the life of the city folk, he planned the yearly visit to correspond with the yearly world summit at the United Nations. He would visit friends and Callie attended the open sessions where she became increasingly sure of the dangers ahead for the world population.

It was during one of those open sessions that she began to consider the morality of allowing the suffering and death of the very poor. The speaker had projected a graph on the large screen that indicated the amount of food that could be produced with current resources in the world. He overlaid a graph that indicated the world population, nine billion. If he was accurate in his analysis, over half of the people would die a slow death of starvation in the next two decades.

His speech left a great impression upon Callie. She realized her own sustainable lifestyle, attempting to minimize the imprint her consumption of goods would have on this earth, would not have an effect on reducing death and disease for the world's poorest. Even if the Governors of the Earth had a plan to conserve and fairly allocate resources, it was too late. Too late for the newborn babies, dying in their mothers' arms, their bellies distended with skin taut and thin from dehydration.

This was depressing and even more depressing was that in the news of the day, available to the people who could read and who could afford a computer there was nothing about the impending doom.

Callie's other concern had been the prospect of war between the unions. From the knowledge gained each year at the summit, Callie believed that a war of this magnitude would destroy the world and she believed that the inequity between the 'haves' and the 'have nots' of the earth would be the catalyst that would spark the war.

The war never came. Instead, a pandemic, of a magnitude the world had not seen before, ravaged the people for decades. It was selective by class. Half of the world's population perished from this dreadful pandemic, the poorest half.

The cause of the pandemic was never fully explained by the press to the common man. Fear left its mark and the majority of the population still alive opted to eat only packaged food such as the IF rations and drink the Purefz water Jordan once purchased. Real food and spring water were said to be dangerous.

Only a handful of people on the earth knew the real cause behind the pandemic and they were silent.

After the pandemic, life appeared to improve for the common man. New technology was advancing and resources on the earth were more readily distributed. Callie sadly thought to herself that half of the people on the earth were sacrificed to allow a healthier life for the ones who survived. If the decision to sacrifice was part of some larger plan, was it a moral decision? These dark thoughts continued to haunt her.

Callie's mind wandered back to her early life on Elly's farm, the struggles with Marta and the joys with Sammy. Sammy's two little girls were now ten and twelve. They drank Purefz exclusively. There was nothing Callie could do about it. When they came to visit, they enjoyed pumping the water from the well, but they preferred to drink the bottled water. Callie learned to be quiet about this. The older one would drink part of a glass of water from the water cooler when she sat down with her grandmother because she knew it pleased her. Were they healthy? Would they be able to have children? Would they enjoy a long life? Callie didn't want to know the answers to these questions. It was as if she had become two separate people. One, the grandmother, accepted her child and grandchildren as they were. The other, the community activist, summoned the last of her energies to write letters to the editor about the government. She followed with trepidation the unifying of the utilities into one conglomerate. She encouraged her friends to use the spring water on Flambeau Mountain for their personal consumption.

Sadly these friends, those people from the little community of Flambeau were almost all gone. Most had died in their late forties or early fifties like Janet's husband. Some, like old farmer Linski had lived well into his nineties. Callie had her theories about this. Now there was no one left but Jordan, no one who shared her early life at Flambeau, not even Janet, with whom she could confide. Each death, beginning with her parents' car accident soon after she and Jordan were married, seemed to have left a hole in her heart. Callie looked out of the window in the study and mused that Elly must also have looked out upon her garden and the river beyond from here. The holes left by Elly's and then Marta's deaths were the largest. Could it be, she wondered, that when her heart would become completely full of holes that she too would die? Callie looked absentmindedly at the calendar. It was two days before

Jordan's seventy-fifth birthday, January 12, 2083. Callie smiled. She would bake a birthday cake tomorrow. Today she would tidy up and clean house. They would invite Tubby Nader, Sammy's old friend, and his family for cake.

With a plan in mind, the heartache she felt did not bother her as much. She stood up from the chair, trying her best to ignore the tired old muscles. Jordan was still asleep. She would be as quiet as she could while making breakfast.

Callie finished making breakfast for herself and Jordan. She decided not to remind him of his birthday. Funny that he wasn't awake yet she thought. Rather than wake him, Callie decided to check her e-mail. Her granddaughters were great about sending little e-mails to Callie and Jordan. As busy as they were with school and projects, they usually connected with their grandparents almost weekly. Callie smiled when the file opened. Katie had sent a video of her latest efforts to make cookies from scratch. Ashley had taken the time to set up the camera when Katie started the project. The result was a humorous video of cookie baking by a twelve-year-old who hardly knew there were ways other than cello boxes to get cookies.

This was too funny to watch alone. Callie paused the video and went to get Jordan. As she approached the hallway to their bedroom she took in a quick breath and her heart skipped a beat. She stood for a long time in the doorway before approaching the bed. Her memories were flooded with pictures of Jordan from their early love, through their divorce, to these last rich years together, but she could not cry.

In the years following Jordan's death Callie found it harder and harder to maintain the house, the garden, and to keep her commitment to drawing water only from the well. On days that she felt tired and weak, she refrained from the arduous task of making her way through the brush to the well. On those days, she kept the water for two or three days, boiling it to avoid getting seriously ill. In the summer of 2086, she read about preparations for the centennial celebration for the following summer. A time capsule would be buried in the town center, which would contain the history of Flambeau. To fund the placement of this time capsule, residents of Flambeau could buy space in the capsule for their own family history. It was expensive but Callie immediately purchased space. This would be her way to say goodbye to Elly's land and yet preserve the Bordeau family history for any future generation. Any time spent at Flambeau after that would be a gift. Maybe she would die there, maybe she would leave before she died. Sammy and his wife could sell the land if they wished and the money would help pay for the education of their children. Sammy had already sold the cabin to Tubby Nader and his family. As Callie saw it, the things of value were the family history, the land, and the water from the well that ran through both.

CHIPPEWA FALLS 2191

Amy returned from Flambeau alone in the late afternoon. It had not been an enjoyable weekend. She missed Matt, Susan had been depressed, and Ned was unable to cope so he went hunting. Amy carted the week's supply of well water into their Chippewa home alone. As in her early days of living alone, she was cautious about how she looked as she carried the water inside. She rarely checked the NASA site but she still had the lingering fear.

Matt wasn't home and he hadn't called. Well, that was okay, she reasoned. He would be home before 8:00. He was very disciplined about getting enough sleep for the week ahead. It was 7:45. It was 7:50; and then it was 7:53. Amy's stomach objected to having food on the table and not eating. Hunger gave way to a nervous feeling, a feeling of anticipation, a feeling of the unexpected. When she finally heard the run-about in the yard, it was 8:30. The unease she had been feeling did not leave even though she knew he was home.

The reason for her feelings was suddenly made clear. She heard voices. Matt wasn't alone. She was no longer uneasy, she was irritated. Why had Matt not called to tell her he was bringing someone home, and on a Sunday night when they both had to rest for the stress of the week ahead?

Wally stood on the other side of the run-about, not moving. "Wally!" Amy shrieked, forgetting her earlier thoughts about getting enough rest for the week ahead. She pulled Wally's head down, standing up on her tiptoes to give him a hug and a kiss on his unshaven cheek. Behind him stood Matt, carrying two large bags. Matt smiled sheepishly and after Amy glared at him briefly, she pulled his face down to hers and kissed him. He also was unshaven, and smelling a bit unusual.

Wally could not stop looking around. Matt and Amy's home was not wealthy by any means, however it was a far cry from what Wally was used to. Matt suggested showing Wally to the den, which served as a guestroom. He was given a set of towels and shown the guest lav. Amy causally suggested he might wish to freshen up before dinner. With Wally ensconced in his room, Amy joined Matt in their room. He had already stripped and was in the lav taking a shower. Amy wished she could join him, but there were other things to attend to.

"What were you thinking?" She asked before going back to the kitchen to find some additional food to extend what she had planned for Matt and herself.

"Talk later?" Matt asked. Amy just shook her head.

It was almost midnight by the time Amy had enough information to be really worried. Wally would be staying two weeks, time to get Matt into plenty of trouble she thought. But it was hard to think clearly. She was overtired and needing sleep for the next day of work. Matt, it seemed, had gotten a second or third wind.

"Night you two." Amy couldn't last any longer. "Wally, make yourself at home. Food is mostly in these cabinets and in the food keeper. I'll have some things out that I think you might like and I'll be home by 6:00 to make dinner."

"Please don't go to any trouble on my account." Wally was trying to be on his best behavior with Amy around. He sensed he was intruding.

"No trouble." Amy had no recourse but to lie a little.

The next morning was a tough one for Matt. He didn't want to think about how little sleep he had gotten. Amy and Matt ate breakfast as silently as they could and tiptoed out to their run-abouts.

"What is Wally going to do all day?" Amy finally asked when the door had closed.

"He will just sleep and get his bearings, I imagine." Matt chose not to tell Amy that only a few hours ago, the two collaborators had hacked into the system with Matt's access code.

That evening Matt and Amy took Wally out to dinner instead of cooking in. Everyone was extremely tired. They took a long walk before dusk and when they arrived back at the pod, they were all ready for bed. The following day, Wally was up at dawn with Matt and Amy. He seemed to have taken on a new life in the past 48 hours. "You have a wonderful, wonderful life!" He exclaimed at breakfast. Amy smiled. She was glad to see Wally so very happy, but she was also a bit concerned. What was going on in that mind of his?

One day followed the next with Wally remaining extremely upbeat, different than the Wally they first met a few years ago. Friday, they prepared for the trip to Flambeau. Wally was ready to share what he had learned that week. Matt also had information to share. The information they were about to share was not good so it was surprising how happy they both were.

Once the three of them were wedged into the run-about, Wally said, "Well, Matt Bordeau, what have you found out with the access I've arranged?" Wally chuckled, almost like Amy's old professor. He seemed to think he had made a joke.

"Well, first of all, no one seems to be noticing that I have more access than before. Wally's plan of increasing the access only slightly seems to have avoided any red flags. It is as if there is enough movement in access codes so that my upgrade is unnoticed. That said, I have been able to determine that there are many hidden files in the company's database--I have not been able to open the files with my access level. I was able to determine when the files were created but I have no way of knowing what information they hold."

Wally looked out the window watching the constantly shifting view from the run-about. He did not have a particular interest in uncovering information about the scrubbers and Purefz. His interest was in the embedded chip he created over thirty yeas ago and how the Governors had used and modified it after they reduced his access. However, he wanted Matt and Amy's continued support even if he didn't need it. It was with these thoughts in mind that he replied to Matt.

"I could upgrade your access easily, however we don't know what increase in risk you will be subject to."

Amy had been quiet up until now, "No increase in risk. Please! Matt!"

"Well," Wally continued, "we could wait a few weeks or months. Increase the time between increased access if you still want to learn more. That would probably minimize your risk."

Matt carefully considered this and the urgency in Amy's voice. "I would like to stay at the access I have—at least for now."

Amy sighed in relief. "So what have you learned this week, Wally?"

"So far, the most important thing I have learned concerns the subroutine I hid with the old DOS password. Evidently no one has ever found it. Otherwise I'm certain it would have been deleted."

"So you can get into the executive function of the config sys program?" Matt asked cautiously.

"Yes, and I have done so briefly each day, just to see if I would alert anyone by hacking into the system." Here Wally told a bit of a lie. He had hacked in each day; that was true. However on the first day, he spent a great deal of time in the system, cloaking his access even further than before to assure that the embedded subroutine would not be found if his work flagged closer scrutiny by the international security system. The rest of the week, he leisurely researched the chip functions, learning what the chip was now capable of controlling thirty years after his initial work.

"I also located the program to alter access, as you know, and I have worked on creating a routine for initiating the chip death sequence." Here, he turned slightly to look at Amy and gage her reaction. "Should that become necessary," he added. Part of Wally's story was true, but he didn't detail how little time it took for him to do this work and what he spent the rest of his time doing.

The three-some were quiet the rest of the way to Flambeau, each with their own thoughts. Wally was given a brief tour of the little abode and his gear was placed in the study. He watched with mild curiosity as Amy crawled under the brush to obtain water. He found her belief in the value of the well water unusual. He chose to keep his opinions to himself and not jeopardize his relationship with Amy. Keeping with the Friday night tradition, the three got back in the run-about and headed to Ned and Susan's house for dinner.

Amy wondered how Wally would respond to their friends. Ned and Susan were more similar to the people Wally had spent the last thirty years with, but from what Amy had seen, Wally wasn't a real socialite. She hoped the evening would go well.

Wally wondered how he would fit into this group of young people almost fifty years younger than himself. In general he hated to put himself out to be pleasing to anyone, thinking of himself as a bitter old man. But there was little time to dwell on these thoughts, for within minutes the run-about pulled up to a modest abode with a small yard and garden.

"I thought you said they lived in town." Wally questioned the seemingly country look to the yard and home.

"This is the town," Amy answered. "Flambeau is a very old town with an interesting history. I'll have to tell you about it sometime." It seemed Wally was already somewhat confrontational and he hadn't even met their hosts.

Ned came out to greet them, giving Amy a hug and saying hello to Matt and Wally.

"Wally," Matt began a formal introduction, "this is our friend Ned."

Ned stepped forward, taking Wally's hand in his own. "I'm glad to meet you!" he said with genuine warmth in his voice.

Wally smiled his reserved smile, "Thank you for inviting me."

"It isn't often we are honored to have someone of your

generation visit us in Flambeau. My wife, Susan, is inside, putting the final touches on our meal. I think she is a little nervous."

Wally was taken aback by this. He thought of himself as the underdog and these four as more upper crust.

Ned continued, "Please come in."

Amy interrupted, "Ned, show Wally the garden first before it gets dark. He might have some ideas for Susan from Rita's garden." In truth, Amy wanted to see how her friend had been doing this week, before the men came in.

Amy found Susan setting the table. Her special dishes from her grandparents, some cracked, graced today's table. Susan had put a small vase of flowers from the garden in the middle of the table. Wonderful, unusual smells emanated from Susan's kitchen. "Hi!" Amy said cheerfully.

"Hello." Susan stopped her work to give her friend a hug.

"How's it going?" Amy asked, looking carefully at her friend for any signs of sadness.

"Surprisingly well. I seem to have climbed out from wherever I was. I still feel sad, but strangely hopeful."

"That's good!" Amy said, relieved at the change from last week in her friend.

Ned brought Wally into the kitchen to meet Susan. Wally inhaled deeply. "Goulash?" He said with his eyes closed.

Susan laughed. "Nice to meet you too, Wally! You have a keen sense of smell. It is goulash!"

Wally opened his eyes and looked at Susan. A memory from the past flooded his brain and he couldn't speak. He just smiled.

The goulash was delicious. Susan had made spaetzl to go with the saucy tomatoes. They all ate until they could hold no more. Ned and Matt cleared the table letting Susan rest. Wally smiled at Susan, sharing the memory that had struck him when he met her. "The one love of my life looked much like you look and she also could cook extremely well. I rarely think about her, but you've brought her back to my mind."

Amy realized she was not part of this conversation so she stood up to help the guys and to serve the dessert. She wondered at the attraction between the two: Wally, who could be so crotchety and Susan, who was always sweet and kind. When Amy returned to the table, she could see that Susan had been crying and Wally was now standing at the window, thoughtfully watching the sun setting through the stand of pines. At first Amy bristled at the thought that Wally had said something thoughtless, but that made no sense whatsoever. Perhaps she would never know what had transpired between them.

Everyone sat back down with dessert and coffee. Coffee was a new drink in Amy's life. It tasted bitter, but she enjoyed it. Susan returned to her cheerful self. The four young people talked of many things, keeping the topics on the light side. Only Wally was quiet. He seemed not to follow the conversation unless Susan spoke. And at those times he watched her carefully. Amy thought he watched her as a young man watches the woman he loves.

The next day, Ned and Susan came to Amy's abode. Ned and Matt and Amy pumped water from the well while Susan went into the study to keep Wally company, When they decided to walk up to the spring on Flambeau Mountain, Wally declined and Susan chose to stay back with Wally. As the three-some trudged through the wooded areas, they talked about the seemingly strange relationship between Susan and Wally.

"She said," Ned confided, "that Wally seems like her father or grandfather. She said that he gives her the feeling that all will be well in our life. Strange isn't it? From what you said earlier, I thought he would scare her out of her wits."

Matt and Amy could only shake their heads in amazement. Neither had anticipated the friendship that was so evident between the young woman and the old man.

When the three returned to Chippewa Falls on Monday, Wally spent every minute working on his old program, logging into the system through Matt's access code. He shared some of his work with Amy and Matt in the evenings after supper. Much of what he was doing he kept to himself. If Amy was concerned for Matt's safety, she didn't say anything.

Wally's curiosity concerning the chip and the programming was satisfied by Tuesday evening. He had made as many changes as he believed were necessary for him to continue his access without Matt. He had found the insidious fertility control program. He covertly altered the programming of Susan's chip in a way he believed would be helpful to her and Ned.

Wally spent the rest of the week looking at the bigger picture, how the Governors of the Earth were controlling resources. He learned that each of the world wide corporations-utilities, food, manufacturing, transportation, and communication-each had a board of directors and from these boards a representative was elected to sit on Governors of the Earth Council. It was these five, most powerful people on the planet who controlled everything. The initial intent of the embedded chips, to keep world peace and to keep crime to a minimum was now only a minor function; the major function was to reduce and control population commensurate with natural resources. Wally struggled with this. Why not just let reduction of resources control population naturally? Why had the governments of the twentieth and twenty-first century been so blind, investing in wars for resources rather than investing in the conservation of these resources through the technology that was so obviously available to them at that time? Was there a God who controlled the Five?

The evening before Matt brought Wally back to his trailer, Wally told Matt and Amy many of the things he had learned from the access Matt had given him. Looking directly at Amy, he confessed to altering the programming of Susan's chip, changing her fertility status. He confessed to upgrading the level of access for both Susan and Ned, giving them a slightly higher standard of living for their food and transportation. Amy bit her lip as Wally confessed to this. She could not help but hope for better lives for Ned and Susan. She only hoped this chip altering would remain undetected by World Security.

What Wally didn't tell them was that he had been successful in creating a code for his own chip that could mimic Matt's chip and allow him access without Matt's knowledge or presence.

Life appeared to resume as before for Matt and Amy after

Wally's visit. A year passed with the healthy birth of Susan's daughter. The birth of this child brought a newfound joy to the lives of all four young people. Ned and Susan never questioned the miracle of this birth nor did they question the upgrades to their social status. They now had access to using personal run-abouts and they had some additional computer access that they didn't have before.

Matt rarely had time to dig further into the data from the research on the safety of Purefz water. He and Amy did not talk of this any longer. They talked of happier things and they learned that Amy was pregnant. The baby would be born in late spring. Initially Amy was furious because she believed Wally tampered with her chip program. But the anger subsided as she became attached to the unborn child she was carrying.

In this time of pleasure and planning for a future child, Matt and Amy planned a vacation with Ned, Susan, and baby Sarah. The trip to the cabin provided them with time for hiking, time for working in the forest surrounding the cabin, and time for simply being alive in nature. It was good to be away from technology and work responsibility.

On the Monday following their vacation, Matt returned to work to find a memo from his boss to stop in the office. "Why is the central agency needing to know more about you? While you were gone, the place was crawling with world security checking all our data files and interrogating anyone working with you on the project. The top headhunter was mad as hell that you were gone. He is coming back next Monday and you'd better be ready with some good answers. What the hell is he looking for anyway?"

Matt feigned ignorance and lied about looking into files. "I was trying to track the development of the old scrubbers and saw the files in question. They were locked and my access did not let me look at them." Matt looked steadily at his boss but his mind was racing. Susan's child, the Nader family's upgrade, Amy's pregnancy, and now this. What else had Wally done?

Unable to focus on work, Matt walked home and changed into running clothes. It was the middle of the day, not a good time for running under the direct rays of the sun. Without thinking where he was going, Matt found himself near the hospital. His legs carried him into the building, into the office where Amy was sitting at her console.

Amy started to smile and then seeing Matt's face she perceived something was gravely wrong. She automatically logged off, gathered her things and left with Matt without saying a word.

While Matt showered, Amy made a quick call to Susan. The holographic image of the two-month-old cherub appeared before her. "What's wrong?" Susan asked. Amy has never connected with her in the middle of the day. "Are you feeling okay? Are you having morning sickness?" Susan's genuine caring almost caused Amy to break down and tell her everything. But it was too soon; there were too many unknowns. Amy didn't know why she called.

"I just wanted to see that beautiful little baby." This was partially true, as Amy could not get enough of little Sarah after having spent a week helping Susan care for her.

Matt finished his shower and the two ate in silence. In a few hours they would confront Wally. In another few hours they would make a plan that would change their lives and the lives of the Nader family forever.

THE DECISION

Wally listened quietly as Matt explained everything his boss had said. The real problem, Wally realized, was not the increased access he had given Matt, but rather his own drive to dig into the files to learn everything he could about all the operations of the Governors. World Security only knew that it was Matt's chip access that hacked into the system. They did not know that Wally the long forgotten engineer, was responsible.

Amy was past being angry with Wally, instead focused on the safety of her friends and on the safety of her unborn child. She listened and tried to understand what Wally was saying, what they now had to do to protect their lives. Amy had no doubt that World Security would not only demote their access, but would cause them to disappear from the earth and in the process, the gray matter of their brains analyzed to see exactly what they knew. It would be a painless yet horrible death, experiencing the synaptic connections that are memories taken from you one at a time until you are left with only the connections that support physical life. It would be a death much like the death from Alzheimer's. The last functions to go would be swallowing, eye movements, hearing, breathing, and finally the heart would stop beating. Your mind and soul would be no more. The disposal of your body would be the last step. Amy forced herself to concentrate on what Wally was saying.

"You first need to convince Ned and Susan of the danger to themselves and Sarah. If they do not believe you, and go along with the plan, World Security will eventually find their connection to us and not only will they die in the process, but their memories will be read which will lead WS to you. After they are on board with the plan, they may not tell anyone but they must prepare for an extended time at the cabin. Have them help you collect all foods and supplies for at least three months from your Flambeau abode and their home and stock the cabin as well as you can. They should try not to purchase excessive amounts of anything that would trigger inquiry. Before you leave here, I'll gather some of Rita's dried foods for you but I will not tell her what is going on. It could jeopardize her life, also."

"On Friday, you both need to get to Flambeau early. Ned and Susan will need to be prepared to leave as soon as you arrive. They could leave earlier, but it will be difficult to synchronize this from my end and it will be safer for all of you if you are together. Remember, when I actuate the death sequence on your chips, your run-abouts will probably not work any longer. You call me from Flambeau when you leave and I will give you exactly one hour.

"What about you, Wally?" Matt asked. "What will happen to you and your chip when you trigger the death sequence of our chips? Will you also trigger the sequence on your chip?"

Wally shrugged. In truth he had not made up his mind about what he would do about this one sticky detail. He knew he had outlived his programmed life expectancy. He knew that if his chip died, he would die also. He didn't want Matt and Amy to know this piece of information. "With your chip untraceable, there is no link to me. I'd better stay on to see what happens. When you return from the cabin, you will need a place to live. Rita and Jim and I will organize that for you and also food. I really don't know if you will have any transportation. There isn't time to find any antique bikes from the 21st century, you may be walking until you re-invent the wheel for yourselves." The enormity of their plight became more and more overwhelming as Amy visualized the loss of the simple things she took for granted. She realized she would be giving birth in the cabin with no medical support. With those dark thoughts Amy and Matt returned to Chippewa and to Flambeau for the three last days of preparation.

SOUTH ST. PAUL 2192

Thursday night Wally sat in darkness in his trailer, looking out his window. It was cold outside, a cold, dark February night. The light from the window of Jim's trailer allowed him to see his old buddy, Jim Razor. Jim and Rita were passing the time playing sheepshead, a card game centuries old. Wally closed his eyes and tried to visualize Sara, the woman he loved who once loved him. He could not bring her face into focus. Instead, in his mind he saw Susan, glowing with parenthood. He saw Amy, curious and determined. He saw Ned, hard working and proud. He saw Matt, tormented and worried.

Wally completed his bedtime rituals with deliberate consciousness, combing his hair and brushing the yellow stumps of his old teeth. He turned back the covers on his bed and sat down, thinking. He sat for a long time, hunched over on the edge of his bed. His heart beat slower and slower while he sat motionless in his old socks and thin pajamas that were no protection from the draft.

He was unaware of the chill, slowly crawling from the soles of his feet, around his ankles, over the tops of his knees. His hands and arms became cold, but still he ignored this so focused was he on piecing together the reality and morality of what he had done so many years ago.

Wally considered that the resources of the earth had been dwindling for over a hundred years. Why had not the leaders of the world protected the resources? Were they too stupid to project what would happen? At the later part of the 21st century, the world population peaked at nine billion people with resources to feed only half. Then the pandemic ravaged for decades, reducing the population by fifty percent.

Even with this reduction, the resources of the world were inadequate. There was a slow starvation and annihilation of entire cultures for lack of food and water. With over four billion people on this earth fighting to stay alive, the government had to do something.

Wally thought about the resources of the world he now lived in and the implication for the world's population in this year 2192. There was very little oil, very little natural gas, and very few precious metals to be mined. No fertilizer could be produced to grow vast quantities of food necessary to sustain the one billion people currently on this earth, and even if the fertilizer were available, there was not enough naturally occurring ground water and not enough water from the much improved scrubbers for irrigation. Once fertile farmland was now desert with less and less food being produced. The sun baked and dried areas of the earth that had once been temperate rain forest. A deadly viral bird disease migrated to other animals and mutated into other forms killing animal food sources and humans. Humans continued to die slow and painful deaths from starvation.

Wally mused that he had only half listened whenever Amy spoke about Purefz. She had been so sure, ever since her graduate years that Purefz water was to blame for the increase in cancer, decrease in birth rates, and mortality rates from other diseases. Her belief in Callie Nelson's well and the spring water of the Flambeau Mountain was all consuming. As a researcher, she had correlated the advent of the wide use of Purefz beginning in 2070 with the statistics of insidious cancers and declining longevity. Wally had not agreed with her analysis at the time. It had not interested him so consumed was he with his own, personal access, to find out how the Governors were using the chip he designed. However, Amy's information was important. When he went over this information now, he realized that these documents alluding to the reduction of the population by contaminates in the water supply proved to the Governors that this alone was insufficient to reduce the population to a sustainable amount.

Wally's thoughts turned back to the part he inadvertently played in population control. He provided the opportunity for the Governors to develop a more humane way to control population with the addition of fertility and lifespan programs. Was this morally acceptable? Mother Nature's way may not be as humane, but was it more human? Who decides wealth and opportunity? Who is allowed to procreate? Who should decide who lives and who dies? And if there is no decision, will natural selection take its course with starvation, disease, and aggression? Wally sat for a long time with these thoughts.

It was his own access through Matt's chip the past year that had alerted world security to the possibility of sabotage from the Chippewa Falls scrubber and had placed Matt in danger. Even with Matt's chip no longer functioning, it still might not take World Security long to connect the dots that would lead them to a small trailer with a refurbished console and an old man who had long outlived both his life expectancy and his usefulness to the Governors.

Now, sitting on his bed in the chill of the night, Wally considered the sum total of what he learned. He started to breathe more quickly and his heart raced. He had come to his decision.

FLAMBEAU 2092

Four years after the placement of the time capsule, Callie wrote her final letter dated June 21, 2092. As she had promised, she sealed the letter in plastic, protected it with additional waterproof materials and with difficulty, dug six inches down and placed the container on the north side of the casing of the well. The larger flat slate marker had been waiting in readiness for this moment.

Once she finished, she pumped a little water to rinse her hands.

She backed out of the small door and closed the door for the final time. Then she slowly made her way around the property stopping at her favorite spots, the oak tree she planted with Sammy when he started kindergarten, another oak she planted to mark the place of Elly's ashes, the third oak for Marta, and the fourth for Jordan. She placed her hand on the bark of each tree feeling both the roughness and the forgiving texture. Each tree was smaller than the one before. Callie stopped in an opening that she had chosen for her own tree. There would be no one here to plant this tree. And, more importantly, there would be no one who knew or cared about her little oak woods. If Sammy ever returned and rediscovered his kindergarten tree, that would be his journey, his memory, not hers.

Callie looked at her watch. It was almost time for Tubby's wife to pick her up and drop her at the transport station. She opened the door to the house, and inhaled the familiar smells; felt the spirits of Bess, Elly, Marta, and Jordan. She closed the door without locking it and sat on the bench under the big oak by the well to wait.

Eileen L. Ziesler

2192

Wally stood up from where he had been sitting on the edge of his bed, immobile for the past two hours. He strode up to the old console he had rigged up, logging in as 'Matt' the way he had done a hundred times in the past year. He worked what seemed like only a few hours, surprised at how little time it took to undo thirty years of programming. Wally smiled when he finished. It was 6:05 AM. It was Friday. He ate with relish two pieces of apple pie Rita had baked and drank a glass of water. He cleaned up the dishes, washed his hands, noted the time, and then went happily to bed without bothering to brush his teeth or to log out.

Matt woke with a start on Friday morning when the new day's sun spilled into the room, surprised that his chip's internal organizer hadn't alerted him earlier.

Amy was already up, staring at the unresponsive console in front of her.

Ned cuddled little Sarah, hoping Susan could get a few more minutes of sleep before the end of the life they'd always known in Flambeau.

Matt's boss, nervous about Monday's meeting had walked to

work early Friday morning in the cold brisk air and found the doors to the building would not open for him.

One billion people on this earth. One billion dead chips. Wally Walczak rolled onto his back still smiling. His face was toward the sun as he took his last breath.

James waited patiently at the bottom of the escalator just beyond the passenger-only zone in the baggage claim area. He guessed Elly would be one of the last passengers to deplane. He saw her before she saw him which gave him time to anticipate the change that he knew from childhood would come over her face when she spotted him. There it was, her face lit up and she let go of the escalator railing to wave at him. When she was within earshot she called out, "Have you finally named this baby?" He waved to her and smiled, not wanting to shout above the airport noise. "Well?" She asked impatiently as they embraced, "What is this baby's name?"

James released himself from his mother's hug and smiled at her. "Callie, we've named her Callie."

Questions

We can recall the past, and with the stories we hear from our own families, we can almost imagine what our life may have been if we had lived 50 or 100 years ago. It is much more difficult and maybe impossible to imagine one's life in the future. How do you imagine you would be living a life fifty years from now?

Following World War II, there was a push for housing for the returning war veterans–a push to build affordable housing with green lawns that required water and fertilizer and powered lawn mowers. These new homes were built for comfort with controlled interior systems for warmth and/or for cooling. They required additional electricity provided in part by the creation of dams such as the Hoover Dam, also providing a reservoir for the additional demand for water. Today, these policies had the effect of creating a water shortage. How will this water shortage bring about new policies, and what effects could these new policies have in the future?

In the twentieth century fear mongering has run rampant, starting with the fear of a war with Russia over Communism. This fear was alleviated when the Berlin wall came down. The war on drugs followed and this fear was diminished as marijuana became legalized. Taking its place as the number one fear, was the fear of weapons of mass destruction and the beginning of the war on terrorism. As this war progressed, it evolved into a fear of various religious sects and thus we have the war of religious divide. We would suggest that the next fear for western economies is the fear of losing domination in the global market. Is it possible that a global state will be created to alleviate these fears or might it be necessary to control fear in the population by implanting a chip, providing a drug induced state, or by some other form of mind control–such as imagined in the late 19th century by author H. G. Wells in The Time Machine?

At the beginning of The Legacy, the woman in the airport terminal concourse seemed to be lost in thought–perhaps in visions of the distant future. What are your visions?

………..to be continued.

Eileen L. Ziesler